The
GOOD WIFE
Strikes Back

**Center Point
Large Print**

**This Large Print Book carries the
Seal of Approval of N.A.V.H.**

ELIZABETH BUCHAN

The
GOOD WIFE
Strikes Back

CENTER POINT PUBLISHING
THORNDIKE, MAINE

This Center Point Large Print edition
is published in the year 2004 by arrangement with
Viking Penguin, a member of Penguin Group (USA) Inc.

The text of this Large Print edition is unabridged. In other
aspects, this book may vary from the original edition. Printed in
Thailand. Set in 16-point Times New Roman type by
Bill Coskrey and Gary Socquet.

ISBN 1-58547-419-3

Library of Congress Cataloging-in-Publication Data

Buchan, Elizabeth.
    The good wife strikes back / Elizabeth Buchan.--Center Point large print ed.
        p. cm.
    ISBN 1-58547-419-3 (lib. bdg. : alk. paper)
        1. Politicians' spouses--Fiction. 2. Married women--Fiction. 3. England--Fiction.
    4. Large type books. I. Title.

    PR6052.U214G66 2003b
    823'.914--dc22

                                                                2003022649

For Margot

Her price is far above rubies.
—Proverbs 31:10

Acknowledgments

Many thanks are owed to Vanessa Hannam and Deborah Stewartby for their kindness, generosity and patience in answering my questions about life as a MP's wife. Any mistakes are entirely mine. I am also extremely grateful to Emma Dally for sending me *Complete Wine Course* by Keven Zraly (Sterling Publishing, New York). I borrowed details for (my) Casa Rosa and the visit to the Etruscan tombs from Frances Mayes's *Under the Tuscan Sun* (Broadway Books), from Iris Origo's *War in the Val d'Orcia* (Nonpareil Books) and from Tim Parks's *An Italian Education* (Avon Books). Also information and anecdote on being a Member of Parliament from Gyles Brandreth's *Breaking the Code* (Trafalgar Square). With apologies also to Jane Austen. A huge thank-you is also owed to my brilliant editor, Pamela Dorman, to Claire Ferraro, Lucia Watson, Carolyn Coleburn, Judi Kloos and the rest of the superlative team at Viking Penguin. Also to my agent Mark Lucas, Janet Buck and, of course, to Benjie, Adam and Eleanor.

Chapter 1

IT IS A TRUTH universally acknowledged that one person's happiness is frequently bought at the expense of another's.

My husband Will, a politician to his little toe, did not entirely get the point. He maintained that sacrifices in the cause of the common good were sufficient in themselves to make anyone happy. And since Will had sacrificed a significant slice of his family life to pursue his ambitions as, first, a promising MP, then a member of the Treasury Select Committee, then minister, and—latterly—as one who was tipped to be a possible Chancellor of the Exchequer, it followed that he should have been supremely happy.

I think he was.

But was I?

Not a question, perhaps, that a good wife should ask.

On our nineteenth wedding anniversary, Will and I promised each other to be normal. To this end, Will carried me off to the theater, ordered champagne, kissed me lovingly and proposed the toast: "To married life."

The play was Ibsen's *A Doll's House*, and the production had excited attention. Although I could see that he was aching with tiredness, Will sat very still and upright in the seat, not even relaxing when the lights went dim. An upright back was part of the training he had imposed on himself never to let down his guard in public. Although I am better than I used to be, I am still laggardly in that department. It is so tempting to slump, hitch up my skirt and laugh when my sense of the ridiculous is tickled—and there was much in our life that was ridiculous. Politicians, ambassadors, constituents, coffee mornings, chicken suppers, state occasions . . . a wonderful, colorful caboodle replete with the ambitious and the innocent, the failures and the successes.

Of necessity, Will laughed with circumspection—so much so that, once, I accused him of having lost the ability through lack of use. There was only a tiny hint of a smile on his lips when he explained to me that one small error of attention could undo years of work.

I sneaked a look at him from under eyelids that still stung from the morning's regular date with the beauty salon. Dyed eyelashes were a necessity because, when I do laugh, my eyes water. In the early part of Will's career, when I was being scrutinized and weighed and measured from head to foot by sharp eyes in the constituency, Mannochie, Will's watchful and faithful political agent, had been forced to whisper discreetly, "Train tracks, Mrs. S," which meant my mascara had smudged. There was no option but to laugh off that one and whisk myself to the nearest mirror for a quick repair job. This was part of the bargain struck between Will and me. In short, to look good as the minister's wife was to be good.

Dressed in pale, shimmery blue, Nora made her entrance onto the stage and her husband asked anxiously, "What's happened to my little songbird?"

Will reached over for my hand, the left one, which bore his wedding ring and the modest ruby we had chosen together. It was small because, newly engaged and glowing with love at the prospect of shared happiness and mutual harmony, I had not wished him to spend too much money on me. Hindsight is a great thing, and I have come to the conclusion that modesty is wasted when it comes to jewelry. The touch of his hand was unfamiliar, strange almost, but I had grown used to that, too, and it was not significant. Beneath the unfamiliarity, Will and I were connected by our years of marriage. That was indisputable.

At the end of the play, still in her pale blue, Nora declared, "I don't believe in miracles any longer." The sound of the front door opening and closing as she left the house was made to sound like a prison gate clanging shut.

Someone in the audience gave a little cheer. It echoed above the perfectly groomed heads in the stalls, and there was a rustle of collective embarrassment at this demonstration of female solidarity.

When Parliament sat, Will lived in London during the week, in a mansion block in Westminster and it was London where he did his deals in the Members' tearoom, and struck alliances. In the old days, he came down to Stanwinton at weekends to nurse his constituency and his family, in that order, and I came up to London infrequently. Now that Chloe, our daughter, was eighteen, I was free to come up to London most weeks, but tonight we were driving home.

I watched the cold, eerie city lights give way to the shadows of the suburbs. At home, I often played the game of not-turning-on-the-light-until-the-very-last-minute. I loved that moment of transition between light and dark, and the textures of light and shade. I had learned that if I remained quite still something surprising might swim up out of the spaces in my head. Sometimes only a fleeting thought. Sometimes a revelation or a conclusion. Its chief element was of surprise and I found myself increasingly craving the delight of discovery. It was the moment to consider peace, happiness, expectation, . . . but, lately, I suppose, to reflect on a certain, creeping restlessness and a growing sense that it was time for a change.

Will cleared his throat—I recognized the signal—and began to talk about his project of the moment: the controversial European initiative to tax anyone with a second car. "There's no question, but we have to do something before the world chokes. We can't stand by and do nothing; we must show that we mean what we say." He turned. "Fanny? Are you listening?"

"Of course," I said. "Look at the road, Will, not at me."

"Well?"

But I was thinking of the days when my energy had been devoted to Will's political life and objectives and wondering why I did not feel the same. It was not as though we were old. I still loved Will, although sometimes ripples of irritation and exasperation made me forget I did—but that was marriage. Our life still held many possibilities.

"Fanny . . . ? Do you agree with what I am doing?"

"I don't think it stands much of a chance," I replied. "I don't think people always want to be told what is good for them."

"So I'm on my own on this one?" he said with the tone of one well used to arguing a case. "Fair enough."

An hour or so later, he nosed the car into the drive, unsnapped his seat belt and reached for the red box filled with papers, which required attention, that was never far from a minister's side.

"I hope you enjoyed the evening." He hefted the box onto his knee and added, "We've made it Fanny, haven't we? Nineteen years . . ."

I felt a sudden, intense disquiet. Or was it bewilderment? Where had those years gone? One of the saints, I think it was Theresa, wrote that the soul has many rooms. So does a life, and a marriage. Motherhood, too, and I had been curious to shine a light into each one. But having struggled through the muffling intimacies of being a wife and a mother, I was now asking: Which room was mine alone? Into which still, private room could I retreat?

I smiled at him. "It was a lovely evening." Then I leaned over and kissed him.

When we let ourselves into the house, I realized that I'd made the mistake, unlike Nora, of continuing to believe in miracles. The commotion that greeted us—Meg shouting and Sacha, her son, cajoling—meant only one thing. Will's sister had been drinking.

"Why?" I murmured. "Why now? She's been off it for months."

Will's face had tightened into the expression of frozen distress that I knew so well and dreaded. "I'll deal," I

13

said. "You go and check on your papers. Otherwise you won't get any sleep." I pushed him gently in the direction of the study. "Go."

I went down the passage that ran the width of the house and waited a moment or two at her door. The noises had stopped.

"Sacha?"

"Upstairs, Fanny."

I found him in Meg's bedroom, manhandling his mother's inert body onto the bed, and hastened to help. Meg was hunched on her side. I smoothed her hair back from her forehead. She was as fair as I was dark, and much smaller boned. "Has she had a lot?"

Sacha arranged her legs into a more comfortable position. "I'm not quite sure." He added with an effort, "Sorry."

"It's not your fault." I bent down to retrieve a whiskey bottle from the floor. It was still three-quarters full. "I don't think she's had that much . . ."

"But enough."

"She's been brilliant lately, and didn't touch a drop while you were away." Sacha's nu-metal band was struggling to get off the ground, and he was frequently away traveling the circuit.

He flinched and I could have kicked myself. "It *isn't* you. It isn't you coming back. . . . It's the time of year, or an unexpected bill or—"

"She rang my father today. He wants to renegotiate the alimony. That's probably it."

"Yes. That's it." Meg had never got over Rob walking out on her when Sacha was tiny. "Talking to your father is always tricky for her."

"I know," he said. He spoke far too wearily for a twenty-four-year-old. I slid my arms around my surrogate son. He smelled so clean. He always did, however many smoky, drink-filled places he'd worked in. "Don't despair."

"I don't," he lied.

"Shall I sit with her?"

Sacha propelled me toward the door. This was between him and his mother and, now that he was older, he tried to keep it that way—because it was so terrible and so intimate.

I turned to look at him. "It *was* only once, remember," I said. "There's been months and months of nothing."

In Meg's kitchen, her lost battle was marked out by a trail of half-empty coffee cups. The one by the phone was still full, and signaled the moment of defeat. "I hate you for knowing when to stop," she had once told me.

I harvested the cups and washed them up, scrubbing angrily at their brown, scummy rims. Through the window, I watched a vixen slide along the darkened flower bed. She was thinner than a London fox. They say that foxes are safest in the city, but I wonder if they are plagued by a genetic memory of the past. Do they miss the smell of corn in high summer, the crispness of frosted grass?

I left the mugs to drain and found Chloe slumped at the kitchen table beside a glass of apple juice. I bent over and kissed her. She smelled of shampoo and her soft cheeks were slippery with face cream.

She rubbed her eyes. "Couldn't really sleep," she

said. "Is Aunt Meg OK?"

I trod warily. Will and I had been clever enough to hide the worst of Meg's excesses from our daughter. Chloe was still too young to be told the absolute truth, but too old to be lied to. "Fine."

She looked anxious and a little bewildered. With her fair hair and dark eyes, she was a smaller, infinitely more delicate version of Will. One day she would be beautiful and that promise gave me deep, unqualified pleasure. "Did you and Dad enjoy the play?"

"It was brilliant; we had a lovely evening."

She polished off the apple juice. "It's nice that you two went out together."

"Did you do all your homework?"

She shrugged irritably. "Brigitte stood guard and I told her to get lost . . . but I did it."

Brigitte was our temporary au pair-cum-housekeeper, who took her duties very seriously.

"Tea?"

She shook her head.

"Bed, then." I pulled her to her feet, hustled her upstairs and settled her. I hunkered down beside her and whispered, "Everything's fine."

Chloe closed her eyes. "Do I really have to go to Pearl Veriker's funeral tomorrow?"

"Dad says we must. No argument."

"It's not fair," Chloe hissed. "Just because you have to do all these ghastly things, you make me as well."

"Go to sleep."

I hovered for a minute or two outside her room. Poor Chloe. She would learn that every shared life, every sep-

16

arate life, has bloodstained patches and tattered remnants of compromise. Sometimes, too, the dull ache of small martyrdom.

Will was already in bed and I slid in beside him. "Chloe woke up. I've tucked her back in."

"Good." He hesitated. "Is she . . . is Meg all right?"

"Sleeping."

"What triggered her off do you think?"

I thought about it. "She and Rob talked on the phone about money, but I suspect that it had something to do with our anniversary."

Our conversation went round and round on the subject of Meg. As it always did. Will scratched his head. "I would give much to think that Meg was happy and sorted out." He turned to me. "She has a lot to thank you for, Fanny. So do I."

My feelings for Meg could be ambivalent, but being thanked by Will was sweet.

He stirred restlessly. "What do you think is best, Fanny?" he said. "Do you think we should arrange more help for her? Could you manage to do that?"

"I could, but it might be better if you could talk to her. Maybe she needs a bit of your attention."

He thought about this. "I haven't got the time at the moment. But I will when I can. I promise."

I used to dream of a big, generous, blowsy household where children rustled and murmured in the bedrooms— two, three, even four of them. And every night, I would do the rounds. "This is Millie," I would say, smoothing fair tangles away from her face. "This is Arthur," removing the thumb from his mouth. "And *this* . . . this one is Jamie, the terror."

But it had not happened that way. After Chloe there were no more babies. My body pulled and strained to obey my longings, but it could not do what I asked of it. Sometimes they haunt me, my nonchildren—those warm, sleeping, rosy bodies, the children-who-never-were—and I listen out for them playing under the eaves.

"I don't mind," Will said to me once. "We have Chloe, that's enough. We look after her. I look after you. You look after me, Fanny. *Be content, please.*"

"Don't you mind at all?" I asked.

He touched my cheek. "I mind for you. I mind anything that hurts you."

Yet, as it turned out, my household was full, and we had been happy. First Chloe was born, and I was catapulted into the terror and mystery and exultation of a love that would never die. Then Meg came to live with us; Sacha too, after his sixteenth birthday. The au pairs came and went; the party workers slipped in and out, each leaving a ghostly imprint on the atmosphere, their rustles and murmurs dissolving into the general murmur of life.

Chapter 2

BEARING A TRAY WITH a breakfast of mashed banana, toast and tea, I knocked on Meg's bedroom door. There was a muttered "Come in."

The room stank of whiskey. Meg was lying on her side, and I drew back the curtains.

She flung an arm across her eyes. "I suppose yet another apology is needed."

"Only if you wish."

"I don't." She struggled upright.

I handed her a cup of tea. "Get that down you."

Between mouthfuls, she asked, "Is Sacha OK?"

"He kept watch. He's probably asleep."

Meg gave a wry smile. "Sacha says he writes his songs late at night. He says his mind is more receptive and fertile then."

"Does he?" I knew what Sacha meant. When I was feeding Chloe as a baby, those small hours of the night provided strange, heightened interludes where, the baby at my breast, I was free from busyness, and at liberty to grope my way toward some sort of clarity and knowledge.

"Why do I do it to him, Fanny?"

It was not the first time Meg had asked the question; nor, if both of us were honest, was it likely to be the last. I followed the uneven progress of the cup to her lips. "Would you like more help? We can organize it."

She cut me off. "Nope. Done it. It's up to me now. Battered, unreliable old me."

"Please don't, Meg."

"Don't worry," she said quickly. "It won't happen again."

I sat down at the end of the bed. "What about Sacha and Will?"

She grimaced.

"Shouldn't be drinking tea on an empty stomach. It doesn't like it." I cut the toast into squares and handed her one.

Meg edged the cup onto the bedside table. "So many people to fuss and worry over, Fanny. It must positively warm your heart."

"*Stop* it."

"Sorry, didn't mean it."

At times like this, Meg took pleasure in driving me, or whoever was coping with her, to the edge, but we both knew the boundaries of our coexistence. Meg wanted love and a place in the family. Like Will with his passion to change the world for the better, I wanted to help, and somehow, muddling along, we had managed to keep a balance.

She looked up and said softly, "I'm a good cause, the kind you like. The best, because I'm unredeemable. So none of you can blame yourselves when the worst happens." She dropped the half-eaten toast back on the plate. "Go away, Fanny. Go and be busy and keep everything in order."

I removed the tray from her lap. "Rob rang this morning."

"So? I talked to him yesterday."

"He forgot to remind you that it's Sacha's birthday at the weekend. He wanted to know what you were doing about it."

Meg buried her face in her hands. "What have I done?"

I bent down, picked up her discarded sweater and trousers and placed them on the chair. "Will and I are busy today. We'll see you later."

"It's all Rob's fault," she muttered. "If he'd stayed

married to me, I might have got through."

At my wits' end, I whirled round. "Meg, you *drove* him to it. He fell in love with Tania out of exhaustion."

"I'm sick," she said flatly. "He should have tried harder. You shouldn't give up on sick people."

"Have I ever given up on you?" I asked.

"You've *wanted* to. Be honest."

We stared at each other. Meg was the first to drop her gaze but only because she knew she was the victor. She knew she had made it impossible for me to walk out of the room.

I drew up a chair, manipulated the banana onto the spoon and handed it to her. "Eat."

A smile hovered at the corner of her mouth, but her eyes darted toward the whiskey bottle in the wastepaper basket before she parted her lips.

Meg and Will's parents killed themselves in a spectacular car crash. The tangle of wreckage made it almost impossible to say who had been driving but, in some respects, it was irrelevant. Both were alcoholics, and the blood tests indicated that neither of them should have been at the wheel.

The children were cared for by grandparents too aged to cope. Four years older than Will, Meg had ended up cooking, cleaning, protecting and directing. She teased out Will's halting French verbs, wrestled with his algebra and, by the time he left home to train as a barrister, had forgotten about herself. "It was as if there was a vacuum inside me, sucking up the person that was me," she confided, soon after she moved in with us, "and

I could only fill it one way."

When she married Rob, another barrister, the drinking had been sly, furtive, but apparently under control. After Sacha was born, and the strains of marriage to a busy man became clear, Meg began to slip. Eventually, Rob said he could no longer live with her. Then he informed her he'd found someone else who would look after him and Sacha properly.

"It was the 'properly' that really hurt," said Meg.

"Meg became my mother and my father," Will said, when he asked me if she could come and live with us. "She gave up everything to make sure that I was all right."

He raked his fingers through his hair in the way that both amused me and made my stomach flutter. Any mention of his early life always made Will go still and quiet and he did now. I remember cupping his face between my hands. "You're with me," I reminded him and watched the dark eyes warm into life under my touch.

An hour later, all three of us were in the car on the way to Pearl Veriker's funeral.

We were a little late and Will drove fast. "You are very quiet. Are you all right?"

Chloe was sitting in the back, picking at the cuticles of her left hand, which, at the last count, sported five silver rings, including the thumb ring that Sacha had brought back from his last gig up north. "Mum's cross with Aunt Meg," she said.

"Not cross," I said.

"Could you cheer up then?"

Chloe fiddled with her seat belt. "Why did you make me come, Dad? It's ridiculous."

"Chloe, I'm talking to your mother, or trying to. Is there a problem, Fanny?"

When I married Will, I was too young to know how the little evasions and dishonesties shore up the everyday. Our partnership was to have been a translucent stream into which we would both gaze and from which we would both draw nourishment. This had been the blueprint, but I had no idea that casting my net into that sparkling water would also yield . . . not the plump, pink-fleshed truth but a shoal of tiny white lies and, occasionally, a sharp-fanged black one.

"I'm fine," I said.

"Good," said Will. "I have a favor to ask. Could you sit in on the next two Saturday surgeries? The Diary Secretary has double booked."

I closed my eyes. My Saturday morning would be spent listening, on Will's behalf, to small histories of everyday injustice—hospital negligence, an intolerable neighbor, an erroneous gas bill.

"Can you, Fanny?"

I opened my eyes. "Of course."

Will parked the car in front of the church, and Chloe groaned theatrically.

Pearl Veriker had been chairman of the party association and, in the early days, had been the bane of my life. Her coffin must have been heavy, for the undertakers had difficulty maneuvering it down the aisle. An arrangement of red roses and green euphorbia rested on its top, and the vicar was robed in gold and white. Pearl, a born bully, was going to meet her Maker in a suitably colorful manner.

I sat between Chloe on one side, who continued to pick at her cuticles in a mutinous fashion, and Matt Smith on the other. Matt Smith was the new Chairman of the Association, and sported degrees from Warwick and Harvard University and a lot of experience in think tanks. He dressed in linen suits, collarless shirts and lace-up boots and talked about shifting voting patterns and focus groups. He was, he maintained, a professional.

Above the altar there was a stained-glass window of a procession of pilgrims making for a distant Paradise. The halos that hovered above a couple of the men suggested that they had already made it to sainthood. Others, women, had long since given up hope of reaching the final destination. I had sat in the church many times. As a bride, I had liked the bold-looking knight who led from the front. Now I preferred the tiny dog that lagged behind the nun. But I worried about all of them. The mother in me knew they would need some clean clothes, a pillow and a milky good-night drink.

My hat, large brimmed, black and not *too* witty—purchased in Harrods especially for these occasions—was a little tight. "Darling, your head has swelled from all the praise," Will had said as I struggled to put it on before leaving the house.

He had been taken aback when, not knowing quite why, I turned on him and blazed, "I've earned it, Will."

He'd backtracked fast. "Yes. Of course you have."

Aware that I was being scrutinized, I adjusted the

brim, which brought my view of the opposite pew into better focus. It was part of my function to be scrutinized, and I had chosen my outfit with care: a slim-fitting black suit that did not shriek extravagance, modestly heeled shoes, and a warm, friendly lipstick. The effect was smart, clever (but not *too* clever), and spoke of a woman of confidence and conviction who had been broken in to the job. A Good Wife. I knew this because it had taken several attempts, and not a few discarded outfits, to get it right.

Will nudged me to attention. It was kindly and affectionately, rather than imperiously, meant. We functioned on nudges, my husband and I, little jabbing reminders of our duty, our tasks, our partnership. In the early days, I gave the nudges, too. Now, for various reasons, I was more of a nudgee—but I reckoned that, in time, that would change too.

I let my hand rest against his thigh, knowing that, with this subversive, suggestive touch, I would unsettle him.

The congregation sang, "I Vow to Thee My Country," and Will delivered a graceful address. I listened with only half an ear. The private secretary had previously rung me and asked for my contribution. "She had a great heart," I suggested, for in the end I had grown fond of her.

"Fanny," Will commented later. "Was that quite the right term?"

Again, I had turned on him without warning: "Don't say anything more, Will . . ."

He did as he was asked but he was a little bewildered, a little rattled.

After the service, Chloe vanished—to meet Sacha, I suspected, for the cousins shared an affinity and they craved nothing so much as each other's company. Thick as thieves, said Meg. Will and I went home, and Mannochie came, too. This was normal. Along with everyone else, Will's agent had been absorbed—somehow—into the running of our household. "He's your *real* wife," I joked with Will, more than once.

I went upstairs to change, paused on the landing and leaned on the window sill. Like many things, the view out of the faux Gothic window had changed since we first moved into the house. One of the two fields we overlooked had been sold for development and was now home to twenty four-bedroom houses. The second field had survived for the time being, and the rooks still cawed and swirled above the clump of beeches.

Occasionally, we were invited into other homes where interior decoration was taken more seriously than in ours, houses that provided the frames for rich, rare materials that breathed expense, with walls that gleamed with authentic paints. Ours was plain, straightforward fare, a last-minute stab at Victorian Gothic, ugly in places, painted in colors from the local hardware store. It was utilitarian and solid; I had never loved it, never sought to pretty it up or to make it smart. We jogged along, the house and I.

The one exception was our bedroom, which I had taken pains to make as fresh and elegant as possible. I wanted it to be the place where Will and I felt entirely at ease, which gave us pleasure to be in—the place where we could shed the busyness and preoccupations of the day and make contact after our absences.

I sat down at the dressing table and brushed out my hair, flattened from the hat. Increasingly, the mirror recorded the evidence of forty years (plus a little bit more), but that did not depress me too much. I wanted to feel that I had lived fully and, if I was lucky, to have found a certain grace. I leaned forward and inspected my face. The eyelashes were fine.

On the way out, I pulled the bedspread straight. It was especially lovely—a traditional American quilt, sent by my mother, Sally, it was aged and faded but still exquisitely stitched, and never failed to delight.

Downstairs in the kitchen, Mannochie was making a pot of tea and Will was talking on the phone. By now Mannochie felt he was one of the family so it was no surprise when he offered me cake from my own tin. "Brigitte made it especially for you two," I said. I cut two slices and dropped the knife into the sink, well out of reach. Otherwise, I would have given in to temptation and had some, too. And a girl, no a *woman,* had to watch her figure. I watched Mannochie bite into it and imagined how the sugary crumbs would dissolve on his tongue.

"How's your son?" I asked, which I knew would please him.

Mannochie failed to suppress a smile. "Turning out to be quite a gymnast. And the fastest runner in the school."

Information on the Mannochie home life was not often released, even after an unexpectedly late marriage, which had produced a pale, thoughtful child who fetched up from time to time at the house to be fed fish fingers at the kitchen table.

Will put down the phone and discussed Matt Smith. We agreed that Matt was a very different kettle of fish from Pearl, who had been from the old school.

"He's keen on putting forward women and minorities," offered Mannochie.

I looked at Will. "You'd better watch it."

Will sent me another of his private signals—a tiny lift of the eyebrows—that meant: "Share the joke." Or "You're right." Or "Thank you." Or sometimes all three.

It was eight o'clock on Monday morning and downstairs line two, the line reserved for constituents, was buzzing. This was not unusual.

"You answer." Will's voice was thick with sleep. He hunched over in the bed and dragged the duvet round his shoulders. *Go away, world.* He did that rather well.

I had pulled on my jeans but not yet reached the sweater stage. The morning chill brushed my cheeks as I padded downstairs. Many things were required of me but dealing with a constituent before I was dressed was not top of my list of enthusiasms.

"Mrs. Savage . . ." The voice was familiar.

"Hallo, Mr. Tucker. Where are you phoning from?"

"From number-nine heaven."

Mr. Tucker changed his location according to which medication he had been taking. "Mr. Tucker, are you alone?"

"You're never alone, Mrs. Savage. I want to complain about the lack of angels in Stanwinton."

This seemed a rather admirable complaint. "Do you

28

remember, Mr. Tucker? We dealt with that one last week."

Voices in the background urged Mr. Tucker to put down the phone and come along. "Good-bye, Mr. Tucker. It was nice to talk to you."

Mr. Tucker resided on a planet of his own but, as Will pointed out, a vote was a vote. "You mean, the staff taking care of Mr. Tucker will vote for you," I said. " 'That *nice* man Mr. Savage . . . never too busy.' "

"Exactly. Anyway, an MP should listen to the dotty as well as the sane."

"I thought you only had to do that when Parliament's in session," I said.

Cleaning materials were strewn all over the hall floor, which indicated that Maleeka was already in. Maleeka was my angel and my savior, and other wives—especially my friends—hated me for her. You can envy another woman's beauty or her mind, but you only truly hate her if her house is clean and shining. Of distant Arab extraction—hence her name—Maleeka was a Bosnian refugee whose husband had been left behind to fight, and she had fetched up in Will's surgery begging for work. Will sent her on to me. "Mrs. Savage, I have two daughters and four grandchildrens to make food for," she said. What could I say except here was someone who really needed my help?

During the first week of her regime, she smashed two china figurines and dropped bleach onto the landing carpet. The navy blue pile now sported three almost perfect white circles. "Look on them as symbols of our commitment," I told Will who had been a little slow to

29

appreciate the point.

Yet if dust, disorder and mess flickered through the rooms of the house and had to be routed on a regular basis, Maleeka maintained a firm perspective on the family chaos. "Izt *safe* here," she said. "Izt good."

I picked my way through a flotsam of bleach, polish and dusters and tracked their source to the kitchen, where she was kneeling with her head in the oven—a position not a few wives have, from time to time, considered. "Izt bad, Mrs. Savage." Her voice was muffled. "Very bad."

She meant the oven but the remark had a general application.

I boiled the kettle and made some toast. "Come and eat, Maleeka." I knew she went short of food so the rest of the family had enough. *Tengo famiglia,* as Alfredo, my Italian father, would say. "Hold the family safe, Francesca. We may be sinners and failures but that is one thing that we must do." On that point, Maleeka and my father were perfectly matched.

She was on her third piece of toast when Will appeared, followed by a cross and late Chloe.

"Dad, could you give me a lift?"

He glanced at his watch and Chloe said: "Oh, don't bother," and slammed out of the back door and ran for the school bus.

"She could have said good-bye." Will looked hurt. "And she's had no breakfast."

"It's all right. I put a yogurt in her bag."

However late we had been to bed, Will always managed to look freshly minted and ready. It was one of his infuriating characteristics. Maleeka crammed the remainder of the toast into her mouth and leaped to her feet. "Mornings Mr. Savage. I get on."

After breakfast, Will and I did a check on our diaries. "Can you make drinks for the European and Commonwealth finance ministers on the seventeenth? And dinner for the same lot on the twenty-first of July?"

"I've got a homeless persons meeting on the morning of the seventeenth. But if the traffic is OK, I'll make a dash for it."

Will tried not to smile. "Don't be nasty. Will you be sure to chat up Antonio Pasquale? Use your dazzling Italian. I need to make sure that he's on board. But you will go carefully?"

"Will, look at me. What do you see?"

He leaned over and cupped my chin with a hand. "You, of course." He wore his busy-busy expression but his eyes were soft and, as usual, I melted.

What did I see? His hair was shorter now than it had been when I'd first met him, but he had a much better haircut. His jaw line was rather tauter than his waistline these days . . . but no, I won't go into that. And those dark eyes still lit up, from time to time, with a combination of idealism and the hint of vulnerability that he was careful to show only to those he loved.

Not bad, I thought appreciatively. Over the years Will had shed a certain innocence. But so had I—so had everyone. We were warier, more realistic, pathetically grateful for the small triumphs of a policy implemented, a constituent satisfied. We knew our limitations better— oh, much, *much* better. We knew, too, for we had discussed it, that as that innocence slipped away, personal ambition had grown in direct proportion.

"How long have I been here for you?"

He had the grace to look disconcerted. "I just have to be sure. We can't afford any wobbles. Otherwise we get dumped on."

He meant the press. Not for the first time, I thought how curious it was that treachery and dissent were longer lasting in their effects than loyalty . . . or fidelity.

No, scrub that. The last thought caught me unawares, which it did from time to time, but I had learned to live with it.

"Trust me," he said.

"Should I?"

He yawned theatrically. "Am I being pompous?"

In politics, or anywhere where power was the prize, it was hard to keep the layers of oneself glued together, and it was hard not to run with the hares. I understood that perfectly.

He got to his feet. "For goodness' sake drive a pin into me if I get fat, boring or pompous." He looked briefly appalled. "On second thought, perhaps you'd better not."

"Would it be that easy to burst the bubble?"

He bent over and whispered, "Only you know the answer to that."

Outside in the drive, the ministerial car nosed to a halt with a discreet toot of the horn. Will shoved his papers into his briefcase. "See you Friday."

I sat quite still. Will's hand pressed into my shoulder. "Fanny . . . the question of Meg."

"Is she a question?"

Meg had never been a question. She had always been a fact. A hard fact that sat at the center of our marriage.

The pressure on my shoulder became almost intolerable. "No," he replied. "No, she isn't."

I went upstairs to our bedroom, which smelled unaired and threw open the window. A man in a bright orange jacket was walking up the road. He looked neither sad nor happy. Just indifferent.

I realized that's how I felt.

I made the bed and pulled my mother's quilt over it. With a forefinger, I traced the tree hung with red cherry blossoms. One of its flower bracts had been unevenly sewn and I often wondered why. Had it been a gesture of rebellion, misery or that same indifference?

Will's clothes from the previous week were stacked on the chair and I set about sorting them. Nowadays, his ties were made of silk and his shirts were soft and expensive. I sat down on the bed to remove the battens from the collars and buried my face in the material. It smelled of Will, the Will I had always loved.

"Fanny, are you there?" Without knocking, Brigitte stuck her head around the door.

Guiltily, I dropped the shirt. Although she was only a temporary feature of the Savage household (I had employed her to help out for a couple of months during the summer), I was thoroughly in awe of Brigitte who came from deepest Austria and was a fully paid-up member of the Green Party.

"The shopping list, Fanny, I cannot find it."

"Of course." I reached for the notebook that was always beside my bed, tore off the top page and handed it to her.

Brigitte scanned it. "You forgot the polish. I don't forget. Or the bread." She gestured with her large, capable hands in a way that expressed her determination to ensure that the Savage ménage remained provisioned. "I'll take the laundry."

She brushed past me, swept up the clothes and marched downstairs, where the sound of raised voices indicated a brief territorial squabble with Maleeka.

Chapter 3

As we were now in the countdown to Chloe's final, crucial exams before she went to university, she and I sat down with the calendar. We marked off the days when she was at school and when the school released her to study at home.

We constructed a routine for the home days. Up at seven A.M. ("Mum, have mercy.") Breakfast, followed by three hours of hard labor, with a break for coffee mid-morning. Lunch twelve forty-five prompt, more study, a break for tea and then sign off work at six o'clock.

"Looks good." She pinned the timetable to the already overflowing notice board. "You will keep me on the straight and narrow?" Her voice quivered, just a little.

"Try and stop me." When Chloe set her heart on something, and she had set her heart on doing well, she usually did it. "She's being terrific," I reported back to Will. "It's just a question of peace and quiet and no interruptions."

"Sounds like heaven," he said.

With the prospect of a few quiet weeks ahead, I made my own plans, which included writing up my notes from my researches into Chilean wines, which I promised my father I would do before he embarked on his monthly orders for his wine business, and turning out the china cupboard and dispatching Brigitte to the supermarket with a long list.

It was a Chloe home day and the kitchen was steamy and fragrant with frying meat and garlic. Occasionally, I cocked an ear for signs of life upstairs, but it was reassuringly silent. I packed up a stew and a chicken pie and divided macaroni and cheese into two dishes and slotted them into the freezer. Then I called up from the foot of the stairs: "Tea break, Chloe."

She emerged slowly out of her room, and my heart turned over for she looked so white and tired and terrified. "Sweetie pie, what's up?"

Abruptly, Chloe sat down at the top of the stairs and dropped her head into her hands. "I hate history."

I ran up and sat down beside her and drew her close. She snuggled against me and giggled. "Bit of a squash, Mum."

I stroked her cheek. "Is it exam nerves? Or did you read too late last night?" I longed to protect my daughter from all the things that, in the future, would cause her pain. I nuzzled the top of her head. "Tea. And then why don't you wash your hair and I'll dry it?"

Chloe's hair reached her waist. We had endless conversations about whether she should cut it or not, and enormous amounts of effort went into its grooming. At present, she had two hairdryers, a pair of straightening tongs and a cupboard full of shampoos.

"Would you, Mum? Thanks."

I led her down to the kitchen and made us tea and I was about to inquire—tentatively—whether it was the Russian revolution or Henry VIII's marital adventures that had given her such trouble when she said, "Mum, do you think I could have a facial? You know, to help me look good for the summer?"

"I don't see why not."

She inspected her bitten nails. "I will have to take more care of my appearance," she said. "Would Dad increase my allowance?"

We were in the middle of a comfortable conversation about beauty routines when Mannochie stuck his head through the open window. "Can I come in?"

"Oh, for God's sake," said Chloe crossly. "I so am fed up with that man. He so lives here." She flounced out of the kitchen and, a few seconds later, the world-war thump thump of one of Sacha's records started up in her bedroom.

Mannochie came in and apologized for interrupting. "Will asked me to drop in since I would be passing," he explained. "It looks as though he's in a spot of bother for not registering a perk in the Commons book and the newspapers are going to publish details tomorrow."

"What perk? I don't know of any? You and I know that Will is as straight as a die."

"Apparently, he accepted the use of the Chairman's chauffeur-driven car on a fact-finding sortie to a weapon's factory in Watford. And back."

"And *back?*" I was amused. "How much worse can it get?"

But Mannochie did not think it was funny. He was of the opinion that the bad publicity could be damaging. "Will is only one of several involved but cozy relationships between ministers and the selling of weapons can always be whipped up by the press. He would like you to come up to London. Bit of hand holding, that sort of thing."

"Let me get this straight. Will is in the soup for having accepted a lift to *Watford?* He's slipping. It should have been to Bangkok." I got to my feet. "I'll ring him and tell him I can't. I have Chloe to think about."

Mannochie appeared to weigh up the pros and cons. "I am only passing on the request. . . ."

I made a brief mental note of the number of times a bit of hand holding wouldn't have gone amiss with me. "I can't leave Chloe at the moment, Mannochie."

His phone trilled.

"Will . . ." Mannochie looked up at me. "Yes, I'm here. Fanny feels she must stay with Chloe." He put his hand over the receiver. "Will says, please will you come?"

"I can't. Tell him Chloe needs me here."

Mannochie relayed the message, but Will was obviously agitated and, after listening in for a moment, I asked him to give me the phone.

"Darling," I said. "It's tricky. Chloe needs one of us here. She's getting a bit wobbly."

"Couldn't Meg cope? I'm sure Chloe wouldn't mind,

just for a night. She wouldn't want you to let me down."

"I don't think this is something for Meg, and I can't let Chloe think she's second best right now."

I indicated to Mannochie that he should help himself to tea, and went into the hall for a bit more privacy. "You can tough it out," I said soothingly. "You always tough it out."

"Of course I can tough it out. I just prefer it when you tough it out with me."

I was conscious that Chloe was hovering at the top of the stairs.

"Was there a problem?" she asked later as I helped her to dry her hair.

"Dad wanted me up in London. He's run into a spot of bother."

"But you said you wouldn't go, didn't you?" She looked up at me, urgent and appealing. "You said you had to be here to help me stick to the timetable, right?"

I switched off the dryer and ran a comb through Chloe's damp hair, which still curled at the ends. "Perhaps you haven't noticed, but I am here."

By the next day, the furor had died down, and Will's small transgression had paled to insignificance beside the greater transgressions of a couple of his colleagues who, it appeared, had been taking money in return for asking questions in Parliament.

The first words I ever heard Will utter were: "No more government waste. No more schools that betray their children, or hospitals that kill their patients. Ladies and gentlemen, I see these wrongs, daily, in my work as a barrister. I know how the trusting, the innocent and the deprived can suffer. I know how much they need a champion."

He stopped, thought for a moment. "Ladies and gentlemen, I consider politics to be a means of building a bridge between what we feel to be just and right in our private lives and putting them into practice in public life. . . ."

It was a bitter January afternoon and I had nipped into Stanwinton town hall to escape the cold, rather than wait at the station for the train I was due to catch, and stumbled on the meeting. I read the papers, of course, but I had only a vague knowledge of politics and my interests were focused on learning about wine—a huge, huge subject—and helping my father to run the business. I had a social life, parties to go to, films to see, business travel with my father . . . what did I need with politics?

Will was speaking as the adopted candidate for his party. At the very earliest, a general election was not due until the spring, but he was making himself known in what I later learned was a carefully constructed program.

I remember thinking: Does he mean what he says? But as I gazed at a tall figure with hair the color of corn in high summer, and at features that were lit by humor and passion, I became convinced that he did, and I was possessed by a sudden, intense hunger to find out who he was. I mean, who he *really* was.

Every so often, the flow of his words slowed a little, as if he wanted to consider absolutely the honesty of what he was promising. He shoved a hand into his pocket. Removed it. Placed it on the lectern. Every movement exerted a strange, hypnotic pull and I could not take my eyes off him. I made up my mind there and then that he was beautiful—fine and well made, yes, and the extremes of coloring intriguing. Yet there was also something else. . . . A hint of sensuality, a slight suggestion of ruthlessness, a subtlety that excited me.

I remember, too, that after the speech, as I made my way boldly toward him to introduce myself, I was stopped by a woman in red.

"Can I help? I'm Will Savage's sister."

She looked me up and down. "I'm afraid he will have to go in a moment," she said and shrugged. "Tough schedule." But she smiled conspiratorially, and her face came alive in a way that matched her brother's. "I'm sure he would like to meet you."

A minute or so later, Will accepted my outstretched hand and said, "I hope you found the meeting interesting." But his eyes widened. It was the shock of recognition. Yet there was no surprise on my part. You see, I already knew. I knew.

From time to time, it happened. I saw something— and it could be trifling—a handbag or a piece of clothing in a shop window—or I encountered someone and sensed that the form, shape and texture of that object or person, matched an element in me. It was neither greed nor imperial conquest: It was, rather, a kind of possession with which I could not argue, and I had learned the sooner it was acknowledged the better.

I think he knew that, too.

Meg touched his elbow. "Will . . . the time . . ."

He pushed her away, very gently, but firmly.

"Look . . . this is odd . . ." He paused, and my feelings—wild and hopeful—rippled and pulsed like electricity. "What I mean is . . . when can you meet me tomorrow?"

Six weeks later, I took him home to meet my father.

Halfway up the drive of Ember House where my father lived, Will slammed on the brakes. "Just a minute, Fanny . . . have I got this wrong?"

Will was twenty-eight and I was twenty-three, and both of us were aware this was a moment of great importance—more important than taking off our clothes in front of each other for the first time. Both of us were nervous.

"You didn't mention that you lived in a stately home." Will wound down the car window and gesticulated wildly at the drive. As it happened, the drive was looking at its best, flanked by clumps of anemones and crocuses, which were so much nicer than the pushy, blowsy azaleas that took over later and drowned it in pinks and reds.

I was already sensitive to how seriously Will had to consider his image; not something he cared for, he hastened to assure me, but the party apparatchiks were manic about certain aspects of how he presented himself to the electorate, including being careful to look ordinary—"to connect with the people." For my part, I was conscious that I knew nothing yet about this new, strange world.

At our snatched meetings . . . sandwiched between his commitments in the barristers' chambers and at court, plus the photo calls, sponsored walks and chicken lunches, and mine—client meetings, negotiating with suppliers, choosing the wines for the seasonal tasting cases—Will explained that he was committed to working for a society where people made their way by merit and not by privilege.

I hastened to reassure him. "The big house was knocked down in the fifties, and replaced by a much smaller one. The drive is the only bit left of the original grounds. My father bought it at a knock-down price when he set up the business. Nobody wanted it, the poor thing. You needn't worry." I was gabbling. "We're not rich, not at all. We're practically poor."

Will gave me one of his intense looks. "No need to go to the other extreme."

I blushed, and my pulses thudded.

Falling in love with such suddenness and abandon had cut the ground from beneath my feet. It left me breathless and palpitating. It puzzled and—almost— frightened me, this violent, sweet, sharp, desperate emotion.

Will's knuckles whitened. "I hope I make a good impression."

Now I was the confident one. "Just don't pretend to know about wine, that's all."

He grinned. "Political suicide."

Father waited for us in the sitting room with Caro, his mistress of ten years. After Caro had come into his life, the interior of the house took a turn for the better. Caro had given it a more settled touch: a cushion here, a chair repositioned there, a pot of white hyacinths in the spring, or a lamp that cast a subtler light. They were only minor, these touches, but so effective.

"I hope you don't mind," Caro had said to me when she first arrived. I was fourteen and, at that time, almost feral in my dislike of this newcomer to the house, and my terror at how quickly things could change, just like that. Caro had laughed and flipped back her hair, which had been long and naturally blond then. She'd been so sure of her position as the woman likely to marry my father that she was careless of my reply.

Five years or so later when we had become friends and Caro was no nearer her goal, she turned to me and said bitterly, "Alfredo never notices what I do."

I saw myself reflected in her large, pleading eyes, and I was angry with my father and sick at the thought that I had made her unhappy in the past. But it was not a subject I could talk to him about easily.

It was a cold day, and my father was in his usual position in front of the fire. I led Will up to him and introduced them.

"Ah," he said in his driest fashion, and my father could, at times, be so dry, and my heart sank, "the politician."

In reply, Will could have said, might well have said, "Ah, the self-made man," which would have described my father perfectly, but his polite rejoinder managed to include Caro, who was sitting on the sofa. Will was good like that.

At dinner, we drank a Sauvignon Blanc from Lawson's Dry Hill in New Zealand. Will barely touched his, prompting a slight frown to appear on my father's face.

After eating, we had coffee in the sitting room and

discussed how Will would fare at the coming election. Every so often, Will glanced in my direction. My father was polite, but I could see that Will's worldly ambitions were of no real interest to him. It was Will's other ambitions, the ones that concerned me, that my father was weighing up in his fierce, protective way.

I took refuge in the practical and reached for the coffee pot and refilled the cups. As I bent over my task, I blessed fortune, luck, whoever, whatever, had been responsible for my decision to take refuge in the town hall where Will was speaking.

He came over to stand by me and held out his hand. "Fanny?"

I took it and sprang to my feet. Will turned to my father. "We have something to tell you. Fanny and I have decided to get married."

My father rocked back on his feet, as if he had been dealt a blow. He looked at me and I knew that I had hurt him by not letting him into my confidence.

"We decided last night," I explained.

"It's too quick," said my father. "You barely know each other."

Will slid his arm around me. "Swift, but sure."

Will sneaked into my bed in the small hours and I spent a wakeful night. It was still early when I decided to get up. I slid out of bed, leaving Will folded onto one side, one hand flung out. Foolishly, lovingly, I bent over and checked his breathing.

On the way down to the kitchen, I passed Caro's bedroom, which was opposite my father's. The door was open, the light was on and I put my head in to ask if she wanted some tea.

Clothes were littered across the bed, and Caro was shoving others into a suitcase. She raised her head and we stared at each other. I, rumpled and sated—she, beautifully dressed but desolate.

"Caro, what are you doing . . . ?" I closed the door behind me. "Why are you packing?"

Caro picked up a green sweater and folded it. "Fanny, the one good thing in this mess has been our friendship. That has been . . ." she blinked back tears. "It helped. Otherwise . . ." she shrugged. "It has been a waste of my time."

I removed a pile of shirts from the bed and sat down. "What on earth has made you decide this now?"

She fiddled with the sweater. "I've had enough. I've given Alfredo enough rope to hang an army on the subject of our getting married. And it's not going to work. I know it's stupid to worry about a piece of paper, but I do. I'm pretty ordinary that way."

I snatched the sweater away from her and pleated it between my fingers. The material was soft and expensive. "Caro, you've been together for such a long time."

She raised an anguished gaze to me. "All good things come to an end."

"Would you like me to talk to him?"

She shook her head. "No point."

"But you've been happy. I know you have."

"Let's see . . ." she ticked off the points. "Your father is kind enough to allocate me a very nice bedroom and a place at the table. I can order groceries and ask the cleaner to hoover the carpets. But that is it,

45

Fanny." She repossessed the sweater. "You won't understand yet, but it is not enough to look decorative when your father entertains. I want a real, live, working partnership. So . . ." She got up and packed the green sweater. "I am drawing a line under the last ten years. I am relying on you to tell him."

"But *you* must tell him."

At that, she sparked with anger. "No, you can give him chapter and verse." She wrenched one of her suitcases shut. "What's more, I am giving you your most useful wedding present."

I had no idea what she meant.

With a foot, she nudged the suitcase toward the door. "I'm showing you how to leave, Fanny. Remember it. It's a good lesson."

Will was sorry for them both, but rather approved of Caro's bid for self-definition, arguing that it was no use being carried along by others against your will.

He looked rather cruel (interestingly so) as we discussed it, and I hastened to say that I was sure there would be plenty of room to breathe in our marriage.

Chapter 4

"IS ANYTHING WRONG, FRANCESCA?"

My father was the only person who ever called me by my full name, and very little of what I felt or did escaped his scrutiny, which was sometimes critical, but always loving.

"Not really." I looked up from our scratch lunch of

mushroom soup and cheese in the dining room at Ember House. It was only five miles from our house and I wrestled him into the diary at least once a week.

The clock ticked reassuringly on the walnut sideboard and the blurred reflection of the blue and white fruit bowl beside it had the depth and stillness of a painting.

I speared a gobbet of dolce latte with my knife. How could I admit to this nagging, troubling dread of my daughter leaving home? Or the creeping . . . dullness? "Once Chloe's A-Levels are over, things will be easier."

"Are you quite sure?"

I managed a smile. "Just a cloud passing over the sun, Dad." I peered at him. Were there new lines on his face? And was his tweed jacket looser than the last time I saw him? He had always been bony. All his energy had gone into running his wine business—and into me, his only child. "Talking of which, I think you could do with some vitamins."

"Stop fussing," he said happily.

He tapped a finger against a bottle of Le Pin Pomerol—the gentlest and richest of clarets. "Think about this instead."

I don't know what my father thought about my situation, for there were some things about which he remained uncharacteristically guarded, but he didn't care who knew about his pride in Battista Fine Wines. A highly respected, idiosyncratic operation, it catered to a growing number of wine lovers who trusted my father to select a range of vintages on their behalf.

"Raoul put me on to it," he added, and shot me a look.

Raoul was the son of one my father's closest business

contacts, a premier Bordeaux negociant family called Villeneuve, and a friend. He had also been my first lover—but I don't think about that.

Yes, I do. Sometimes. I strain to catch the exact sensation, recapture the sear of my startled reaction. Not because I still want Raoul, but because I haven't quite worked out what went wrong exactly. I have not quite arrived at a resolution in my mind.

"How is he?"

"Expanding the business. Busy with family."

I smiled. "I'm glad," I said.

My father was an Italian refugee, brought to England from the village of Fiertino, north of Rome, by his widowed mother who fled the war and settled in the Midlands. The Villeneuves were wine aristocrats who lived in an exquisite château. My father and they made contact during the fifties and a close alliance developed despite their differences. That was the way with wine people.

After I had Chloe, and found it difficult to juggle all my commitments, Raoul took my place at my father's side for a while before returning to his family business. We still kept in touch. We still talked on the phone . . . oh, about many things.

We discussed why the French drank their vintages young and hopeful. We discussed oak casks, sandy soil, the amount of sun for that year, the use of technology in Australian and American wine making. The results? "Simplistic," concluded Raoul, the Frenchman. But perhaps that was not a bad thing. Clean, stable, sediment-free wine suited our age better than the muddy, sometimes fractious yields of the Old World.

We agreed that the finest wine defied categorization. Any reasonably intelligent observer, we said, could point to the best soil, position and climate, the necessity of keeping vigil until the grape trembled at the peak of ripeness and say, yes, that was the formula. But good wine, great and successful wine, like a marriage, was a glorious fusion of nature, substance and will. It was a product of patience, understanding and knowledge, of great passion and love, which could never quite be regulated or predicted. One sniff, one drop balanced on the tongue, is all it takes to exult the mind and flood the senses with the delirium of discovery.

My father poured two glasses of the Pomerol (the perfect collaboration of a Belgian vintner's inspiration and the merlot grape), and waited for me to ready my palate.

I accepted the glass, sniffed, took a mouthful, held its crimson ravishments on my tongue.

"Describe," he instructed.

"Flamboyant . . . and yet concentrated. A rich inner life."

My father was amused. "You, too, Francesca, I hope."

After I left school and I first began to work for him, traveling and learning, talking to clients, wine represented a mysterious combination of provenance, production and perception; I yearned to unlock its secrets and become proficient in its lore. But then I fell in love with it, and learned that wine was life, and for life. It was sun and warmth—it could be bitter, unfair, disappointing, but the possibilities of greatness always remained.

After we had finished eating, I went over the paperwork that I did for my father on a regular basis. It wasn't much, but it was the compromise we had worked out and it meant I kept my hand in.

"It's time you came back to work properly," said my father. "Now that Chloe's leaving home. I need the help, and you must be ready to take on the business one day." He looked expectantly at me from across the table. "After all, it's in your blood."

I felt an answering beat of excitement. I could best describe it as the quiver that accompanied the waking from a long and deep sleep. My father had hit on the right thing to say. Wine was in my blood.

He stacked together the papers in his brisk way. "Anyway, it's time I went back to Fiertino and I think you should come with me. We have left it too long."

"How many times have you said that?"

He looked a little shamefaced. "I mean it this time."

When I was three, my mother, Sally, absconded with Art, a real estate agent from Montana, where she still lived, and where I'd visited her every other summer until I married Will.

Unless it was absolutely necessary, my father never mentioned her. "She went," he said, "and that is that."

I picked over the imperfectly healed scars for years; my mother took with her far more than the clothes she had stuffed into two suitcases. For a start, she removed my belief that things were automatically strong and permanent. She shattered my father's notion of constancy and of the family, and I don't think he got over it. She left us warier and more fragile.

In place of a mother, my father summoned Benedetta

50

from Fiertino, and she lived with us until Caro took up residence in Ember House, which had been the cue for a thunder-browed, red-eyed Benedetta to pack her bags and return to Fiertino. Benedetta was a third cousin by marriage who sprang from a particularly tangled branch of the Battista family tree. She was dark haired, not as slender as she would have liked, and, while she ruled the house, held my father in check, which few could.

Bedtimes were usually reserved for my father's inexhaustible supply of Fiertino stories, which, it must be said, were a little different each time he told them. I enjoyed pouncing on the discrepancies. "But, Dad, you said the oxen were gray, not white." At which point he would tap my hand and say, "Don't be too clever, my darling," and continue.

"Fiertino is only a little town, but a town all the same. Ask Benedetta. She will tell you. It is in a valley north of Rome, which was originally lived in by the Etruscans, an ancient people who loved the good things in life. Chestnut trees grow on one slope; on the other, wheat, olives and vines. It has a square with a large church at one end, and a beautiful colonnaded walk around it, which gives very necessary shade from the sun. Our family, the Battistas, lived in the *fattoria,* the farm, just outside the town, and your grandfather was the *fattore.* He supervised the granaries and cellars, the oil presses and the dairy. We had our own vineyard and grew the Sangiovese grape."

Like the horn of plenty, the stories never appeared to be finished and Fiertino, and the idea of it, became synonymous with drowsiness and sleep. I heard about hot sun and the harvesting of olives, of the family house, the *fattoria,* which echoed to the shrieks and exchanges of large, extended, uninhibited family. I knew that the town had suffered badly in the war. I heard the story of the three-legged goat, the miraculous olive tree, the runaway Battista bride, and of the young wife who was murdered by her much older husband for taking a lover.

"You see, there is the code," my father said. He spoke in the present tense.

Curiously, we had not been there together. In fact, my father had returned only once, as a young man. We traveled everywhere else in the world, and we did business in the north of Italy but my father had never cared to go south to Fiertino. Partly, I suspect, this was because of Benedetta, who had wanted to marry him. But *that* was another story.

I checked my watch, and rose to leave. "OK. If you are serious this time, how about September, when Chloe is in Australia? I should be free then." I corrected myself. "I'll have to have a word with Will and Mannochie, but I'm due time off . . . ."

My father brightened in a way that caught my heart. "If you think that's possible, there's nothing I would like more."

I tried a bit of role reversal. "There is one condition. That you go and see a doctor for a checkup. I'll make the appointment. Then, I promise, we'll go to Fiertino. Just you and I."

My father looked guilty. "I've already been."

I raised an eyebrow. "And?"

"Just a shade of concern about the heart. He's given

me pills. So everything is fine . . . everything except I'm getting older, that's all."

Driving home, I turned on the radio and music filled the car.

"Quick, Fanny, before Benedetta sends you to bed. Tell me, which are the grapes grown in Tuscany?"

I pressed my cupped hand to his ear. "Sangiovese," I whispered.

"Good girl. Now, the big reds of Piedmont?"

"Dolcetto, Barbera, Nebbiolo . . ."

Wonderful Benedetta. Many times she scolded my father for heating up my poor little brain. *"Santa Patata, Alfredo, you are a cruel man." Santa Patata* was the nearest the devout Benedetta would allow herself to swearing. "The child is too young."

She need not have worried. My poor little brain was quite capable of sniffing out an opportunity to draw attention to myself. Anyway, I was being invited onto my father's territory. What the French—what Raoul—would call his *terroir.*

I know that *terroir* really means topsoil, drainage and climate. But to me it suggested something more profound and interesting—the territory of the heart.

Chloe greeted me from the kitchen as the front door clicked shut behind me. "Mum, I'm hungry."

"Grandpa sends his love." I opened the fridge door and extracted a fish stew.

"Not *fish,*" she said.

"Good for the brain. It's fish fish fish from now on."

53

Chloe bit her lip. "I feel about as keen on these exams as I did on Pearl Veriker's funeral."

"Just one last effort, sweetie, and then you're free. You'll be off to Australia and fretting about something different." I put the stew on to heat. "Do you think Sacha would like some?"

"Probably. He's been helping me to study." Chloe extracted knives and forks from the drawer. "He's so kind. He just *knows* things."

"Lots of people know things."

Chloe carefully positioned a fork on the table. "I do love him, you know, Mum."

"Of course," I said swiftly. "He's your cousin." I wanted to say, "Please be careful. Don't get into dangerous territory." Chloe did not lack friends—far from it. They swarmed in and out of the house, demanding coffee, meals, television, beds for the night, and yet it was Sacha to whom she turned. Darling, lovely Sacha, who dressed in leather and wore his beautifully clean hair in a crop that emphasized his bony but fine features.

"Chloe . . ." I began.

She cut me off. "Is it ready, Mum? I'm so hungry."

While Chloe and Sacha ate, I sipped a glass of cranberry juice—which my friend Elaine insisted cleansed the system. They discussed exam tactics and analyzed Chloe's little wobbles.

"All you need to do," said Sacha, "is to have a good idea when you've seen the question. Don't bother thinking up the ideas now, otherwise you'll try and fit the questions around them and that doesn't work."

As a principle for life, this seemed sound.

Chloe sent him one of her melting looks, and ate a huge plate of fish stew. I worked away at my system cleansing and thought how lovely it was just to be sitting here peacefully, listening to them.

Meg came into the kitchen. She looked groomed and well pressed, and her fair hair, in shades of light caramel, was twisted on top of her head. "Darlings," she said. "You should have summoned me from exile. I would have liked to join you." She sat down at the table. "It's been a bit of a lonely day. Everyone was out."

I was refilling my glass but I knew her gaze rested on me. "Be quiet," I wanted to say to her. "Please be quiet."

"Still, chores are good for the soul. And we all know that my soul needs a bit of a workout." Meg's expression held a touch of complacency and plenty of mischief. When no one made any comment, she said, "I *have* been good today."

Sacha sprang to his feet and the chair screeched across the tiles. "Why don't I make you a cup of coffee, Mum?"

Meg tapped the table with her exquisitely shaped nails—her hands were quite lovely and she kept them immaculate. "Coffee is so . . . *brown* . . ." she said. "But I guess I have to settle for it." Again she looked in my direction—and a shock of loathing suddenly pulsed through me. "Joke," she said.

Hatred is a curious emotion. It can be dulled with weariness, then spring into sharp, destructive life. Or, and this never fails to astonish me, it can sometimes go hand in hand with what can only be called affection. That's how I found it with Meg.

55

If I concentrated hard enough at such times, I could win the battle with myself. I looked directly at her. "That's a nice sweater," I said. "Is it new?"

She gave a little nod, as if to acknowledge my very small victory. "You look a bit frazzled, Fanny. Isn't it time you and Elaine had one of your outings? Weren't you planning a trip to Edinburgh? I can hold the fort here."

My emotions performed a neat volte-face. "That's a nice offer Meg."

"Oh Mum," cried Chloe. "Not till my exams are over. *Please* . . . don't go away. You said you wouldn't."

I laughed and slipped my arms around my beloved and quixotic daughter. "You know, I'm not going anywhere for the time being."

For some reason, Will's late-night call came through on the business line. "This is Mrs. Savage," I said. "And it's far too late to be phoning."

"You're completely right," said my husband. "You shouldn't be talking to strangers at this hour."

"You'd better put the phone down then." The words issued tartly from my mouth before I could stop them.

There was a second's silence. "It's not like you to sound so fed up. What is it? Have I done something?"

"Sorry."

Will tried again. "Can I help?"

I resisted the temptation to tell him he sounded as though he was dealing with one of his crankier constituents. "OK. This is the daily report. There are three photographs of you in the local press. One is not good, the others are fine. There is also a piece about the Hansard report, which shows how hard you're fighting for the constituency even though you're a minister."

He sighed rather wearily, which made me feel churlish. "What *is* wrong, Fanny?" he asked.

These days when I looked at Will, I no longer perceived the golden light that, when I first fell in love with him, had bathed him from head to foot. Now I saw differently and Will was only an element in a larger context: family, home, commitments. At fortysomething, I had learned many things, not the least to reshuffle the priorities. Perhaps that was better, certainly more rational. All the same, I mourned the golden light, I missed it, and the intensity of my hunger to find out what Will *was,* my passion to possess him, and for him to possess me.

"Fanny . . . ?"

I wanted to say that I wished he were at home more often. That he *should* be at home more often, before it started not to matter if he was or wasn't.

Instead I stuck to routine exchanges of information. "Meg is fine. Chloe is seesawing between terror and elation. Sacha is being . . . Sacha."

This appeared to satisfy Will. "Busy day tomorrow," he said, and I wondered if he realized that he said that most days.

"So have I." I wondered if he noticed that I said that most days.

"Good night, darling. Hope you are feeling more cheerful in the morning."

"Good night," I said.

Chapter 5

ON OUR HONEYMOON IN the Loire valley only five months after our first meeting, Will laid his head on my breast and said, "Your heartbeat is louder than a drum."

"And how many heartbeats have you listened to this closely?"

"Very few." He smiled. "Promise."

"That's good," I heard myself saying. "I don't want to have shared you with too many." I luxuriated in the feeling and the smell of him on my skin. "Do you think our heartbeats match?"

"Of course." He wrapped his arms tighter around me and said he had known they would as soon as he spotted me. "Five seconds is all it took. All right, perhaps *ten*."

"I saw you first." I kissed the damp, faintly salty hollow of his neck.

"Hussy," he said and made me lie still, and I looked up into the dark eyes and saw a life ahead, filled with possibilities, and thought how lucky I was.

On the third day of our honeymoon, we had lunch in one of those plush, well-manicured but sleepy villages by the Loire. It was hot for early June and the heat shimmered off the stone streets. The big, sleepy, shiny river murmured beneath the clatter of cutlery and chink of glasses.

Will did not eat much. Eventually, he dug into his pocket for his cigarettes. Officially he was a nonsmoker, and would never do so in public—except in France, which was "different." In fact, he was very fond of white-filtered American cigarettes, and it made me smile then that a testament of our intimacy was having smoke blown in my face.

I fussed with the waiter over the wine—I had never rated the Chinon red, which colonized most of the list. Will watched me and then said, "I love seeing you with your wine. You know such a lot, and you know exactly what you want. You're your father's daughter."

We had agreed that if Will was elected to Parliament, then he would give up the law and I would continue to work at Battista Fine Wines. The finances seemed to work, at least on paper, and I was looking forward to trips to Australia and America with my father.

The waiter poured out the wine—a raspberry red, which looked pretty enough.

"I love you, Mrs. Savage." Each time Will said that to me, and he did so often, it was as if he had only just thought of the idea, which made it the most delicious, the most delightful, the most necessary thing in the world for me to hear.

I turned away and gazed at the river. I did not know Will very well yet. Yet I knew beyond any doubt that our marriage was right. This absolute certainty made me feel both old and tremblingly young.

"Will you think about going to the Val del Fiertino with me sometime, to see where my family came from?"

He stubbed out the cigarette. "I can't think of anything I'd like more." His expression clouded for a moment. "I don't have much family, except Meg and Sacha of course." He brightened. "I'm looking forward to adopting yours."

I caught the echoes of his past distress. "Do you want to talk about it?"

He lit a second cigarette. "My grandparents were too old and bewildered by what happened to really get a grip on things. They blamed themselves for letting my mother marry my father, and blamed themselves even more when she began to drink, too. I'm glad they never knew about Meg."

This was delicate territory, and one we had not yet fully explored. "When did Meg . . . ?"

"I don't know. She kept it secret. I never smelled it on her. I never suspected. It probably wasn't a problem until she married Rob. Just a drink at the end of the day. But I was busy with other things—school, exams, the desire to get away. I'm ashamed to say but I didn't think much about Meg. She was just there. It was only afterwards that I realized how much she'd done for me; and what it had done to her."

I remember . . . what exactly? A tiny ripple of unease; the merest suggestion of a shadow, to dull the vivid quality of our companionship. The glasses on the table, the sun on the white stones, river sounds . . . us, together . . . all this happiness, and yet?

"Will," I said, and the breath caught in my throat, "we must never turn into Pa and Ma Kettle."

He grinned. "Do we look like Pa and Ma Kettle?" His eyes narrowed. "I've just had a thought."

"What sort of thought?"

"It involves going back to the hotel . . . now."

But when we got there, there was a message waiting for him. Will read it and then he put his arms around me and said excitedly, "Mrs. Savage, we have to pack. The election is on July the fourteenth and there's no time to waste. Not even a day, not a minute. If we drive fast we can be home by midnight."

In our room, I looked down at a pile of unsent postcards on the table under the window. Virgin postcards of pretty French villages and sleepy French rivers. "I haven't even written these," I said.

He snatched them up. "You can write them in the car."

I sat down on the bed. Talk of a summer election had been batted back and forth, but most pundits had reckoned that the government would wait for the autumn. I thought I had schooled myself very carefully for a moment like this and I knew that if I married Will I would be called on to make these kinds of sacrifices. But disappointment made me temporarily speechless.

He took on board my stricken expression. "Fanny . . . I know the timing couldn't be worse, but this means everything . . . well, not everything exactly. *You* mean everything to me, of course . . . but we have worked for this moment. You do see that?"

He looked so anxious, so determined, so serious, that my heart melted. How could I possibly make a fuss on this most important occasion of Will's life? When all was said and done, what was a honeymoon? Not vital, compared to what Will was setting out to do—which, put at its simplest and boldest, was to solve the problems of the nation.

"Fifty-fifty deal," he said. "I promise, the first moment we can, we'll have a second honeymoon."

More than anything, I wanted Will to be happy. I held

his hand and agreed: "Fifty-fifty."

Before we left the hotel, I sat down and wrote on one of the postcards: "Dear Fanny, having a wonderful time. Wish you were here. Love, Fanny." When we checked out, I asked the concierge for a stamp and dropped it into the post box in the lobby.

On the drive north, Will jiggled frantically with the car radio. Once he insisted that we stop at a motorway service station and leapt out to phone Mannochie. I watched him from the car. He placed his free hand on the glass, and leaned against it, leaving a cloudy imprint. After a moment or two, he took it away and wrapped his arm across his stomach.

That little display of nerves affected me more than I could say, and I was shaken by just how precious he was to me, and by how important it was that he was allowed to try to achieve what he wanted.

Twenty-four hours later, I entered party headquarters on Stanwinton's high street. It was stuffed with chairs, overflowing wastepaper baskets and photocopiers, and seethed with people.

Will was immediately claimed by a party apparatchik and Mannochie materialized at my elbow. "You must meet the chairman of the association and you must get on with her."

"Will I be put in the stocks if I don't?" I asked, and realizing that it did not sound very funny, wished I hadn't.

"At the very least." Mannochie piloted me up to a woman who was ordering pamphlets into neat rows.

"Pearl, this is Fanny."

A heavy woman, she pulled herself to her feet. "About time."

We should have met before—*candidates wives have to be vetted*—but Pearl had been in the hospital when I had been available. Tall and long nosed, she did not trouble with fashion. Her cotton shirt clashed with her skirt, and she wore flesh-colored tights with white, fret-worked leather lace-ups. Her scrutiny, however, was intelligent and merciless. Eventually, she held out her hand. "Since we will have a lot to do with each other, I will call you Fanny."

If I had hoped for consolation over our ruined honeymoon, I was to be disappointed. She continued, "I hope you are wearing comfortable shoes." She glanced down at my bare legs and short denim skirt and grimaced. "I'm sorry, but it would be better if you wore tights and a longer skirt. The more far-reaching and revolutionary our ideas, Fanny, the more unthreatening and respectable our appearance should be. You should have been told."

She meant I should have known. I flushed at my ignorance. "I'm sure Will will brief me."

"Have you sorted out where you plan to live in the constituency if we triumph?"

"We'll stay with my father at Ember House when we come up."

"Won't do." Pearl shook her head. "You can't be seen to be living off a parent, and it's important that it looks as though you have roots here."

"Apparently, we need a quiet, modest, cheap house in the constituency," I informed Will in the privacy of the bedroom at Ember House.

He swung around, one sock off, one sock on. "We will be living here if we win."

"Will, I had not really clocked that one."

He peeled off his remaining sock and dropped it to the floor. "I did explain."

"You said only that it was possible. I don't want to live here; the bulk of my Battista business is in London. Also, I've lived here most of my life and I know what it's like."

"Fanny." Will came over and sat on the bed. "Look at me. This is important. We're going to have to give up some things. Remember what we believe in. All the things we've agreed." He slipped down on his knees beside the bed. "No one said it would be easy."

I heard him utter the words, and witnessed the features light up with his conviction and belief. "Will, we don't have to live here. We can come down, lots."

"There can't be any half measures. This is a battle, a war, of sorts. I see it so clearly now. We have to fight it all the way."

I gazed into the dark eyes that so delighted me. "Will, could I point out that *truth* is the first casualty of war."

"Mrs. Savage, that is not being helpful."

"You must never say anything," Pearl Veriker instructed me, "that is not your role."

"Never, ever say what you think," echoed Mannochie. "Particularly not on local issues."

If I gained Mannochie, I lost Will, or rather my private Will. The public Will was surrounded by aides with clipboards, potential voters and voters who hated him. He was admired and criticized in equal measure. One thing was a constant, however: Wherever he went, Will was noticed.

Forewarned and silenced, I climbed onto battle buses and attended endless rallies and meetings. In turn, I was welcomed, abused, told to sod off, threatened and chased by an Alsatian. Sitting well back on the platform, I attended meetings and came forward to stand (silently) beside Will to take the applause. Suitably dressed, I attended photo calls with my arm linked through Will's and the results were not bad.

"It's so lucky you are good looking," said Pearl. "Your husband obeyed orders."

I stared at her and she patted me on the shoulder. "A little pleasantry, Fanny."

If Pearl was cracking jokes of a sort, then I could only suppose that she and I were making progress.

I was told to accompany the canvassers as back up and, obediently, I pounded the streets for hours at a time with eager party workers. More often than not, it was the women who answered the knock on the door and I caught glimpses of interiors where baskets of wet laundry waited to be hung out and where children's bicycles and strollers cluttered the hallways.

We visited blocks of flats where the walkways reeked with urine, and quiet, net-curtained homes in neat, tree-lined streets. We trudged up gravel drives to capacious well-maintained villas, which had been built by the industrial barons at the turn of the century. Their occupants were the worst for they couched any hostility in a more polite and deadly form.

No one, it had to be said, was much interested in actual political debate. The chief talking point was not whether taxes would go up or not, or whether the government should spend more money on health and education; it was: How much were beer and cigarettes going to cost?

"What do you lot actually do?" said one heavily jeweled, heavily made-up woman to the group in her front garden. She made to shut the front door in our faces. "*Who* did you say you were?"

Mannochie cornered me one evening. He looked embarrassed. "Fanny, could you keep your thoughts on local transport to yourself."

I was startled. "Do I have any?"

"Apparently you do and were overheard talking about them at the Guides' coffee morning."

"I said I thought there should be more buses at night."

Mannochie looked concerned. "Precisely. You are playing into a lobby."

By the time polling day arrived, my shoulders were stiff and my feet swollen and I had been drip fed facts and statistics by the bagful and learned the hard way some of the rules of political engagement.

Will worked right up until the end, and he asked me to bring in a change of clothes. I packed up a suit and shirt, and picked up his best black shoes and slipped my hand inside. Burned into the inner sole was a private imprint. My shoes held one, too. Will's second toe was longer than his first and I rubbed my finger over the indent rubbed into the leather. It was my secret, and my secret knowledge.

We arrived at the town hall at midnight. The last two ballot boxes had been brought in, and the final count was on. The tellers bent over the trestle tables, forefingers and thumbs encased in rubber guards. The piles mounted, shifted: A couple were recounted, the tally noted.

Someone touched my arm. "Hallo," said Meg. "Sorry I didn't get here earlier." She was flushed and bright-eyed, impeccable in a red linen dress and pretty shoes. "I couldn't miss little brother's big day."

At one-thirty, Pearl Veriker chivvied me into a side room. "Looking good, Fanny. Let's check you out."

Skirt long enough? Tights? Makeup?

"Where's your wedding ring?" Her gaze fixed on my naked left hand.

I fished it out of my pocket. "It's given me a rash. I'm not used to it yet."

"Wear it, Fanny."

I pushed it over my red, swollen finger. To my astonishment, the itch and burn of my rebellion was no less urgent. As surely as an ox, I was being yoked.

I pulled myself together and went over to talk to the party workers. Their average age was well above mine, but there were one or two younger ones. "Isn't it funny how the other side always seems so much uglier than your own," breathed a sharp youth next to me.

I was pouring orange juice into plastic cups when I happened to look up. Will's eyes met mine for a long moment. He was asking me to keep faith. Short-lived and unfocused, my rebellion died.

• • •

At three o'clock in the morning, I stood beside Will on the platform as the returning officer read out the votes and Will was declared the new Member for the constituency of Stanwinton. We stood side by side, both of us lightheaded and almost incoherent with joy. There was pleasure and pride—and an explosion of joy in my chest. The future seemed as if it could be tackled.

Down below, the indomitable Pearl sat down suddenly and pressed her handkerchief to her mouth. Mannochie was clapping, and a couple of the party workers danced.

Will slid his arm around my shoulders and kissed me, and I promised silently to do my best for him, always.

Meg pushed her way up to the platform, her red dress a bright blur and linked her arm through his. "Darling Will . . ."

The photographers flashed away, someone else cheered, Mannochie continued to clap.

Later that day, the official photograph was published in the *Stanwinton Echo*. It had that grainy, blurred look that local papers sometimes have and it was hard to make out some of the figures on the platform. A smiling Will stood tall and straight. He looked young, happy and full of promise. Beside him was a slender, fair-haired figure, wreathed in smiles. Not me, but Meg.

Chapter 6

MEG ASKED, AS A special favor, if she could fetch Chloe from school on the day of her final exam. Chloe burst through the kitchen door. "Mum? They're over. Finished." She was pale, shaking and elated.

I stroked her hair and gave her a hug. Then I led her upstairs, made her take a bath and fetched a mug of tea.

Face turning pink in the steam, she slumped back in the water. "My nice mummy." She was silent for a while. "I can't move. I can't think. I can't do anything."

I put a towel to warm on the rail. "Shall I wash your hair?"

The shape of her skull was so familiar, so beloved. The shampoo made the strands feel curiously wiry. Very carefully, I rubbed and rinsed, and wiped teardrops of foam away from her eyes. I knew what this moment meant.

"Now my life begins, Mum," she said as I toweled her dry, the way I used to when she was tiny, unformed and all mine. "How about that?"

When I woke a few days later, I put out my hand. If Will was there, my fingers usually made contact with his warm back or the curve of his shoulder. It was a private early morning reminder to myself, too often neglected, that we should be kind to one another.

Today, Will's side of the bed felt particularly empty and cold.

I got up, dressed in jeans and a T-shirt, drew back the curtains and watched as a summer day shook damply into life. Two figures were walking down the road. They moved slowly, dreamily, seemingly transfixed by each other.

Chloe stopped by the laurel hedge, and I could see

that there was nothing childlike about her any more. Sacha bent over and whispered something in her ear. She replied and turned to him, her arms snaking up around his neck. Sacha nuzzled her head and said something else, which made Chloe giggle.

Conscious that I was spying, I stepped back from the window.

Chloe ambled into the kitchen as I was making coffee. "What are you doing up so early, Mum?" She sniffed. "Coffee. Great. Can I have some?"

"Have you been out all night? Did you have something to eat?"

Chloe shook her head and her long hair flew around her shoulders.

"Sure we were up all night." Sacha, who had followed her in, fetched the cups. "No big deal." He smiled at me teasingly. "Can't you remember?"

"Dimly," I replied, with a touch of acid. "How was the club?"

Their eyes met and a private message was exchanged. "Brilliant." Chloe's voice was a note higher than normal.

I cut the bread and slotted two slices into the toaster. "I hope you didn't do anything . . . silly."

Chloe's eyes flashed me a warning. *Don't go there.*

"Yup . . ." Sacha unzipped his leather bomber jacket and arranged it over the back of the chair. "The club isn't bad. The boys and I might just do a gig there to help out."

Chloe hunched over her coffee. There was a faint flush on her cheek and a hint of a smile on her lips.

The toast had stuck and I pulled it out, spraying

crumbs across the floor. I put it in front of them. "Have some Tuscan honey. I got it in the supermarket."

"What's wrong with English honey?" She feathered her impossibly long eyelashes. "Or anything English, for that matter? It's all Italian pasta, Italian ham, Italian this, that and the other." Again, she fluttered those eyelashes as Sacha watched, seemingly enraptured. "You and Dad ought to go this year. Get it out of your system, Mum."

I fetched the dustpan and swept up the crumbs. "As it happens, I am planning a trip with your grand-father."

Chloe raised her eyes to the ceiling. "So you say."

While they ate and drank, I sat at the table and puzzled over the agenda for the Stanwinton homeless persons' committee. Eventually, Sacha got to his feet and lifted his prize jacket off the chair. "Bedtime," he said and disappeared.

"What about you, darling?"

Chloe drained her coffee and hunkered down beside me. "You mustn't interfere, Mum. Not any longer."

I slipped my arm around her. There was a smudge of honey at the corner of her mouth, and I wiped it away with my finger. "He's your first cousin, Chloe."

Chloe's happy look vanished. "He's my first every-thing, Mum. He's my blood and bone. He knows me. I know him. You don't understand."

"He's your first cousin," I repeated. "There are other boys . . ."

Chloe straightened up. "Forget it, Mum," she said, in a flat voice that was new to me. Then she, too, was gone.

I looked up and out of the window where, like

71

bunches of bruised plums, summer rain clouds were gathering.

Later in the morning in the garage, Chloe and I sorted through bags of discarded clothing for charity.

I upended a bag, and a mountain of grubby sweaters, trousers and shirts spread across the floor of the garage. Their smell—musty, used, depressing—made us recoil.

"Ugh," said Chloe. "Throw them away."

"We can't. They might be useful. Someone might need them."

Chloe inspected a second bag. "Actually . . ." she pulled out a pink cardigan that looked suspiciously like cashmere, "there's quite a nice one here."

I gathered up an armful of clothes and plodded into the kitchen, where Brigitte was cleaning the sink. "Could you put these through the machine?"

She took a step back too. "These are not nice."

"They'll be better when they're washed and ironed."

Brigitte loaded them sulkily into the machine and banged the door shut.

Chloe handed Brigitte the detergent. "It's a funny old life," she said. "Do you think it's OK if I keep this cardigan?"

I gave Meg a lift to the doctor on my way into town. She snapped the seat belt into place. "Sacha tells me that you've . . . been talking to Chloe about Sacha. I gather you don't approve of him and Chloe being together so much . . ."

I eased the car out of the gateway and into the road. I

72

should no longer have been surprised by the way information circulated in the house. "Does he discuss everything with you?"

"Mostly. We've always talked. As you know."

It was unfair, but the remark set my teeth on edge. "Chloe edits any confidences she grants me."

"Tell me," Meg searched in her bag, "is it my son you object to, or my genes?"

"I love Sacha, and Chloe shares your genes."

Meg flipped down the passenger sunshade and used the mirror to apply bright red lipstick while I wrestled with a one-way system that had been expressly designed to send drivers mad. "You know, Fanny," she said, "we were once better friends."

I felt her stare burn into my cheek. "Meg," I said, rashly. "I've been thinking that it's time to make a few changes."

As ever, she was as sharp as a knife. "You want to chuck me out?" Then she gave one of her laughs. "I would if it was me." She pushed her hair behind her ears, an uncharacteristically nervous gesture. "Does Will know what's on your mind?"

"I haven't discussed it at length. But Chloe will be leaving home fairly soon, and I thought maybe . . . maybe it's time for a smaller house."

"Will wouldn't like that. He'd never chuck Sacha and me out." She shot me a wary look. "And you wouldn't either, would you Fanny?"

"Won't Sacha be leaving home too?"

Meg flung the lipstick into her bag. "Yes."

Rather as my mother had departed from Ember House

virtually empty-handed, Meg had arrived in Stanwinton with almost nothing, just a suitcase and a small bag of Sacha's clothes for his weekend visits. "I couldn't cope with choosing," she'd said.

Years later, when I talked to Rob at Sacha's eighteenth birthday party, he told me he had begged Meg to take it all—furniture, clothes, china—but she'd resolutely refused, telling him she wanted space for her grief. Rob had been puzzled by this, but, in a curious way, I felt it made sense.

Meg raised her hands in front of her. "Look, only a little tremble. I'm improving. The other night was just a lapse. I am going to try for another job, you know."

"Sure." I drove into the surgery car park and dropped her by the entrance.

Meg gripped the door handle. "But I'm not quite well enough to cope on my own."

I leaned over to close the door. "Meg," I called after her. "I didn't mean it."

After the committee meeting, I drove up to London. It was raining again. I peered through the windshield. My father made a big thing of the Italian summer and, not for the first time, I realized why. Oh . . . to be there, where it was so hot in the valley that if I sat under an olive tree and looked up, the leaves would resemble flickering tongues of fire.

Will had left a note on the hall floor of our London flat where I would be sure to tread on it: "See you at the embassy. Don't forget Pasquale. Plse don't be late."

Of course I was. I made the mistake of taking a bath

and, as I soaked, the phone rang twice. The first call was a journalist from a broadsheet saying they were planning a piece on possible future senior figures in the party and could they interview my husband? I told him to contact Will's office. The second was Will's private secretary, warning me that if I spoke to anyone from the Italian delegation I should steer clear of anything remotely political. The word had been passed around to all the wives. "What do I steer on to?" I wanted to know.

"There has been a recent find of Etruscan bronzes that are considered very fine," he replied.

I traced a pattern of hearts on the steamed-up mirror in the bathroom. "Talk me through the bronzes."

"Unfortunately, Mrs. Savage, they're well . . . rather erotic. But you can keep off the detail. And . . . Mrs. Savage . . . if you could avoid the words 'car' and 'tax' . . . the negotiations are at a rather tricky stage."

Hobbled conversationally, and late setting out, I took a taxi to where Will was waiting for me. He smiled and kissed my cheek, but his grip on my arm was almost painful. "You're late."

"Traffic." I laced my fingers through his and made sure I got in with my list of topics to discuss. "We must talk about Chloe."

He squeezed my fingers and then dropped them. "What about her?"

"Her and Sacha. I'm a bit concerned."

"Meg says that's nonsense. They're just very close, as cousins sometimes are."

"You've talked to Meg? I've been trying to ring you all week, but you were always busy . . ."

"Hallo Ted." Will transferred his attention smoothly to one of his fellow ministers.

A good champagne was served in a long, narrow reception room. Obedient to my briefing, I talked about weather and flora to an ambassador, who was dressed in a multicolored tie, and about wines to a junior consul, who informed me he had been brought up on beer. I took Antonio Pasquale aside and astounded him with my grasp of Italian and Italian wine. When we said good-bye he kissed my hand and I knew I had done a good job.

Back in the flat, Will made straight for the drinks tray, which was unusual, and poured himself a glass of whiskey. "I'm whacked. Pasquale's wife was a night-mare."

"We ought to eat something."

"Too tired."

"So am I." I kicked off my shoes and curled up on the sofa. "Tell me what's happening."

Will sighed. "Haven't the energy."

"Oh." I studied my feet, encased in their light, evening tights.

"I'm sorry, darling."

I reached for the cushion and hugged it. "How would you feel if Dad and I went on a trip to Italy?"

Will snapped to attention. "When?"

"While Chloe's away. September probably. We haven't settled on anything yet."

"Without me?"

"Yes."

Will put down his glass and came and sat down beside me. "Of course you must go. I know what it would mean

76

to you." He paused. "But do you have go this year? There is so much going on . . ." He took away the cushion and put his arm around me. "I need you on board." I sensed the energy flowing back into him as he concentrated on bringing me back into the fold. "Just at the moment, I'm not sure I could manage without you." He took another gulp of the whiskey. "Perhaps I'm being selfish." When I did not reply, he said sharply, "Fanny, are you listening?"

I raised my eyes and saw my old Will—the clever, funny, passionate, committed man with whom I had fallen in love, and I wondered what he could see in me, and whether or not he was looking.

"Ours is becoming a curious marriage," I heard myself say. "I've been trying all week to talk to you about our daughter . . . where do I come in the queue?"

"Don't be silly." This was said with a flash of irritation.

"It's true."

He caught my chin. "Is this because I talked to Meg? She just happened to phone at the right time, you idiot."

"Partly." I shook his hand away and started to pick at the braid on the discarded cushion. "I mind about that."

He sighed. "I honestly don't think there's any need to worry about Chloe."

"But I do worry about her. And I worry that I have to worry about her on my own."

"When she is traveling around Australia, she'll forget Sacha; she'll meet other people. It's not so odd at her age to have a passion—if she does—for someone unsuitable."

He was probably right, but I'd had enough politician's

explanations for one evening. I heaved myself to my feet and went over to the window and looked out at the dull summer night. "I would like to go away with my father, Will. I don't think he is all that well, and I'd like to spend some time with him."

"Rather than with me . . ."

I turned round and glared at him. "I'm going to forget you said that."

Will set his glass down on the table with a snap. "Did you really suggest to Meg that she move out?"

"Not exactly," I replied. "The idea was proposed, but not voted upon."

"Don't you think you should have discussed it with me first? She's upset and unsettled, and it can't be good for her."

"Discuss things with you? What an excellent idea. I've been trying all week. Shall I see if Mannochie can squeeze me into your schedule at some point?" I made for the door. "But right now I'm going to bed."

As I walked down the corridor, he called after me, "I can't hurt her, Fanny. I can't abandon her."

Chapter 7

WE HAD OUR SECOND honeymoon. I made sure of that.

It was quite natural that, with all the drama and excitement of getting elected, Will should forget his promise, so I took matters into my own hands.

"Get up, Mr. Savage . . ." It was a Friday morning in early September—plenty of time yet before Parliament reassembled and Will was scheduled to make his maiden speech—and he was sleeping. I was already up and dressed in trousers, sweater and walking boots. I leaned over the still prone body and shook it hard. "Come on. . . . We're going on a honeymoon. A weekend one."

One eye flicked open immediately. "We're going on . . . what?"

"You owe me one remember? Get your walking clothes on, we're off to France to walk in the Alps."

He struggled upright. "You can't do this. I need my sleep."

"Oh yes, I can. And oh no, you don't. And before you ask, I've run it past Mannochie."

I threw back the bedclothes and pushed him out of bed, and he was so taken aback that he was very good and did what I told him. Two hours later, as we checked in at the airport, he said to me, "You're quite mad, Mrs. Savage."

Throughout the short flight, I was aware that Will was watching me covertly. I put down my magazine. "Is anything the matter?"

"Nothing. It's just that I've seen another side of you, Fanny. That's all, and I'm getting to know it." He made a face at me. "The efficient side."

"Listen, Will, I've been organizing traveling and suchlike since I was in diapers. Dad and I do it all the time. It's second nature."

"Of course," he said. "I was forgetting."

Our hotel was tucked up the side of the mountain. It was a modest, but friendly place, and the meals were generous. The bed was enormous and covered by an even larger duvet, which, for some reason, reduced us to giggles. Each evening, a thermos of herb tea—a disgusting brew of vervain and dandelion—was left by the bed. "For health and strength," the manager explained when we signed in, with a slight leer which seemed perfectly acceptable as it was part and parcel of the honeymoon experience.

Shall I say, the disgusting brew came in useful.

That weekend, that lovely weekend, was one of our most intense and happy. That is how I recollect it.

For two days, Will and I walked until we dropped. We were lucky with the weather, not always predictable in September. But the sun shone incessantly and, in the thin, clear air, its rays seemed to burn right through our clothing.

We plastered on the sun cream, packed up our day sacks with ham baguettes, fruit and water, and plotted a route on the map.

"This is my territory," said Will. "Women don't have any spatial awareness." He grinned at me. "Have you noticed that at all, Mrs. Savage?"

I did not give him the pleasure of rising to the bait. Actually, Will's map reading was impressive. He had an instinct for direction, and made those connections necessary to pilot us between map and landscape as if it was second nature. If the connections between him and his electorate remained as instinctive and as productive, then we would be all right.

And between us.

The exhilaration of being up in the mountains spurred us into greater ambitions. On Saturday we walked seven hours and, to our astonishment, returned stiff, but only

80

mildly fatigued. We went to bed, drank the dreadful tisane, and slept.

Will woke me at dawn. "This *is* our second honeymoon," he reminded me.

On Sunday, we were out on the mountain by eight-thirty. The morning chill made us shiver, and we kept close together as we began the ascent. By the time the temperature rose, we were walking through alpine meadows sprinkled with autumn crocuses and gentians. At ten o'clock we stopped to drink coffee at a café in Ste Marianne de Ventoux, a tiny village at the foot of the col, which had a well whose waters were reputed to be miraculous. Neither of us were superstitious but, just to be sure, I hauled up the bucket and dipped my finger into it, and marked both Will's forehead and mine.

On the way out of Ste Marianne de Ventoux, we stood aside to allow the goatherd to bring his animals down from the high pastures into their winter quarters. He was a lean, elderly man with a whistle hanging around his neck. He moved purposefully down the path toward the village, no doubt looking forward to a proper home and fire for the winter.

Up here in the mountains, there was no blurring of the seasons. No looking up from a desk and thinking: Goodness, it is summer and I had not noticed.

I suggested to Will that, each year, we should make the effort to get away somewhere where we could be reminded of weather, and of what really ruled the world. He replied gravely that, yes, of course, he would consider *anything* that would make me happy and sweet tempered.

I smacked him on the bottom. In retaliation, he tickled me and no progress at all was made for half an hour.

At lunchtime, we reached a plateau and sat down on a slab of rock. It was hot and so silent, and there were no shadows, for the sun was at its zenith. I lay back. The heat of the rock fired my back and the rays on my face were like a furnace.

I thought of what Will and I had walked into. He and I had to manage the business of life. This included the quiet activities of paying bills, researching the right mortgage, discussing with earnest good intent such vital but unexciting subjects as shelving and cupboards, or which washing machine. It meant having friends over for meals, talking to neighbors, negotiating with a bank with whom you were so irritated that you felt like saying "stuff you," knowing that the power in these transactions only flows one way.

Then there would be the significant and affecting decisions. When to start a family? Shall we have a cat?

These small pieces: often only half decided, happened on, accepted by default . . . would make up the framework that held us.

"What are you thinking about?" Will sounded dreamy and sleepy.

"Us."

"And . . ."

"We have to learn to manage each other."

He murmured. "We love each other, that will do."

Will made his maiden speech in October when Parliament reassembled after the long vacation. The night before, we argued over which color suit he should wear. I opted for the gray. He preferred the blue. Did it matter? Apparently. Colors (or so the apparatchiks had suggested) conveyed subtle meanings. This was, I felt, a little puzzling for I had assumed it was the message that was the important thing.

"I know it's nonsense," he maintained stoutly, "but just this once, I think I ought to listen to what the advisers advise."

I rubbed his shoulders, which felt like tensed steel. "Hey, take a few deep breaths. Loosen those muscles."

I did not tell him that my own nerves were conducting a nauseous dance in the pit of my stomach. All I had to do was to watch Will get to his feet and talk about the social benefits of cheaper housing, and impress his peers. But this first showing would affect his future— and mine.

"I must not muck this up, Fanny."

"Spare a thought for your sister and me," I pointed out. "We get to look down at all the bald spots where we sit in the strangers' gallery."

He gave a muffled snort.

Will's speech went off well.

At least, I think it did, for when Will got to his feet, cleared his throat and began to speak easily and fluently, my attention veered off into another sphere.

It was nerves, I know, but I found myself thinking about trees. Tall ones, like the sycamore, whose stout uncompromising leader branches emphasize its winter nudity. I thought of poplars swaying in the summer breeze, and feathery acacias and the astonishing reds of the maple. But the trees that spoke to me most particularly have always been the cypress, the *Cupressus sempervirens,* the dark exclamations dotted over medieval and Renaissance Italian paintings. And the box, which is not strictly a tree. Box was probably introduced to this country by the Romans, and its stems and roots are so heavy that they sink in water.

Meg caught my eye, and I colored up guiltily. I had promised to hang on Will's every word, in order to assemble a useful Situation Report.

You spoke too quickly. Your hands were too busy, they distracted the listener. Don't look at your feet.

Etc.

"To the manner born," whispered Meg.

Meg misinterpreted my lack of response as lack of control. Furthermore she would be thinking of Will. Indeed, I suspected, that she thought of little else. Her Situation Report would be immaculate and very helpful.

She laid one small hand with its exquisitely shaped nails on my arm. Today, they were painted pink to match her lipstick. "You have to learn to lighten up, Fanny," she advised in a low, concerned voice. "Develop a sense of humor. Then you will cope better."

I gritted my teeth. Quite apart from the insult to my perfectly operational sense of humor, did she consider I was *that* lacking in the requisite qualifications? Was my ignorance and inexperience obvious? "I will bear it in mind," I muttered.

Meg pressed on. "Please don't be offended," she said. "You are so nice, Fanny, and I am only trying to help." She smiled understandingly. "I've been at it a bit longer than you."

Outside the House of Commons, a photographer was on the prowl for a national newspaper, and he inveigled Will and me to pose for him, and Will and I were snapped, hand in hand, framed in the doorway.

"Parliament's newest Golden Couple," ran the caption in a weekend paper. The camera had caught Will looking grave but irresistible. I less so, I concluded, after glancing briefly at the photo, for I had a wary look on my face, startled almost.

At any rate, Mannochie, who had bedded down overnight on the sofa in the flat, pronounced himself pleased. "This will go down well in the constituency."

Will studied the photograph for longer, it seemed to me, than was decent. "Better of me than you," he pronounced.

"That's what I think." I concentrated on frying up the bacon. "But I'll pass."

"Certainly you do," said Mannochie.

Will still had his teeth into the subject. "I can't afford to photograph badly. Ever. Back me up, Mannochie. One bad showing and it takes years to eradicate."

We perched on the sofa and chair in the sitting room, ate bacon and toast, drank coffee and rifled through the morning papers. Will and Mannochie discussed tactics and, at great length, diary commitments.

I looked up from the paper and tossed a fact into the date discussion. "I shall be in Australia in December."

As one, both men turned in my direction.

Will said: "You didn't mention it to me, Fanny."

"Yes, I did. You've forgotten."

Mannochie brushed the crumbs surrounding his plate into a tidy little heap. "Stanwinton is big on Christmas. It's part of the civic pride. There's a frenzy of fund-raising, which the sitting MP always supports. Then there are parties for the local children's homes, the ever-greens and the disabled." He smiled apologetically. "Attendance really is compulsory."

I addressed Will. "Fine. You will be there."

Will fumbled for a second piece of toast and buttered it. "Fanny. I am not sure how to put this, but I need you with me." He looked especially desirable: slightly rum-pled, boyish and pleading. It made me want him very badly.

I shook my head. "Dad and I have set up a lot of busi-ness. We're due at the Hunter Valley, we are guests of honor at a dinner in Adelaide and Bob and Kevin are coming over from the Yarra."

These names meant nothing to either of the men. They were part and parcel of my and my father's terri-tory and we had done business with them for years. "You want me to smile sweetly, kiss cheeks, sing carols, pat sticky hands?"

"That was the deal." Will's gaze shifted from Man-nochie to me.

Will and I had discussed the theory of our division of work plenty of times, and I assumed that I would be at liberty to choose when to go on duty—when to be a good wife. "This is business, Will. These are long-term commitments."

Mannochie picked up his egg-stained plate and edged toward the door. "Will, Fanny, I am sure you need to talk things over . . . Fanny, perhaps it would be a good idea if we went through the diary for the year. That way, we will avoid future clashes."

This was the cue for our first quarrel . . . which went along the lines of: Why didn't you say something earlier? And me saying tartly back at him: You don't listen to what I say. Then Will demanded how could I have made him look a fool in front of Mannochie?

"Very easy," I said, quick as a flash.

That made Will grin. After that, the atmosphere calmed down and we began to talk properly. It was clear we had not agreed on demarcation lines and we needed to sort this out.

It was not that Will demanded that I give up my work for his. "No, not at all," he said. He scratched his head with the Biro. "Your work is important, and it has to be slotted in. It's just, I would have liked you to have been there for the Christmas run-up. Just this first year."

This caused me to lie awake for most of the night, sifting over the pros and cons of the respective demands on our time.

The subject suddenly appeared so vexing that I ended up making myself tea at four o'clock in the morning. While the kettle boiled, I ran my fingers over the glass jars with red screw tops that I had bought soon after we married.

Kitchens should be larger than this. They shouldn't be mean proportioned and stingy with storage.

Not like the big house in Fiertino, if my father was to be believed, where a larder led off the main kitchen where the pâtés and dried meats and tins were stored.

"There were rows of bottles in there, in wonderful colors," he told me. "Fruit and pickles and walnuts . . . if you could bottle summer, it was on those shelves. My mother checked the larder every day. It was a habit, and it was unthinkable to her she did not make that daily check. 'It is important for the family,' she always said. 'I have to make sure there is food; otherwise, I can't sleep nights.' "

I thought often of that larder, glowing with jewel-like reds and yellows, a place of surety and comfort and pleasure.

Meanwhile, I was going to make do with two small shelves in the kitchen and fill my glass jars with rice, nuts, pasta and lentils. I had already arranged my wine manuals on the spare bit of worktop by the toaster.

The cold sliced into me with the cruelty of a knife.

What had I done?

If you pick the grape too early, it is hard and bitter and will never yield. Is that what I had done? . . . tumbled into this marriage before I had had time to grow into my skin, to ripen? Had Will's lean body and dark eyes, his passionate convictions, his need for me, seduced my wits and dulled my brain?

With senses reeling, flesh quivering, I had been a fool who had bartered my freedom for . . . what?

The kettle boiled.

Next door, a bedspring creaked and feet hit the floor. Will appeared at the door. "Fanny . . . you must be freezing." He squeezed into the kitchen and slipped his arms around my waist. "You *are* freezing. Here, let me make the tea." My doubts fled at his touch.

88

We took the tea back to bed and we drank it, with my cold feet resting on Will's legs to warm them up. "My fault," he said.

"It's my fault, too."

Then he took away my cup and put it down on the bedside table. He stroked my hair and I had a minor revelation as to why arguments were so necessary, for making up was extremely sweet.

"Mannochie and I will manage," he said cheerfully.

"Are you sure?"

"Almost."

That made me laugh. I slipped my hand under his T-shirt and rested it on his exciting bare flesh.

Chapter 8

AT THE VERY LAST minute, Will was ordered to join a Parliamentary fact-finding tour of Europe researching data for the car-tax scheme, which put paid to his plan to spend a couple of days at home with Chloe before she left on her travels. He broke the news to her over a Sunday lunch. "Sorry, darling. I hope you understand."

Chloe continued to eat. "It's OK," she said.

I couldn't bear the disappointment on her face. "Will, couldn't you just manage an afternoon?"

"It's OK." Chloe did her best to look as if she did not care.

Will shot me a look and I mouthed at him, "She's upset."

"Chloe," he said, "I feel miserable about it."

She stood up, and I suddenly saw a much older Chloe

in her expression. "But not quite miserable enough, Dad," she said. "So let's leave it, shall we?"

She left the room, closing the door with a distinct bang.

I looked at Will. "She's been planning this for ages. . . ."

Will looked really distressed. "I wish I didn't have to go."

"Oh, well." I began to clear up the plates. "It's done now."

He winced, and studied his shoe laces. "Fanny," he said at length, without looking up, "I have a favor to ask . . ."

"Don't tell me," I said. "Let me guess."

Surgeries took place in a small, airless room in the town hall. Tina, the constituency secretary, had tried on countless occasions to open the window but it was stuck shut. She bustled in with shopping bags and dropped them on the floor. "The whole lot is bound to thaw, but the old man likes his dinner pronto . . ."

She was a compact, motherly sort of woman, who had a habit of clicking her tongue as she listened to some of the worst cases. Her husband was out of work and, to make ends meet, Tina sold makeup from door to door, but she never complained. Today, she sported a shell-pink lipstick upon which I hoped her future finances did not depend, but she wore it with an air of "never surrender" I could only admire.

"My old man thinks we should have a bodyguard to protect us against the madmen out there," she said.

"Mannochie will defend us, won't you Mannochie?"

"To the death." Mannochie sounded even drier than normal.

First in was Mrs. Scott, a regular at the Saturday surgeries. Over the years, Will had struggled to sort out her damp flat and the family next door who terrorized her. She was tiny, twisted with osteoporosis, and totally alone.

"Oh, it's you, Mrs. Savage. The minister busy? Something important?"

Touchingly, Mrs. Scott considered Will's seniority a personal plus and lapped up status from her acquaintanceship. Today, she had an arm in a sling. "Tripped on the stairs and the council won't do anything about it. I want you to sue them for me."

I did my best to run through what Will might be able to arrange for her, and how she might cope with her frightening neighbors. Mrs. Scott's mouth was drawn tight with pain and distress, and I feared that I was not helping that much. "Check with council," I wrote on my notes, reminding myself that if politics had any meaning it should be here, at the grass-roots level. It was here you could see, touch and smell where the limits of the possible to help and advise began and ended, but in my heart of hearts, I knew perfectly well that this would be just another addition to an already clogged system.

"Mrs. Scott, should we get a doctor to come and look at that arm?"

A spark of her old spirit returned. "Last time a doctor set foot in my place, Queen Victoria was on the throne." She delved into her bag. "I've brought you something. I was going to give it to the minister to give to you."

She passed over a soft piece of netting edged with beads. "It's for your milk jug," she said. "I made it."

I spread it out on the desk. The beads were lapis-lazuli blue with gold flecks and very pretty. I felt a lump in my throat.

She watched me. "Not all a waste of your time, eh?"

I shook my head. "This must be your best one, Mrs. Scott."

Before she hobbled out of the door, she sent us her parting shot. "It's gone in a flash. Life. I wouldn't mind, you know . . . if it hadn't been such a rotten one."

Tina clicked her tongue and typed away while Mannochie patrolled the doorway to keep the madmen at bay.

Surgery over, I drove into town and met Chloe in the backpacker's shop. My father and I had friends throughout the Australian wine-producing areas, and we had suggested that Chloe stay with some of them. But Chloe was being Miss Independent; all she would permit us to arrange was a week in the Hunter Valley. "Stop interfering, Mum," she begged.

We bought her walking boots and sandals, padlocks and insect repellent. "There must be more," I said. "It's not safe to go improperly equipped."

"You should listen to yourself, Mum. I'll be fine."

I longed to reach inside my daughter and tease out exactly what she was thinking; to be allowed to smooth away any ruffles of apprehension and to be a wise mother. Instead, I found myself clucking and fretting. "I'm allowed to make a few suggestions," I said defensively.

Chloe picked up a travel wallet, designed to strap on under the arm. "Do you think I should take this?"

"Yes," I said quickly. "And sun stuff. Masses of it for when it gets hot."

"Mother. They *sell* sun cream in Australia."

She was very quiet in the car home, and picked at her frayed cuticles. "Sacha says Aunt Meg told him you're thinking of moving house. You wouldn't do that without me, would you? Not till I come home?"

"Aunt Meg shouldn't have said anything."

"Why not? I'm grown up now, Mum. Why can't I discuss these things? Especially if it's true . . ."

"It was just an idea." I drove a bit farther. "But you know, I wouldn't mind a change, and you will be leaving home . . ."

"I hate it when grown-ups say things like that."

I reached over and touched her cheek. "Where's the girl who couldn't wait to be eighteen? The one who was always saying: 'Don't treat me like a child?' "

She hunched over and said irritably, "You're so silly sometimes, Mum." She gazed out of the window at the speeding landscape. "Are you and Dad getting on all right?"

I negotiated the bend with extra care. "Why do you ask?"

"I don't know. I just am."

"We're fine."

"Something you said to him on the phone."

"Hey. My phone conversations are supposed to be private."

Chloe looked pityingly at me. "Get real, Mum, this is a family."

I laughed with genuine pleasure. "That's good."

We laid out her purchases on the bed in the spare room and Chloe disappeared to update her traveling companions on the phone. A stream of excited chatter filtered from her room.

I went downstairs to the kitchen. My father was coming to supper that evening. I removed my wedding ring and hung it on the hook by the notice board. From time to time, it still made my finger swell—hormones, my mood, the time of year?—and it bothered me when I was doing the chores.

Brigitte poked her head around the door. "I'm out," she said. "OK." It was a statement, not a question, and underlined by the banging of the back door.

"I don't think she's a happy bunny . . ." Meg joined me in the kitchen. "She's been on the phone a lot, and she wasn't very nice about you, earlier."

I knew perfectly well that the au pair network ran an information service. I had never quite got over meeting comparative strangers who knew the exact state of my underwear, but who also knew that I possessed detailed top-secret information on theirs.

I began to chop up stewing steak and an onion, which made my eyes water.

"You've turned into a good cook, Fanny," observed Meg. "Who would have thought it?"

Silence.

She watched me lay the table with cutlery and water glasses. "You've laid too many places."

"Dad's coming."

She nodded. "Good." Another silence. "You seem cross."

"I am." I put the final water glass in its place. "I can't trust you, Meg, ever, not to repeat things. You shouldn't have told Sacha, which in the way of things in this family means Chloe, about the idea of moving house."

Meg looked defiant. "Doesn't she have a right to know?"

"You've upset her."

"Fanny," she pointed out, gently, "Chloe is a big girl now."

That Meg was right made me even crosser. "Will and I would prefer to be the ones to choose when we discuss something important with her."

"If you say so." Meg filled the water jug and placed it in the exact center of the table where it overshadowed the little vase of pink and white roses I had put there earlier.

Halfway through the meal, I looked up from my plate. Meg was flirting with my father, which he always enjoyed. "Meg is funny and smart," he once told me. Sacha and Chloe were deep in conversation. The candles on the table threw a dreamy light over the roses and the water jug. Will's chair was empty, of course, and I thought he must miss this.

Chloe laughed and, in the candlelight, she glowed with the kind of beauty that you can only possess when the most interesting part of your life lies ahead of you. My father raised his glass in my direction. It was a little habit of his. It told me that he loved me, and always would.

I raised mine back.

I was banished from the washing up and ordered to put my feet up. The phone rang as I was enjoying this moment of peace. It was Raoul. "Fanny," he said, in his excellent English, "I haven't heard from you for far too long."

"I was thinking the same. How's business? How are Thérèse and the children?"

"Business could always be better. The French market is not flourishing."

I knew perfectly well from my father's records that the French suppliers were more than holding their own, but Raoul liked to play the role of professional doomster. "Don't tell me claret is out of fashion."

"People are drinking more and more of the New World wines . . . if it goes on I will have to get another job."

I appreciated the performance. There was no possible chance of the Villeneuves turning the château into a safari park. Besides, if you cut Raoul, he would bleed Petrus or Château Longueville.

We talked for half an hour or so—a happy, meandering conversation, which flowed neatly past any specter of unfinished business.

Eventually, Raoul said, "Alfredo tells me that now Chloe is off, you are considering coming back properly into the business. Really, Fanny, this is exceptionally good news."

"I'm thinking about it. It all rather depends on what Will's up to. He's . . . um . . . hoping for big things."

"It would make you very happy," he said simply. "I know it would."

I allowed myself the merest moment of reprise, of what-might-have-been-possible. "Dad tells me that Château d'Yseult has been bought by the Americans. Has that caused a stir?"

"I think we will get used to it," Raoul said. "Or, rather, I think we French have to get used to it."

Chloe's flight was on the thirteenth of July and I struggled against feeling superstitious.

The day before, we drove over to Ember House to say good-bye to my father. Before lunch, we walked around the garden and came to a halt under the beech in which, many years before, my father had built me a tree house.

"Don't look down," I called as Chloe insisted on climbing up to see if any of it was still safe.

"Don't worry, Mum."

Don't look down. "You taught me that," I said to my father. "Excellent advice."

"She's just like you," he remarked fondly.

"Was I as pig-headed?"

"Probably. I can't remember."

I bent down to tip a stone out of my shoe. Tucked into the beech's roots was a vivid green carpet of moss and the remains of the miniature cyclamen I had planted. Cyclamen should never be in pots. They belonged outside in the cool dampness of an English spring. "I feel rather desperate about Chloe going, Dad," I confessed

97

finally. "I know she must, but . . ."

He tucked my hand under his arm. "It isn't the end, believe me. Look at us. But I shall tell you a secret. Chloe may be going, but you are still on duty for the rest of your life."

It was not a new idea, but a comforting one.

Chloe scrambled up to the second fork in the trunk where, I knew, the bark was smooth and flecked with lichen, and the branches were wide and generous. Perfect for the lonely, perennially grubby girl who had made it her den all those years ago. Chloe hooked her leg over the branch and settled back. "I'm probably looking at exactly what you looked at."

"Probably."

She squinted across at the remains of the tree house's platform. "The planks look rotten."

"Be careful." A breeze rippled the leaves. I knew that sound so well. In the end, I had known the pathway up that tree better than the stairs in the house.

"Did you know, Dad, I drank my first bottle of cider up there, and practiced swearing?"

"Of course," he said. "These and many other unspeakable sins. I used to prowl underneath, just to make sure you were all right."

"Really? I never saw you. I always thought I was the clever one."

"And so you were, my Francesca." He patted my hand and looked extremely pleased with himself. "And so you were. But I wasn't a complete fool."

I hunkered down to remove a stone from my shoe and my hair fell back over my shoulders. "It is extraordinary how like your grandmother you are growing, Francesca, and Chloe has a little of the look of her, too. But perhaps more like Lucilla?"

"Lucilla?"

"Did I say Lucilla? I'm getting muddled in my old age. I don't know what I'm talking about."

This was unlikely as my father was as sharp as a tack but I shot a look at him. For some reason, he did not wish to explain who Lucilla was but, however much I tried to ignore it, he was growing older. Fright drove a painful stiletto into me. "If I'm going to come back to work properly, why don't you offload some stuff onto me today? I can take it home."

"Why don't I?" His touch on my arm felt suddenly brittle, but the ease of his surrender worried me more.

"Guys, I'm coming down." A moment later, Chloe landed beside us. "Got moss all over my jeans, Mum. And this is my *traveling* pair."

It was not strictly necessary for me to brush and pat Chloe clean but, since I would not have her for much longer, I allowed myself free rein. It gave me the excuse to smooth back her hair and run my hands over her shoulders to check they were not too thin. Savor and memorize, I told myself. *Imprint* the feel of her.

Will—of course—was unable to see Chloe off. According to the schedule faxed through by his office, he was in Spain. "Send her my dearest love and . . . Fanny, make sure you give her some extra money. From me. I'll pay you back."

Nor could Sacha. "At a gig."

99

I drove Chloe and her rucksack to the airport where we met Jenny and Fabia, her traveling companions.

The three girls tried their best to pay attention to their three mothers while the final lecture—*stick together, watch out for spiked drinks and lecherous, possibly murderous, men*—was delivered in anxious, staccato bursts.

I drew Chloe aside. "I'm sorry Sacha isn't here."

Chloe averted her eyes with the long, long lashes, but not before I had caught a glimpse of panic and hurt. "Sacha doesn't think good-byes are important. But I think they are, don't you, Mum?"

She fingered her day sack, which contained her money, ticket and passport. "Anyway, he couldn't have come. He was too busy. The gig was important."

"You did pack all the medicines?"

"Yes, Mum."

"You've got your money belt on?"

"You've asked me that twice."

Her role was to be composed and determined. Mine was to fuss, fear and, finally, to raise my hand in farewell.

Chapter 9

HOPING TO CATCH A final glimpse of her—a hint of head, or a suggestion of shoulder—I hovered outside Departures and watched the passengers file through. Some were girls like Chloe, Fabia and Jenny—young, hopeful, eager to be tested and tempered by what the world had to offer.

Five minutes sifted by, then ten. I shifted my bag from

one shoulder to the other. I dug my hand into my jacket pocket and felt the car-park ticket slide under my nail. I was preparing myself. A tooth is numb after Novocain, but the pain is not absent, merely waiting.

An official on the gate sent me a look of boredom blended with mild suspicion. He'd seen it all before. My mobile phone did not take international calls and I ducked into a telephone booth, rang Will and fed more coins into the slot and waited.

"What's up?" he asked eventually.

"I forgot to check that Chloe had her fleece. It's winter in Australia now and she will be cold."

"Is that why you've got me out of a meeting?"

"I just wanted to tell you she's gone."

His voice sounded tender—but also a little exasperated. "I'm glad you did. Listen, you idiot, she can buy something out there. They do have shops."

"I know," I said, miserably. "I know I shouldn't have rung you. I'm being stupid, that's all."

"Well, I'm glad you did," he repeated, and did not terminate the conversation with the usual "must go" until he had talked me through Chloe's potential goose bumps and checked that I had enough money to pay for the car park.

In the car, I cried all the way to Elaine's house and the tears dripped down my face and fell into my lap.

I had met Elaine Miller at a Christmas party at the House of Commons. It was my first outing as the wife of a new MP and I was nervous, but she put me immediately at ease. A tall, whippet-thin redhead whose husband was also tipped for fast-track promotion, Elaine maintained that she disagreed with most things that he believed in and considered politics to be nasty and corrupting. "But what the hell?" she said. "I love him, and I fall in behind him." She gave me a beautiful, honest smile. "I am the original trouper, and I suspect you will be, too."

"Be warned," she added as we scribbled down each other's addresses. "Parliament *hates* women. It makes their lives as difficult as possible."

As luck would have it, Neil's constituency was not so far from Stanwinton, and Elaine and I fell into the habit of escaping children and commitments and stole "trouper-away days" together. Of course, while the children were small, these were limited. "Wait until they are older," we promised each other, "then we'll do something *really* exciting." The promises added a frisson of expectation to the friendship and gave suggestive shape to the future—which, while we stumbled around in a furor of child care and school runs, seemed shapeless and distant.

Simple, unambitious, the trouper-away days were spur of the moment. They imported a touch of fantasy and nonsense in our planned lives: a trip to a garden, or to the cinema where we ate popcorn, or we had lunch and talked. Elaine had three children and planned to start up a knitwear business. "I'm biding my time," she said. "It's an art all women have to develop."

"*All* women?"

This time the lovely, honest smile held a hint of anger. "If you have children. Think about it."

Her house was a replica of mine—rather ugly and not

much loved by the person whose fate it was to live in it most—which always amused us. She was making chocolate cupcakes for the Red Cross charity fete when I walked into the kitchen. There was a deafening noise coming from upstairs.

"That's Jake," she said as she kissed. "Practicing the drums."

"Just like home," I said.

She grabbed me by the shoulders and searched my face. "Very down in the dumps?"

"A bit." I bit my lip. "Actually, very. I don't know what I'm going to do without Chloe."

"Right. Let's make a list," she said briskly. "First of all you will help me make these wretched cakes and then you will ring home and tell them you are staying the night, and blow everyone else." She thrust a wooden spoon at me. "Get going. Earn your keep."

Upstairs, the drum beats rolled and crashed. Elaine sighed and brushed back her hair with a hand that trembled. I asked a little anxiously, "Are *you* all right?"

"Sure."

But, over a supper of spaghetti Bolognese and a bottle of wine, Elaine confessed, "I've had enough of this life."

This was not like her. "What's happened?"

There was a long pause and she dropped her head into her hands. "I think Neil may be having a serious affair this time." Her voice was muffled. "All the signs are there. One of the secretaries in the House. I've been trying not to face it, but I must."

"Oh, Elaine."

She raised her head. "I didn't mean to say anything,

Fanny. Not while you're feeling so bereft."

That was so like Elaine and I cast around as to how I could possibly help and comfort. "Tell me about it," I said, "and then we can work out what's best."

We spent half the night talking and went to bed not much the wiser and with nothing resolved. We could think of any amount of practical things to do—including Elaine packing her bags—but none of them was a panacea for anguish. Stupid with fatigue, I arrived home mid-morning to find my house in an uproar. Overnight, Brigitte had done a bunk. At some point the previous evening, she had packed her bags, dropped the keys onto the kitchen table and abandoned ship.

"Without a word," said Meg, avoiding my eyes. "I didn't hear a taxi or anything."

"She izt horrible womans," Maleeka said.

Brigitte had not appeared to me to be "horrible womans." Irritating, perhaps, but not horrible. Yet when I discovered that her parting shot had been to let herself into our bathroom and help herself to my shampoo and bath oil, her malice felt like sandpaper against sunburned skin.

On Friday night, Will arrived home unexpectedly early.

I was sitting at the kitchen table. Having worked my way through a pile of my father's invoices and shipping orders, I was reading a couple of files I'd scooped up at Ember House. "Ambitious," he had written of one vineyard, "but too impatient." Of another, "Soil unlikely to yield." Of a third, "Terroir limited and undefined." They were so like him, these precise, careful assessments.

"Where am I?" Elaine had cried. "*Who* am I? Where do I go from here?" Her distress had affected me deeply—for all sorts of reasons that were not only to do with my affection for her.

I sorted the papers into Done and Must Do, and surveyed the piles. Come to that, who was I? Certainly, I was not Fanny Savage, wife, mother, wine expert and business woman, which once had been my ambition.

But that had been my choice. I had had my reasons. Love, practicality, the desire to build something strong and lasting beneath my roof.

"Hallo, darling," said Will.

I looked up, surprised, and did not register for a second who he was. He was in his best gray suit and sported a light tan. "I wasn't expecting you yet."

"I managed to get an earlier flight. I thought I'd try and come home early to see how you were." He smiled rather sadly. "I knew you'd be missing Chloe."

I held up my hand and he took it. "That was nice of you. You look well. You found a second or two to sit by the pool."

"Yup." He dropped a kiss on my head. "What are you up to?"

"The usual Battista stuff. I've been talking to Dad about taking on a bit more; I really think he needs the help. What do you think?"

He frowned slightly and flopped down into a chair. "Any chance of supper? Where are the others?"

"I'll see what I can rustle up. Meg decided to go to an AA meeting and Sacha's in London." Something in his pose alerted me to trouble. "Has something gone wrong?"

"Trouble . . . of course." He sighed. "The car lobby is getting pretty vicious over the second-car tax. It's got a lot of money at its disposal and a couple of the tabloids have come out in its favor, banging on about personal freedom." He sounded unusually despondent, and very tired.

I got up and laid a hand on his shoulder. The material of his suit jacket felt smooth, expensive, sophisticated. "Not so very terrible. And there is always trouble somewhere along the line."

"It's pretty bad," he said. "If this goes wrong, I'll look a fool, and it will mark me out as a loser."

He twisted round to look at me, and I knew he was still aching for the chancellorship. I opened the fridge and surveyed its contents. "How about fish cakes and tomato salad?"

"Fine."

"By the way, Brigitte's packed her bags and done a bunk. Last night, without any warning."

Will was not listening. "Do you care at all about the second-car tax, Fanny? I'd rather you told me now if you didn't."

I took a deep breath. "Not as much as I should." I put the fish cakes into a frying pan and chopped up the tomatoes. They were small, cold and tough and I cheered them up with a sprinkling of chives. What was the point in not telling the truth? "You know I've had doubts about the idea."

He was clearly hurt and a little bewildered, and it cut me to the quick. The ingrained habits of love and loyalty resurfaced and I put my arms around him. "Sorry, Will. But I can't summon the enthusiasm for it." He leaned against me and I stroked his hair, relishing its thickness.

"I get a little tired, too," I continued, "of waiting and organizing, and of being on show all the time."

"Not much of a deal, is it?" he confessed. "For you, I mean. But I honestly don't know what I can do about it."

A cool little voice in my head said to me that Will was right and there was no point in pursuing the discussion. There wasn't anything to be done—except to live with it. Or was there? That cool little voice unsettled me even more when it added, sympathetically and most seductively: *Fanny, I think you need a holiday from being married.*

The idea made my knees shake. *Only a holiday?*

Will was searching my face for clues as to what I might be thinking and, unnerved by the subversion, I thought it best to return to the subject of the second-car tax. "I still think people don't want to be told what's good for them, Will."

"Listen to me," he urged and, once again, outlined the arguments for the scheme. I replied, reiterating mine. We found we agreed on one point, disagreed on another. We laughed about a third. Suddenly, our intimacy was back.

"Come upstairs with me, Fanny."

"Yes," I said.

"What a touching scene." Neither of us had heard Meg appear in the doorway.

Will released me and she glided up and gave him a hug. "Good meeting?" he asked.

She looked calm and collected. "Winning the

battle. I hope. No more scenes like the one you came back to . . . when was it? You know, the wedding anniversary scene?" She looked straight at me. "I am sorry about that, Fanny. I hope you have forgiven me?"

"Short meeting," I said.

She raised a quizzical eyebrow at my lack of response and unwound a pink scarf from her neck. "It's very simple and it can be said in two words. 'Don't drink.' Even the stupidest can get that message, and I'm not stupid."

Will regarded her fondly. "No, you're not."

"So what were you two talking about?"

I went to check on the fish cakes. "Second-car tax, what else? But I was rather hoping to discuss the revival of my career."

She tucked her arm into Will's. "I'm not up to speed," she said. "Tell me all about it."

I found myself chopping the last tomato with unnecessary vigor.

The week of the finance ministers' dinner dawned scratchy and unsettled, in keeping with the summer so far. I got myself to the hairdresser and spent two hours reading up the briefing notes on the European Union supplied by Will's office: Transport. Tariffs. Aids. Agricultural initiatives.

In the evening, Will led me into the ministerial car and surprised me by saying, "You look lovely."

"Thank you."

In a full, black silk skirt and matching peplum jacket,

my hair expertly swept back from my forehead, I sat between Antonio Pasquale—we greeted each other warmly—and the charming Italian ambassador. During the first two courses, I was occupied by Antonio and we discussed rubies. He had noted my ring. "Is there not a passage in the Bible that refers to a good woman being above the price of rubies?" He smiled into my eyes. "Your husband should have bought you a bigger one."

I said, "This must remain a secret between us, Antonio—but I agree." Conversationally, we both did well and, as dessert was served and I turned to my right, I was sure he winked at me.

The Italian ambassador was formidably well educated and good looking. "Is something amusing you, Mrs. Savage?"

"I think your finance minister has just winked at me."

"Can I wink at you, too?"

"If you like."

"Your husband has been most energetic lately. He is a notable politician." He leaned toward me. His breath was scented with raspberries and vanilla. "We just need a little more time to think through his scheme. You know that we've stuck on one or two points."

Out of the corner of my eye, I saw Will fix his gaze on me. *Don't let me down.*

Teamwork. The spoon in my hand was cool and hard and the raspberries lingered sweetly on my tongue. Once a team, always a team.

"Why don't you talk to him after dinner?"

"Maybe the Prime Minister. . . . We're not sure how supportive the Prime Minister is . . ."

I smiled. "The Prime Minister is not a personal friend."

"But perhaps you will remind your husband to consider everyone's interests."

I reported this conversation to Will when we got back to the flat. "Point taken," he said, climbed into bed and reached for the red box.

Fatigue was etched into his face. "Will, would you ever consider doing something different?"

"Not really. Though there are times . . . it used to seem so straightforward. Get elected and start improving the world. . . . It isn't that simple, is it? But I don't see myself getting off the treadmill quite yet."

I turned away and pulled the pillow under my head. The box hit the floor and Will put his arms around me. "Fanny . . ."

But the distance had opened up again between us, and I struggled with my feelings of indifference . . . and remoteness. Will had almost—but not quite—become a stranger, a troubling kind of stranger—someone I had once known inside out, but who had slipped into acquaintanceship.

"Oh Fanny," he said at last. He pulled back my arms and caught me by my wrists. "I miss you . . ."

I made an effort and put my arms around his neck. It was a matter of faith, I think, and an effort of will. I had to believe that the passionate feelings we once shared were not completely dead.

It worked.

Afterward, he said, "Fanny, that was so nice."

I smiled and touched his thigh. "It was."

. . .

I lay awake, listening to the sounds of the city.

I would have given almost anything to be walking on a hot hillside where my father told me that the vines plunged deep through clay and sand. I wanted to squint through the sunlight at a horizon where *Cupressus sempervirens* pointed to the sky, and to see olive trees, fat tomatoes on skinny stakes, the bright green of basil.

I ached, too, for Chloe and wondered where she was. Did her feet or her back hurt? Was she fed and were her clothes clean? Would she cope with . . . the experiences that lay before her? Those bewildering, sometimes funny, mistaken, sometimes treacherous encounters with the as-yet unknown. Like mine?

From the branches of my beech tree at Ember House, I had spied on cars as they negotiated the bend in the road that skirted the garden. If I angled my (plastic, shocking pink) telescope correctly, I got a good view of the occupants. Often, when a car slowed, the women passengers flipped down the sunshade to check their lipstick in the mirror. Occasionally, the driver wound down the window and chucked out rubbish. This behavior made me conclude that people were very peculiar.

It was on my eighteenth birthday that I took Raoul up to my eyrie; we clawed and cursed our way up in the dark. For once, Raoul had drunk too much wine, and I was wearing delicate, strappy sandals. The platform groaned under the weight of our bodies, and we embraced clumsily. My thin cotton dress split at the seam when Raoul tugged too hard and he pounced on the tongue of flesh which appeared. "So brown," he

111

murmured, and wrenched off his shirt. Raoul had been wanting this for a long time.

On his first visit to help out in the Battista business when I was sixteen, we had avoided each other.

My father had noticed and made sure that he invited Raoul over again a couple of years later. *You will have to get to know one another,* he said. *These links are important for the wine.*

Raoul was now twenty and sharpened by desires, and I was eighteen and sharpened by curiosity.

Raoul had laid his siege. He had taken me to the cinema, which smelled of cigarette smoke and decaying popcorn, and we sat on plush seats that bit into the soft flesh of my bare legs and he held my hand. He had taken me for walks and told me about the family business and what he would do when, eventually, he took it over. As he talked, I watched him . . . stirred by this suggestion of power, by the differences between him and me.

Stirred, too, by the fact—the increasingly obvious fact—that I held power over him. But of its scope and limits I did not know precisely.

Nor did I know myself.

Inexperience and ignorance made me shrink and Raoul was unnecessarily rough. We had no saving grace of humor, only a grim determination to get the deed done.

"I'm sorry, I'm sorry," Raoul said at last. He lifted a face sheened with sweat. "I love you."

But I pushed him away.

That was unfair of me.

A tree house is no place for seduction. It belongs to

childhood . . . to a different place. Now, it was spoiled.

That night, I quit my tree house in more ways than one.

I turned over in bed and considered the aspects of my life. The rubies and crimsons, the frail gold and amber of wine. My father. Will. Meg. Sacha.

Pushing my daughter toward Departures . . .

Chapter 10

. . . As I HAD PUSHED her into life . . .

The first contraction took me by surprise when I was eating an early supper by myself in the flat.

I was thirty-nine weeks pregnant and, when I reflected on the rapidity of the changes in my own life, it seemed to me that I had known Will for very little longer. I had met him in January, married him in June, and was pregnant by October.

Chloe, as it turned out, was the result of that first quarrel over the Australian wine-tasting trip. We made up in the best way we knew and I had not the least inkling that I was pregnant when I went out and bought a brown leather diary and laid it in front of Will, in order that both of us should know exactly what the other was doing.

"I do want to be a good wife to you," I told him. "I will try my best, but you will have to compromise as well . . ."

"Of course I will," he replied. "What else does a good husband do?"

In the end, because the pregnancy was a little tricky,

the doctors felt it would be unwise to fly long haul and the question resolved itself. I went instead to a series of carol concerts, the Homeless Persons' Christmas tea and the mayor's cocktail party.

The six o'clock news flashed onto the television screen, and Will rang to say that he was caught up in a meeting and not to keep supper. I was feeling soggy, stupid and apprehensive, and it flashed across my mind that Will loved his work more than he loved me. Worse, he understood it better than he understood me, and *preferred* to be doing it rather than having supper with his wife.

"Fine," I said.

"Miss me?"

I glanced at the television. "No."

"I'll take that as a yes. Do *both* of you miss me?"

A smile forced its way to my lips. "No."

Like an animal, I had gone underground. I had become blind and subterranean, blundering through the days. Toward the end, I scaled down my work for Battista Fine Wines and retreated to our flat. On one level, I craved Will's attention—and he had been so thrilled at the news, that he had rushed out and bought a stack of books on pregnancy and childbirth and was meticulous in updating me. "Did you know it's the size of a broad bean?" "Now, it's the size of an ammonite." On another level, I did not. Curiously, at this point Will had almost become superfluous, for I was wrapped up in a female parcel, an enormous, bulky thing with embarrassing aches and pains. The books informed the reader exhaustively about backache, varicose veins and other delights, and illustrated the invasion of the body with copious diagrams. Not one of them, however, was honest about how thoroughly one's mind was invaded. How the broadbean-cum-ammonite sucked dry one's river of wit, energy, calculation and inventiveness until there was not much left.

With Will frequently not around, and without the energy to visit my friends, I was alone quite a lot of time, and I had fallen into the habit of talking to myself. "I feel like softening butter, underdone jam, a melting snowman," I informed the grill pan as I cleaned it after my solitary supper—a task that, these days, represented the level of my achievements.

My father rang to check on my progress. "You're alone? This is not right. Someone should be there. What if something goes wrong?"

"Don't panic. I'm fine."

He sounded angry. "Shall I come down?"

"Will promised to be back after supper."

In the background, his second phone shrilled. "Got to go," said my father. "I'll keep in touch."

A second contraction was intrusive enough to make me gasp. I pressed my hand into the small of my back and walked up and down the tiny sitting area.

More contractions sent shocks through my body. Apprehension turned to fright. A phone call to the House elicited the information that Will had left a short while ago and had left no contact number. I tried his beeper, but it was switched off.

I rang Elaine, who happened to be in London, and she said at once, "Would you like me to come over?"

Friendship was sweet but no substitute for Will. I thanked her and said, "Could you ring my father? Tell him I'm on my way to the hospital."

From then on I don't remember the fine detail, only the general picture, for which lack of clarity I am grateful. The midwife said it was because it happened so fast, which was unusual for a first baby. I do have one fixed memory: of me hovering above a thrashing figure who, with a shock, I recognized as myself. The room seemed to be filled with shadow, and was illuminated only by a dim light. The midwife moved in and out of that shadow. Sometimes she spoke to me. Sometimes I answered.

Soon I changed my mind about wishing to be alone. I wanted someone to hold my hand and pull me back from the strange, disembodied person on the delivery bed. I craved for the touch of someone who loved me, and cried with pain and for Will's absence.

"Look who's here . . ." The midwife materialized by the bed and, wild-eyed, I reared up expecting to see Will.

"Hey," said Meg. "Your father rang." She was wrapped in a black jumper that was too big for her and, despite the heat in the room, she was shivering. Traces of whiskey hung on her breath.

I fought the impulse to turn my face away. "Isn't Will coming?"

"He's on his way," she said. She picked up my hand and I knew she was probably lying. Her cold touch was like a burn, and I wished she was anywhere but here.

Then things began to happen. Meg stood beside the

bed, wiped my face and informed me that I was doing fine. And she was the first to see Chloe.

She was born at twenty-five minutes to midnight, without the aid of drugs. "What a good girl," said the midwife. "What a brave, *good* girl. So much better for Baby if Mummy does it all herself."

She placed Chloe on my stomach, a still pale and muted ammonite. Until that moment, I had been preoccupied with the heroic and peculiar physical achievements of my body. Now there was a moment of hush, of expectation. I looked down. How extraordinary, was the thought that flashed through my mind. This is what a nine-month invasion of my body and an undignified battle on a delivery bed results in.

Chloe turned her face toward me and screwed up her eyes. Her hand reached up into the air as if she were grasping for her life. That tiny hand looped an invisible, unbreakable silken cord, aimed it at my heart and, with one flick of those shrimp-pink fingers, lassoed it forever.

"She's perfect." Meg leaned over to inspect her, and there was a yearning note in her voice. "I think I should be godmother, don't you?"

She left when Will burst into the room a short while later. "I'm so sorry, so very sorry." Unsure of whether or not to touch me, he hovered by the bed. "I'll never ever do that again. I'll never not check."

"Your daughter's over there, Will."

He took a chance and slid his arm round my shoulders and kissed me. He was very, very disappointed, furious with himself. "It was a late sitting. Regulations about child labor in East and British manufacturers. I

117

don't blame you if you are angry."

"Not angry . . . empty."

"I switched off the beeper, forgot and went off for a quick supper at Brazzi's. I've missed out, haven't I?"

His guilt was almost comic, but it was sad too. For he *had* missed out—on that special, perfect moment when Chloe came into the world.

The backwash of exhaustion, discomfort and spent hormones was draining my strength. "Go and look at your beautiful daughter. Then please ring Dad . . . and my mother. I promised her that you would."

"Forgive me?"

Of course I did. Chloe was here, well and safe and, set against that, there was nothing to forgive.

Pearl Veriker found the house in Stanwinton. She sent us the particulars. "This one would do," she wrote, in a determined hand. The *do* was heavily underscored.

It was a couple of miles outside the town, halfway down a lane and flanked by two fields. It was a rambling house, built of harsh red brick in late-Victorian Gothic style, with a couple of outhouses tacked on to the kitchen.

Will was delighted. He pointed out the proportions of the bedrooms and the view over the fields. Downstairs required a lot of work but he was excited by the challenge. "I can build shelves," he said. "And lay floors. I like do-it-yourself-projects."

His energy and enthusiasm were infectious and it was a relief to know we could afford the house and make plans. I stood in the place where he reckoned we should put the kitchen and looked out at the rookery in the clump of beeches beyond the rather ridiculous Gothic window. Black shapes wheeled in and out of the branches. I told myself that the country was a much better place to bring up a baby and felt surprisingly content.

We moved in when Chloe was four weeks old. Still sore and battered, and bewildered by the routines of feeding and nappy changing, I found myself fearful of leaving the safety of our tiny flat, but Will insisted that I would feel better once we had settled.

"I don't feel capable of doing anything," I confessed, and even my voice sounded different. I put it down to hoarseness from my cries but I almost believed it was because I was changing so profoundly.

"That's quite normal," he said.

"How do you know?"

"The books say."

I managed a weak smile. "If the *books* say."

The fields were bristling with stubble as our heavily laden car nosed between them, and the leaves on the beech trees swayed in the breeze. In the back of the car where I sat with Chloe, I looked out on the fields and experienced a dawning sympathy, even affection for them. They might be plain and utilitarian but they were going to be companion presences.

Mannochie was waiting at the front door. "Welcome to you all," he said as he helped me out of the car. On cue, Chloe began to wail and I could not quiet her. "May I?" asked Mannochie, and picked her up. Wouldn't you know? Chloe stopped crying.

"I didn't know you were good with babies, Man-nochie."

"Years of kissing them." Mannochie was rocking her in a way that she appeared to like. "She's lovely."

"Isn't she just?" Will appeared with the first of the suitcases.

I left them to it and stepped over the threshold. The men had been hard at work on the house. The freshly varnished banister felt sticky under my hand as I went upstairs and the virgin carpet a little slippery underfoot. Our bedroom smelled of paint and I tugged open the window, leaned on the sill and surveyed a landscape that I would have to learn about.

My back ached and my mind felt dull and spongy. Was there something seriously wrong with me? I felt drained of life and miserably daunted by the prospect of having to sort out the tiniest details around the house. I was frightened that I, the efficient and busy Fanny, was not going to be able to cope.

I had lost something. My tree house and the freedom I had experienced up in its branches belonged to another country, far, far away—as distant as the one I had lived in when, eager to begin, I had seized the reins of my father's business and embarked on that life. Without doubt, I would grow older—old—and never go there again.

I closed my eyes. Somewhere a baby was crying and resentment flickered. It was gradually dawning on me that a new mother could not be alone, or only for a few minutes at a time, and that frightened me, too.

Mannochie padded upstairs. "Chloe's crying."

"I know." I did not move.

He tried again. "She seems hungry."

I opened my eyes. I should close the window and go downstairs. But I wanted to remain here and watch the rooks wheeling through a gun-metal sky.

Mannochie touched my arm. "Have you been to the doctor for a check-up, Fanny?"

"For which read: Are you going to be able to manage?" I muttered.

Mannochie looked taken aback. "I'm sure you will."

"Fanny!" Will appeared with a screaming Chloe and thrust her toward me. Then he peered at me. "Are you OK?"

"Fine," I said.

While the men brought in the luggage and made tea, I sat and fed Chloe. Enchanted by her, enraptured by her, angered by her, I watched the busy button mouth and the little veins in her almost transparent eyelids. "You're a greedy minx," I informed her.

Chloe took no notice. After she had finished, her head fell back and she slept. Gradually, the jangle of feelings inside me subsided.

Will came up with a cup of tea and watched us fondly. His presence was calming and, suddenly, I felt almost peaceful and happy.

"Here," he said, and settled me against his shoulder, and took Chloe onto his lap. "Just sit for a while. There's no hurry."

"I love you both very much," he added.

Chapter 11

"OK, READY," CALLED THE photographer from the *Stanwinton Echo*. The camera flashed. "Again," he commanded.

I tried to hide my still bulky stomach behind Will.

"Smile and look to the left."

The experience was not as bad as I had feared. In fact it was fun to be the focus of attention and, at any other time, I might have taken to it.

"Could we have the baby now, please?"

The one thing that Will and I agreed on absolutely was sticking to the principle of keeping Chloe out of photographs and publicity. Yet here we were, with Chloe only a month old, in the town hall at a press conference. It was, we agreed, a minor emergency.

A more senior MP had been taken ill, and Will had been press-ganged into a TV discussion panel on transport. In the heat of the moment, he had fumbled over a phrase, which made it sound as if he were taking the opposite view to agreed party policy. Party-wise, it was a big, black mark against him.

After the program, he had driven home to Stanwinton and, during the night, had been very sick. I held his head and mopped up and made him tea.

He drank it gratefully and muttered, "I do this sometimes when things go wrong. Silly, isn't it?"

His confession touched me deeply and I sat up with him into the small hours while we tried to work out the best damage limitation plan.

The morning papers reported on the program and picked out Will for special mention. "Fluency and an independent mind," wrote one (upmarket) critic. "A Prince Charming talks straight," wrote another (downmarket). Mannochie got on the phone and they agreed that some well-focused local publicity would go a long way to propping up his image in the constituency.

One of the reporters now asked, "How do you feel about being the most glamorous couple in Parliament?"

A girl in leather trousers stuck up a finger. "Are you feeding the baby yourself, Mrs. Savage?"

Mannochie intervened. "If you wish to question Will on policy, now is the moment."

The girl made a face. *Policy? Get real!*

Relaxed and smiling, Will allowed the photographers to take as many shots as they wished and answered all their questions. Then I spotted an expression in his eyes that was neither patient nor obedient. It was a private expression that only I could interpret—a signpost to the real Will, the one who was shown to me only—and it made my senses quiver.

Mannochie had arranged that I would give one interview and I retreated with Chloe, who was behaving beautifully, into a smaller room with the girl in leather trousers whose name was Lucy.

She set down a tape recorder between us. "How do you see the role of today's political wife?"

"It's developing . . ." I replied. In the sudden quiet, my exhilaration vanished, my bones almost burned with fatigue and the weight of my broken nights hung heavy under my eyes.

"So not the traditional helpmeet, then?"

"Wives are different from the way they used to be."

"Would you vote differently from your husband?"

"If I felt it was right."

She looked extra sympathetic. "Given that political marriages are, for obvious reasons, at risk, do you think you can hack it with motherhood and a career?"

I resented the implication that Will and I were doomed. "I am not prepared to answer that question," I said. "As you will have noticed, my baby is still very young."

From that moment, the interview limped.

Two days later, the article was published. The headline read: "SKEPTICAL AND INDEPENDENT, THE MODERN MP'S WIFE VOTES AGAINST HER HUSBAND." The text read: "Fanny Savage is one of a new breed—a modern woman with a career and a mind of her own. If she felt it was right, she would vote for the opposition."

Pearl Veriker rang while I was still in bed feeding Chloe, and read the article out over the phone. "That was so unwise, Fanny. A betrayal, even."

With a sick feeling, I realized that Pearl's rule book was more complicated than I had thought. "Pearl, I am entitled to my own views, and this is hardly treason."

But, as with the wearing of tights, it seemed that there was no room for negotiation. In the end, I handed the phone over to Will and listened to him finessing Pearl back into calm.

This particular mess *was* my fault. I knew it, and Will knew it. He slumped back onto the pillow. "We discussed it so carefully," he said.

I rubbed my hands over my eyes. "She got me on the raw."

Will swung himself out of bed, ripped off the T-shirt in which he slept and dropped it on the floor. "We talked about that, too."

"Could I point out you made the first mistake."

"And I've paid for it twice."

I nuzzled Chloe's cheek. She smelled of milk and baby lotion, innocent, innocuous, ordinary, honest things. I visualized my culpability stretching out like a gauzy vapor trail through an endless sky. Had I ruined Will? Set a mark on him—*unreliable*—like Cain? "I'm sorry. I forgot how hard it is not to say what you think."

Will wrenched open the shirt drawer. "Hasn't it been made plain enough to you? Never, ever say what you think."

There was a long, odd silence as we each absorbed the implications of what the other had said.

"Will, don't you think it is slightly strange that, in order to appear honest and transparent, we have to pretend?"

Will picked out a blue shirt and examined the collar. "I know." He looked up at me, perplexed, and more than a little aghast. "I *know.*"

My father was horrified when I rang up, almost incoherent with exhaustion and strain, and reported my lapse.

"This is outrageous, Francesca. How dare that woman speak to you in that way? I'm coming over this afternoon, and I'm taking you back with me to Ember House and you will stay with me for a bit. There is no argument."

I rang Will and told him I was going home with my father. "Just for a couple of weeks."

"What do you mean 'going home'?" He was offended. "I thought home was with me."

"Sorry. Slip of the tongue." But it made heavy weather of our conversation and, not for the first time, I wished we did not have to discuss plans, issues and developments by phone. "Do you mind? It would do Chloe and me good."

"I notice you've just gone ahead." But, in the end, he said, "Of course, you must go. Of course, you must have some help."

I put down the phone. A layer of dust roosted on one of the ugly radiator cases, but I was too tired to fetch a duster. I blew on it instead. The dust lifted and settled back. "Go away," I ordered it. "Pack your suitcase and go somewhere else."

I walked through the door of Ember House and felt the strain and fatigue of the last few months loosen their grip.

"I've ordered in pints of milk," said my father, "to help with the feeding and laid in masses of food."

I managed a smile. "I don't think it works like that."

"Well, it should." He peered. "And that means three good meals a day, and no nonsense about getting thin."

He took Chloe from me. "Look, she's already a beauty."

"And clever, Dad. She has us all running around after her."

He sat down with her on his knee and propped her up. "I won't make the same mistakes that I did with you."

"You didn't make any mistakes," I countered. "You are the best father. A good father."

My father was gently examining the shape of his granddaughter's head. "There were times when I felt like packing the whole thing in and dispatching you to your mother. But, of course, I didn't."

I busied myself with a stack of Chloe's diapers. "Was I in the way?" Suddenly, I was close to tears.

"Francesca, you haven't grasped my point. Once you arrived, I simply couldn't be without you. It was as simple as that. If I am sorry for your mother, which I am not, it is because she did not have you." He stroked Chloe's chubby cheek. "You will find out. If you have children, then you look after them. No discussion."

I observed the interaction between grandfather and granddaughter. No need to find out, for I already knew. I wiped my eyes surreptitiously and got on with unpacking Chloe's things in a room that appeared to be charged with love, the uncomplicated, unconditional kind that I craved.

Chloe opened her mouth and began to cry. My breasts seeped. Quick as a flash, my father handed her back to me.

Home . . . I should say Ember House . . . was solid, peaceful, shabby and, above all, familiar. It allowed me to be sleepy and doe-like. It knew me and I knew it. No surprises. No adjustments necessary. But the best thing of all was the arrival of Benedetta, summoned from

Fiertino by my father, who had asked her to let bygones be bygones.

"*Santa Patata,* you are pale," she said. "You must eat liver. I will cook it for you."

Naturally, she took charge, and it was as if the intervening years had been swept away. She issued orders in the foreground and fussed in the background—laundering Chloe's tiny garments, making sure I slept in the afternoon, whisking Chloe away when she was fretful in the evenings and making sure I had time with Will when he came down on the weekend. "You are my *bambina,* Fanny, and I look after my *bambina's bambina.*"

They were clever, my father and Benedetta. And generous. Despite their past, they united to give me the space and the peace to concentrate on Chloe. I learned that one kind of cry meant hunger, another that she was uncomfortable and bored. With Benedetta's advice, conducted in her broken English and my Italian, which could always do with improvement, I began to understand Chloe's needs—when to feed, when to put her to sleep, when she needed additional soothing. Under Benedetta's tuition, I began to flex the muscles necessary to carry, lightly and gracefully, the weight of change and of motherhood.

The day before I went home was cool and blustery and I went out into the garden.

The smell never changed: damp earth, a sharp, acrid whiff of mold under the trees, the sweeter tang of shrubs growing close by. I left a trail of footsteps on the wet lawn as I made for the beech tree.

I stood under it and squinted up through the leaf canopy and the fractured light. The tree house still looked intact, and I ran my palms over my hips. *Go on, Fanny*. Smiling, I placed a hand on the first branch and hauled myself up. Easy. Then I scrambled up to the platform wedged on the thickest branch. This was less easy.

Up there, balanced on the planks, I felt queen of all I surveyed. The breeze shook raindrops off the leaves and I licked one off my wrist. It tasted clean and cool. Up here, I felt weightless, without responsibility, without the terrors that came wrapped up with a new baby. I felt peaceful. Not precisely how I used to be, but good enough. I eased back against the branch and felt the breeze on my cheek. Soon, it would be time to climb down, brush away the lichen and moss from my jeans and return to the house to feed Chloe.

Gradually, my jangled feelings lightened, lifted and drifted away.

That evening to cheer me up, my father held a little party. I squeezed myself into a tight black skirt, wincing at the pad of fat still attached to my stomach and stood in the receiving line in a pair of high heels which tilted my pelvis forward and pinched my toes. It was quite like old times.

The guests were wine people and I knew them all, including Raoul who was over for a short visit. At first, there was a trace of awkwardness but it soon wore off. "How's the nose?" he asked as he kissed me. As pregnancy was known to affect the nose, it was the first question he would have asked.

"I don't know," I said seriously. "I shall have to see."

Raoul had olive skin, an interesting, sensitive face and he liked to dress well. Today, for some reason, he had a scratch on his cheek, which gave him a bold and buccaneering look.

"What happened?"

"I was hacking down some undergrowth back home and it bit me. But I haven't congratulated you," he said. "I hope when the baby is older you will make sure you pay us a visit. My family would love to see her."

"I would love that, too."

In France, passion for good wine was part of the national psyche—it is what makes the French consider themselves French, apart from their language. Thus the Villeneuves would consider it only their due that they lived in the most exquisite château I had ever seen.

He peered at me. "You look a little tired, Fanny. I know it is hard after a baby to get back to normal."

"A little." His sympathy was sweet, but too close to the bone. I forced back treacherous tears and I looked away, down at the carpet that I had helped to choose with Caro many years ago. It was a blue one, patterned with gold fleur-de-lis.

He came to my aid by saying in a matter-of-fact way, "My father will be retiring soon, and I will be taking over."

How perfect, I thought. Raoul's life is now arranged like an immaculately set dinner table. Well off, position assured. Doing what he loves. Knife, fork, spoon . . . and wine glass.

"What's so funny?" he asked.

I told Raoul and he said he considered that the interesting bit in life would prove to be when one has worked through the hors d'oeuvres and was halfway through the entrée.

"We must discuss it when we get there," I said.

Before I left for home my father and I had a serious talk about the business. "Fanny, I think you should consider taking more time off until Chloe is well launched. There's no hurry for you to come back. I can manage for the moment."

I was not sure if I was hurt or relieved. "Perhaps you're right," I said.

My father looked at me thoughtfully. "I think for the moment, you must concentrate on Chloe."

My father was right, but I struggled to be grateful and sensible. It was as if all my unquestioned assumptions were under attack, and up for renegotiation without my permission.

"By the way," added my father, "Raoul tells me he is going to marry Thérèse. Very suitable." Thérèse, I knew, was the daughter of a fellow wine family, and also very well off, and the union would be suitable, a brilliant merging of business interests. He smiled. "So, it has all worked out, hasn't it?"

Chapter 12

I WANTED TO GO home. I missed Will and, now that I felt stronger, I needed to be in my own domain. The idea of it was growing clearer and more urgent: the notion of drawing the curtains, lighting the fire and tucking my daughter into a cheerful bedroom decorated with Beatrix Potter's Peter Rabbit.

"Now you take care," said my father, holding me close.

"Now, *you* take care." I kissed his cheek, so familiar beneath my lips.

With his instructions about getting some help ringing in my ears, I got into the car and drove away.

The laurel hedge was still the same dispiriting color and rooks dived over the beeches. No change there. I carried Chloe into the kitchen and slotted her into her bouncer. "My best girl," I told her, and her mouth split into such a lovely grin that I could not resist picking her up again. She smelled of baby and was so small and trusting that I knew I would die to protect her from harm.

Elaine arrived with her children at lunchtime, en route from London. She brought lunch with her and we ate store-bought quiche, scraping away the pastry because it was soggy and agreeing that it was more slimming that way.

Chloe bounced in her chair beside us and Elaine's children rampaged in the garden. Elaine herself seemed to fill the kitchen with her energy and crackle. She cast her eye over the battered old stove, the packing cases still filled with china. "Could be nice here; if you made the effort."

I sat back in my chair. "Give me time."

Will sneaked up on Chloe and me as I was giving her the evening bath. He slid his arms around my waist. "Hallo, Mrs. Savage. Please don't go away again."

I twisted round to kiss him. "I had planned to be all

beautiful, shiny-haired and lipsticked for you."

He swept the damp hair away from my neck and pressed his mouth onto the exposed skin and I gasped. "Careful, I'll drop Chloe."

Later on, we sat down to supper and Will produced a bottle of wine. "I want you to approve my choice. I've been doing some homework."

"Have you?" I felt extraordinarily pleased and excited. I raised my glass and sniffed. Rich and warm. Tannin and black currant. "Perfect, Will. Eight out of ten. No, nine . . ."

"It isn't *that* good." His eyes danced above the rim of the glass. "Not one word about politics, tonight. Promise." He took another sip. "So, first off, do you love me?"

We were halfway through our roast chicken when Chloe woke up with a touch of colic. When I finally made it back downstairs, Will was on the phone deep in conversation with a colleague about an upcoming piece of income-tax legislation. I poked at my congealed chicken and listened in to a one-sided conversation about who in the party was likely to rebel, who would not, and the consequences.

Will was talking easily, rapidly, absorbed and intent. The lazy intimacy—the give and take of exchange, the delight in each other's company—of our supper table had vanished. By the time he had convinced his colleague that an extra penny on income tax was vital to fund a social program, I was on a second helping of fruit salad.

Will yawned. "Bed, I think."

At this point in the evening, I needed no persuading. We lay with our arms wrapped around each other and, almost immediately, Will fell asleep.

It seemed no time at all before Chloe demanded her night feed. She was fractious and grizzly and when at last I backed away from the cot, hardly daring to breathe, I was chilled and shivering with exhaustion.

Will had turned on the light and was sitting propped up on the pillows. He looked up and said, "Fanny, I've had an idea, which I've been mulling over. I meant to talk it over at supper." Then he dropped his bombshell. "I've been trying to think what's best for everyone. For us, and Chloe, and Sacha. And Meg. Meg has got to move out of her flat because the area is being redeveloped and she's looking for somewhere else. I know it's a really big thing to ask, a huge thing, but I feel it makes sense . . ."

"You're right," I said, as the implications of his idea sank in. "It is too big a thing to ask."

He picked up my cold hand and kissed the fingers, one by one. "Listen to me. I've worked it out. We could turn the scullery into a kitchen for Meg and give her the rooms above as a bedroom and sitting room. There's plenty of space in this house, and the alterations would be worth doing anyway. I can do some things."

I had heard that before. "Will, you know you won't. . . . Anyway, that's beside the point."

There was a lengthy silence.

Will broke it first. "Families should help each other, shouldn't they, Fanny? Meg is miserable, needs a home. I thought that this might be a way to keep an eye on her."

I let my hand rest in his. "Will, I don't want *anyone* living with us. It's enough being with you and Chloe."

"I know, I feel that, too, but . . ." Up went a questioning eyebrow. "You like Meg, don't you? She says she can talk to you."

Meg had told me the story of her broken marriage, her battle with the bottle and her anguish when Sacha was taken away to live with his father because of her drinking. Meg had become estranged from all she cared about—her ex-husband ("a saint whose patience snapped") and her son (who was only permitted to see her on weekends). I had felt very sad for her, and completely helpless.

"Of course, I like Meg," I said hurriedly. "I like lots of people. I *love* lots of people, but I don't want to live with them."

Will pulled me close. "Listen, Fanny. Here's a chance to practice what we preach. But not just for the sake of a cause, for the sake of my *sister* . . ."

"But, Will, this is a marriage, not a . . . charity."

I sensed he was struggling with the legacy of an old, difficult history. "Fanny, when I really needed her, she was there for me," he said simply. "It doesn't seem fair for me to turn my back on her now . . ." He brightened. "Also, we don't have much money to buy enormous amounts of help, and you need help. Meg can do her bit. You could come up to London to be with me without worrying." There was a pause. "And . . . you will have to go to functions in the constituency."

"No," I said. "No, it is not a good idea."

He looked down at our clasped hands and made a

final appeal. "She's losing her flat and she hasn't got a job at the moment; she can't cope. I owe her so much. In one way or another, her life has turned out pretty badly, and I can't help feeling that quite a lot of that is my fault."

I took my hands back for, as always, his touch was unsettling, and I needed to think. "Will, that's not true. Of course, Meg looked after you and that was wonderful. But it is not your fault that . . . that she didn't look after herself."

He searched for the words to convince me. "That's the theory but, in practice, I feel that if she had not taken me on, then it would have been different. I try to explain, or rationalize her away, but the truth is . . . I can't. So, there it is . . ."

Soon after that, Will fell asleep but I lay awake, puzzling out the contradictions. Should I help others at the cost of myself? I had no illusions that agreeing to Will's request would exact its price. But a desire to help was what he and I were about—what, in part, fueled our intimacy, our closeness—and I craved, above all, to keep that intimacy immaculate and rich with our private pleasures.

It was a long time before I slept.

When I woke, Will was beside the bed with Chloe draped over his shoulder. "She's hungry," he said. "I didn't know what to do with her."

Everything had changed. The room swam and my heart pounded in protest. Every nerve in my body screamed with exhaustion. Downstairs, a basket of laundry required attention. There was not much food in the fridge, and dust still crusted the radiator. I pushed my hair out of my eyes, and pulled myself upright. "Give her to me."

Will laid Chloe in my arms and I put her to suckle. "You win," I said to Will. "Meg can come and live here. But only for a few months, until everyone is straightened out. Just till I'm back on my feet and she's feeling better."

The builders were summoned, and I left with Chloe for Montana to see my mother. We planned to stay for a month. My father did not like it. "Why bother?" he demanded, with a rare flash of bitterness. "You can come and live in Ember House if the mess is that bad."

"Sally should see her granddaughter."

"Nothing stopping her from getting on a plane."

I hadn't seen Sally for three years, and it took me a moment or two to recognize her—she could have been any one of the middle-aged women dressed in sweatsuits or capacious jeans and fleeces who milled around the airport concourse. Sad or funny? My mother was somewhere in that crowd and I wasn't sure who she was.

Finally, I spotted her in a brown suede jacket with hair—frizzy and overlong—settled around a pale, freckled face innocent of makeup. Arms folded, she was leaning on the barrier and looked scared. Big, burly Art was beside her, scanning the arrivals. His baggy jeans and checked shirt were deceptive; he made a good living. Property in Montana was not like property in London, but there was plenty of it and more space.

"Hi," cried Sally, in a voice from which all traces of her English origins had long gone. She kissed my cheek briefly, embarrassed, and turned to Chloe. "Why, *hallo!*"

I relinquished Chloe and Art pumped my hand. "We sure appreciate this," he said. "Sally's been unreal with nerves for the past few days. Haven't known what to do with her."

Out of the corner of my eye, I saw my mother give a tiny shrug.

Sally and I sat in the back of the car with Chloe between us while Art drove extra carefully through the town and out the other side. He did not say much, but his was an easy silence. Sally did not say much either. "Hasn't changed much since you were last here. More houses, which is a pity."

Paradiseville had been so named at the height of gold fever, when it was thought a seam ran through the mountain foothills to the south, and a cluster of tin and wooden shacks had mushroomed down by the river. It had grown from there.

Art gave a satisfied chuckle. "That's fine by me. Good business, don't knock it."

"A person can make a comment," Sally said sharply.

I had forgotten that the Montana landscape was a spectacle on the scale of a grand opera or a wide-screen cinema epic. Nature was big here. It was like walking into a great golden tidal wave into which red and ocher had been splashed. Horses grazed against a backdrop of mountains, where the shadows lay purple and black.

I pointed all this out to Chloe, who took no notice.

To be honest, I remembered the house better than I

remembered my mother. Constructed of off-white painted clapboard, it had a veranda that ran around it and a swinging seat by the porch.

Sally slid out of the car. "I didn't know what you needed, so I asked Ma Frober down the way. She lent me some of her stuff. She's had six." Sally smiled a little anxiously. "Hope it's OK."

It was fine, except that Chloe was jet-lagged and refused to sleep for most of the first night. Her crying rang out through the small house and, as I strove desperately to pacify her, the light was switched on more than once in Sally and Art's room.

After breakfast, I sat on the swing seat with Chloe. Sally plumped up a cushion embroidered with a black horse and wedged herself beside me. She peered down at her granddaughter. "I had forgotten how awful it is." She rolled up her shirt sleeves, revealing freckled forearms. "I was no good at it at all," she confessed. "I've got no advice or handy tips."

"I'm not sure I've got the hang of it yet, either."

"I reckon a person is given only one talent. Mine's for horses. I always thought if you could cope with horses, you could cope with kids. But it doesn't work like that."

Chloe began to fuss and Sally set the seat to rock, which seemed to settle her, and we sat there talking of nothing much, until the sun slid around and hit us. Then we retreated to the kitchen. With one foot on the borrowed baby bouncer, I drank bitter coffee and jiggled Chloe while Sally prepared a meal of stew and carrots for later.

I tried not to stare at my mother, but I could not help

it. So much of her—the shape of her mouth, her high forehead—reminded me of myself. Could I edge closer and try to cross the barriers of time and history? It was impossible. All we shared was a set of genes, and that was not enough.

Now I had Chloe, my perspective on my mother had shifted. I knew what it was like to hold a tiny person against my body, and I experienced what it meant for her to depend on me absolutely. *How could you have deserted me?* was the question that trembled on my lips. But I did not ask it. A silence between a mother and a daughter should be an expression of the comfortable weight of mutual history. *My mother smacked me when I stole money out of her pocket. My mother made me wear a dress with smocking in coral pink silk. My mother promised me a hundred pounds if I did not smoke.* But there was nothing between me and Sally except a gap. Not a hostile gap (we did not know each other well enough for that), but an unfilled space.

Sally chopped a carrot. "How is your father?"

I knew she had steeled herself to ask the question. "Fine. He sends his regards. He wants a full report." I added: "I don't think he ever got over you."

She put down the knife and wiped her hands on her apron. "Yes, he did. He knew perfectly well that we . . . did not suit each other. He wanted one thing, I wanted another. In the end, I chose for him."

"You make it sound so simple."

Sally turned on the stove and slapped down a frying pan. "It was. If two people can't live together, one of them has to go. I'd met Art, so I went. It was better that you stayed in England with Alfredo."

I bent over and checked that the strap holding Chloe was secure. "I used to search for you in the street. I made up stories about you and imagined you might fly into my bedroom at night. I used to try and stay awake in case you did."

Sally went very still. "That's a lot to put on a person." She tipped the meat into the pan and the snap and hiss of frying filled the kitchen. "I wish I could say that I watched over you, but that's not the way it was. Not all women manage what is expected of them, and I don't see why I should be guilty, Fanny. You had Alfredo, who loved you."

"Sure," I said.

"Pass me the casserole, would you?"

I took it over to her. The phone rang and Sally answered it. I spooned cubes of meat and carrots into the casserole, added some stock, and put it into the oven.

The next day I was awake early and stretched out in the old spool bed in the spare room under a patchwork quilt, watching the sunlight slide like melted butter over the wall. Outside, birds sounded in the trees, and a breeze rollicked through the branches. This was a wilder, wider place than home, with a bigger horizon. Sally had left my father for Art, a simple love triangle, but I reckoned, warm and sleepy in bed, that it had been as much to do with the wind in the trees and a distant horizon as anything else.

"Come and see the horses," Sally said after we had had breakfast, and led the way up to the paddock behind the house. There were seven of her shaggy-maned, large-eyed darlings milling around and, at the sound of her voice, they came over to us and jostled for attention. Rapt and confident, Sally talked to each one in turn. "Here, Vince. Here, Melly . . ."

Not sure about them, Chloe squirmed in my arms, and I longed to be as assured in my handling of her as Sally was with her horses.

Sally took Chloe. "Go on. Make friends."

I touched the hot, fragrant hides and soft muzzles. Chloe blinked and Sally guided her small hand toward a steamy flank. "Nice horse, Chloe," she said. "When you're old enough, you must come and visit and I'll teach you to ride."

A sour taste came into my mouth. With a shock, I realized I was jealous of my own daughter. I busied myself with Melly's mane and struggled for control.

The moment passed.

Melly's neck was corrugated with muscle. I ran my hand over it, enjoying the feel of damp horse. "I wonder how Will is?"

"What sort of man is he?" Sally batted Melly's nose gently out of Chloe's orbit. "Would he like it here?"

"I think so. But he was too busy to come this time."

Sally gave me back Chloe and climbed over the fence. Her horses swirled around her and she attached a lead line to Melly's halter, grasped a handful of golden mane and swung herself up. She seemed older in daylight, though the thigh muscles under her denims were toned and strong. "Art gives himself plenty of time. That's the difference." She turned Melly, then trotted her to the end of the paddock and back again. "Just testing. We've had trouble with her hock. But she's fine."

In the distance, Art's car was nosing its way down the track toward us. He wound down the window, spilling country-and-western across the paddock. "Thought I'd make a detour," he said. "Say hi to you ladies."

He drove on.

"Now, that's what I call passing the test," Sally said fondly. "He does that most days." She slid down from Melly's back and leaned against the picket fence, where her horses closed in on her once more.

I felt a download of sadness, even anger, that my father had not passed Sally's test. "You must get tired looking after the horses."

Sally squinted into the sun, which emphasized a fanlight of lines around her eyes. "You get tired of everything. The question is, what do you tire of least? My horses are easy and uncomplicated. They want feeding, grooming and exercising, and they might, in return, love a person a little. But not too much. It's not their nature. I know that. And because I know that, it's fine."

She dropped down lightly beside me. "Do you want to know why your father and I didn't make it? He wanted to go too far, too fast. *That* tired me. I didn't want the big house, the entertaining and the wine snobbery. And I didn't want to sacrifice everything to make money."

"He didn't become *that* well off. Battista Fine Wines is hardly a gold mine."

"I should never have married him," said Sally. "I didn't realize how a person could change as he grew older."

On our last day Art minded Chloe, and Sally took me out on Melly. She rode up front on the big, prancing Quincy, and urged him along a track fringed with trees that were turning every shade of yellow and orange. The earth was moist underfoot and insects swarmed in clouds. In the distance the ridge of hills rose ragged and restless in contrast to the tamed, warm country around the town. Sally pointed toward them. "There are the ruins of a couple of mining claims up there, if you look. Poor devils. They never found a thing."

Quincy's tail twitched and I tagged behind, fussing with Melly's reins and the angle of my foot. Every movement reminded me that I was not with Chloe. I knew she was perfectly all right, that she was safe, yet with every rustle in the undergrowth or shiver of the branches, I found myself listening for my child's breathing. With every thud of the horses' hooves, I strained to hear the sound of her hunger, pleasure or distress.

After supper, I helped Sally to make gingerbread for the Pony Club picnic. "We head up into the mountains, sing a little, eat a lot. It's neat." Chloe was asleep in the little box room and Art was watching television next door, surrounded by papers and beer cans.

Sally dug a spoon into the molasses. "Since you've been here, my housekeeping has gone to pot. But who cares? I've enjoyed it, Fanny. This has been good."

The molasses had to be coaxed into the bowl.

"Mum . . . are we friends?"

"Yup." She flushed harsh red. "I wish . . . But that's my business." She dropped the spoon and folded her hands across her stomach.

"I thought you had no regrets."

"I don't and I do. That's natural." She poured the gingerbread mix into a baking tin. "But I have to say it's mighty big of you to. . . . Oh, what the heck, Fanny? What I did was for the best."

"Hey," I slipped my arm around her shoulders, "I didn't mean . . ."

She looked up at me. "I chose me because I figured that I only had one life and I'd better live it." She lowered her voice. "In a manner of speaking, Art was incidental." She gave a little laugh. "Coincidental, perhaps, because he happened along at the right time. But that's our secret."

I leaned past her and ran my fingers around the bowl. "He's nice, Sally."

"He's a man," she said briskly. "We come in all shapes and his suited mine."

I licked my fingers. "You got away."

Sally offered me the bowl. "Feel free. Like I say, I'm better with horses. And that's what I've stuck with. You need things, you know, to take your mind off the mess and muddle and eating and sleeping and being polite in the home. Men don't expect to think about it all the time. Why should I?"

Just as I was climbing into the spool bed for the last time, Will rang. I wrapped a shawl around my shoulders and went down to the kitchen to take the call.

"Can't wait to see you," he said.

We had not spoken for three days and I felt the lack acutely.

"I miss you," I said. "Badly, terribly."

"I keep turning over in bed and not finding you," Will said.

For a second or two, we mulled over this agreeable, needed exchange.

"Tell me what's been happening?" I begged.

He had several pieces of gossip. "Listen to this. The PM liked the speech I wrote for him and used a couple of the phrases. 'Tough care' . . . you know the sort of thing. Not very revolutionary but it seemed to do the trick."

I told him about riding through the woods and the skeletons of the mining buildings. "They sat up there during the winter, freezing and dying."

"They wanted a better life."

"If you come out here with me next time we can ride up into the mountains."

"Yup," he said. "I'd like that."

Chapter 13

ARRIVING HOME IN THE airport in London, I spotted Will before he saw Chloe and me. He was deep in conversation with a girl with a blonde ponytail and tight leather trousers.

He was smiling and talking, and gesticulating in the way that he had when he wooed a listener around to his way of thinking. This was Will at his most persuasive, and the girl was listening intently.

Despite my burden of Chloe and the luggage trolley, I almost ran up to him. "Will?"

He whirled around. "Hallo, darling. Hallo, my poppet."

The girl melted away. "Who was that?" I asked.

"I've no idea." Will hugged Chloe. "She said she recognized me from television and admired what we were trying to do, so I was just explaining to her how it would work."

I clung on to him. "Am I pleased to see *you!* The last few days went so slowly."

"For me, too."

Will handed back Chloe and took over the luggage, and we made our way out to the car. "It's good isn't it?" he commented, as he strapped Chloe into her seat. "My face *is* getting known."

All the way home, I kept looking at him, ravenous to reacquaint myself with the size and shape and look of him. "Did you really miss me?" I asked.

He turned his head and looked at me and, for a moment, I thought I saw a shadow in his eyes, a wariness that I could not place. "I missed you more than you can possibly imagine."

I laid my hand on his thigh and let it rest there.

Back at Stanwinton the brown leather diary was lying on the hall table. Tucked into it were typed lists and invitations . . . the bowling club tea, the single-parents' jumble sale, the Ladies' Guild Ball . . .

"Mannochie's been busy, I see . . ." I said.

Meg came hurrying out to meet us. "Welcome home, Fanny. Are you exhausted? How's Chloe? There's coffee and sandwiches in the kitchen. Come and see what's been done."

I inspected a badly needed new oven in my kitchen and showed it to Chloe, who thought it extremely exciting when I banged the door shut. In Meg's part of the house, her tiny kitchen sparkled with new fittings and equipment and matching pink towels hung over the heated towel rail in her bathroom. I touched one. It felt expensive and exclusive and matched the color of the bathrobe hanging on the door. I looked out of the open window. The rooks cawed in the trees, the curtain by my hand fluttered a little in the breeze and my inner eye registered this peaceful, supremely domestic vignette and settled it alongside other pictures and echoes stored in my mind.

Meg hovered behind me. "Fanny, I haven't thanked you properly, for agreeing to me living here."

I turned around to face her. "You don't have to thank me. I'm glad we can do something."

"No, but I do have to thank you," she said. "I appreciate it. I need somewhere safe and secure so that I can . . . beat . . . well, you know what I have to beat. I can't seem to do it on my own. I promise that I will be as helpful as I can, to make it up to you. I plan to look for a job as soon as possible." She smiled a little bleakly. "I will try and earn my keep."

I had weaned Chloe in America, a process that had involved a few struggles on the swing seat. I settled myself into the chair in her bedroom and was giving her a good-night bottle. Will came in. Chloe let go of the nipple and turned her head in his direction.

"Did you see that?" He was as pleased as punch. "She knows me."

"Of course she knows you."

"You were away so long that the poor little thing might have thought she didn't have a father. Here, let me." He hoisted Chloe onto his knee and gave her the bottle. Chloe fussed a little, then settled. He cuddled her closer and then said, "Now that we've sold the flat, how do you feel about renting a house in Brunton Street?"

With the birth of Chloe, we needed somewhere bigger in London to roost, and before I left for the States I had put Will's flat on the market. It had been snapped up within ten days.

"Brunton Street? Isn't it rather dark and gloomy and expensive?"

"But it's close to Westminster. I've learned a few things lately, Fanny, and taken soundings. We've got to entertain and make contacts, get our faces better known. Talk to ministers. I think you'll love all that. There are some interesting people . . ." He looked up at me. "I've been to see one with Meg and she thinks it would be perfect."

I threw Chloe's dungarees into the laundry basket. "She does, does she?"

"I thought you wouldn't mind." He peered at me. "But you do, don't you?"

I don't know why that small disloyalty stung quite so much, but I did mind. I really minded. I took refuge in sarcasm. "Would it be too much to suggest that I went and had a look at it, too?"

Chloe had finished her bottle and Will got up, burped her and laid her down in the cot. I wound up the musical mobile and we stood together and watched her drift into sleep.

"Will . . ." I whispered, "you are *quite* sure we can leave Chloe with Meg? We're not putting them both at risk? What would happen if Meg went on a binge and I wasn't here?"

"Very unlikely," Will replied, perhaps a shade too quickly. "There's never been any hint of a problem when she has Sacha on weekends. We must try her. I know she would never let anything happen to harm one hair of Chloe's head."

"I hope you're right."

He slipped an arm around my waist. "Meg would walk on water for Chloe."

Meg appeared the following morning in the bedroom with breakfast on a tray. "I thought you would be so exhausted." She settled the tray on my lap. "I've given Chloe breakfast and Will's playing peek-a-boo with her in the kitchen. I don't know who's enjoying it more."

Meg had taken trouble with the tray. The marmalade had been put into a little dish and there was hot milk for the coffee. I thanked her and enjoyed my breakfast and felt extremely guilty that I wished she had not done it.

We discussed the Brunton Street house as I drove Will on Monday to Westminster and agreed to take a decision that evening. I dropped him at the Houses of Parliament and continued on to the flat to begin the process of packing and clearing it out.

It was a mess, but that was no surprise. I did the washing, watered the drooping house plant, threw out a month's newspapers and vacuumed the sitting area.

For diversion, I rang Elaine. "Lovely to hear you," she said. "Let's meet as soon as poss. I want to hear everything."

We gossiped for a good twenty minutes and Elaine described the preparations for Sophie's coming birthday party. "It's the party bags that are giving me a migraine," she said. "I'm trying to outdo Carol over the way. Rumor is there were plane tickets in hers. I've only got Smarties. Can I live with the shame? Am I harming my daughter for life?"

Still laughing, I rang Meg to check up on Chloe. "She's fine," she said. "Just gone down for her nap." We discussed the weekend when Sacha would be coming to stay. "It's the giving back I dread," confessed Meg. "Oh well," she added. "I deserve it."

"Meg, don't say that."

"Come on, Fanny. What do you think happened? No husband. No son. No job as yet. If ever. Dependent on a brother and his kind wife. Hardly ruling the world. And all my own fault."

I returned to the clearing up of the flat. In America, I had resolved not to let my mind stand idle and I listened to a current affairs program that I would later discuss with Will. This stern objective was subject to a major diversion when I caught sight of myself in the mirror and decided I needed, I really *needed,* some new clothes. The outer woman. This was the cue for longer-lasting debate with myself over the virtues of quality over quantity and plumping for the latter. The easy, vibrant, well-informed, up-to-the-moment me required lots of clothes.

Will phoned. "Just checking," he said, ". . . that you are there."

I clutched the dust-pan brush to my chest. "I'm here."

"Good."

"Miss me?"

"Miss you."

Next on the list in the flat was the bedroom. I switched the radio to a music program that was playing Beethoven's Fifth, whipped the sheets off the bed and gathered them up. My knees buckled and I sat down on the mattress.

Lying on the floor was a plain, white silk camisole, and it did not belong to me.

When Will arrived in the early evening, I was waiting with a meal and an open bottle of wine. The flat was immaculate and the washing machine churned in the background.

I allowed him to kiss my cheek.

He was excited and wanted to tell me about the bill they were pushing through the House. "It's not perfect, Fanny, but it's a big step forward and we're in a hurry to get things done."

That is what I had been. In a hurry to marry Will.

He poured out a glass of wine. "Better still, there's whisper of a vacancy in the Whip's office, and my name has been mentioned." He slapped his hand down on the table. "I'm starving. Can we eat?"

I faced him across the cutlery and china. "Will, who

have you had here?"

He started. "Why?"

"Because I found underwear in our bed."

Will went chalk white. "What are you talking about?"

"You tell me."

Did I want him to deny it, vehemently, convincingly, so that I could allow myself to believe him? Or would I prefer him to look me straight in the eyes and say, I have been unfaithful?

I did not know the answer. Each came with a terrible burden of pain or suspicion.

"Who is she?"

Eventually, Will said, "It must have been Liz."

"There's a choice?"

"She's a researcher and I said she could crash here after she'd worked late one night."

"Don't lie."

He looked away. "All right. No lies. No more lies."

"When?"

"You want the details?"

I looked down at the floor, which I had swept so blithely that morning. "Perhaps not."

Will put his hand over his eyes. "What have I done?"

The sounds in the flat—the muted gurgle of a water pipe, the washing machine—were very loud. "In *our* bed?"

"I'm sorry."

"About our bed, or what you did in it?"

Will flinched. "I deserve that."

There was a click. The boiler switched off and, with it, I felt something did in me . . . the trust, absolute and unquestioning, I'd had reposed in Will.

I felt so foolish, so naive, so ignorant.

"Will," I whispered. "Had you grown tired of me? We haven't been married that long."

"It wasn't like that, Fanny. I can't explain. I have no excuse but, in a strange way, it was nothing to do with you."

"How can we continue after this?"

He dropped his head into his hands. "Please don't say that."

"What am I supposed to say? What would you have said if it had been me?"

"I don't know," he said. "I just know I would have been desperate."

"Well?" I moved in the chair experimentally, because every move I made seemed to hurt. "It might have been different if we had been married for a long time."

"No, it wouldn't," he muttered.

"It was all so easy," I burst out. "I go away with your daughter, and you leap at the opportunity . . . to betray me."

I got up and went and looked at the freshly made bed. The images it conjured up were too much to bear, so I went into the bathroom, sat down on the edge of the bath, and tried to assemble my thoughts. I looked into the mirror at an ashen, unfamiliar face.

I went back to Will. "I'm leaving," I said. "I'm going back to the house, and I'll let you know what is happening when I've made up my mind."

I was neither witless nor an innocent. I knew about sex.

I knew that lapses happened and people survived. The world was built on temptation and Liz had been one of them. I pictured her hurrying busily through the corridors of the House. I saw her making telephone calls, working on the facts—smart and organized, the icing on the cake.

Maybe that was the explanation. Proximity—just as there had been a peculiar intensity of living cheek by jowl with Will when we shared his flat. In the tiny space, we touched constantly. If I went into the kitchen, I brushed against him. If he sat down on the bed to lace up his shoes, he dislodged me. If we passed each other, our shoulders met—sweet, intoxicating reminders of that proximity.

Perhaps that was true of Westminster?

I almost persuaded myself that if I'd worked where Will did, and watched the prowling men, I, too, might have listened to a serpent and eaten of the fruit.

But it was Will who had not kept faith.

Perhaps if we had talked, he might have explained that he had been eased aside by the messy, cozy intimacies between baby and mother, and by our new and deadly priority: the need for sleep.

Maybe to give birth is to remind one of death, and the nudge is too sharp and shocking. I could understand that a tender-fleshed apple offers a moment of sweetness and oblivion. Then again, maybe something *has* to die when something else is born. If so, we should have shared our fears, for I felt their dark presence too.

Chapter 14

I WOKE THE NEXT morning in our empty bed at Stanwinton.

What was I going to do?

Take refuge in motherhood. Take refuge in the slap and polish of running a house. *That* was what I would do. Give Chloe her breakfast. The heating? I'd adjust it. The morning post required sorting. Ordinary life flowed over the rocks and hidden pools and coasted over the dangerous shallows. In danger of drowning, I clung to it.

Somehow, the morning passed. These tasks accomplished, I held Chloe tight and, imagining that we were playing a game, she crowed with delight and looked up at me. Reflected in those huge, innocent eyes I saw a new version of myself—tall and strong, the one on whom she relied.

She bounced up and down and beat at my chest. Then, without warning, she regurgitated her lunch and cried with the shock. I took her upstairs and ran a bath.

Now it was the yellow duck routine, the splashing routine, the song about the deep blue sea and the silly games with the towel.

My distress must have filtered through to her, for after she was dressed, Chloe switched from being a happy little madam to a tyrant who demanded extra cuddles and fussed endlessly when I put her down in her cot. A fretful wail followed me downstairs.

In the kitchen, I cast around for something else to do and my eye lit on a mountain of baby clothes. I seized the iron.

The heat and steam battered them into submission. If only it was so easy to smooth a life into a shape. If only I could infuse the tiny vests and pink tights with the bright anticipation of yesterday. If only I could iron away a strange woman's underwear in my bed.

"Hi." Meg appeared in the doorway. She looked flushed and pretty in a suede jacket and black trousers. "I wasn't expecting you last night."

"I decided to come back."

"I heard you so I didn't see to Chloe this morning. Can I ask why?'

I laid the iron back in its cradle and switched it off. "I want some peace."

"Fanny! You do have some bite." She unbuttoned the jacket and draped it over the back of a chair and I wanted to shout: *"Don't put it there."* "We all have our off-days, God knows." She curled up on the sofa. "My turn to listen to you."

"Go away, Meg." It was the first time I had ever spoken to her like that.

To her credit, she did not take offense. She pursed her lips and surveyed the pile of ironing. "I know how hard it is with a new baby. It takes its toll."

I did not answer.

Meg did not give up. "Have you and my darling brother quarreled? Love's young dream sullied?" She propped her elbows on the table and rested her chin on her hands. "You have my sympathy. Been there. Got the T-shirt." Her gaze followed me as I continued to fold, tidy and stack anything and everything, to keep moving, to keep breathing. "It's not worth it, you know. Getting all bothered." She let the comment slide into the silence. "There's no point in putting all one's eggs into one basket. Take it from me."

The curious thing was that, despite everything, my heart ached for Meg as well as for myself. I picked up the laundry basket with its burden of clean clothes. "I'll make us coffee, and then I must get on."

Meg cocked her head. "Chloe's crying. I'll go and see what she wants. By the way, while you were in London, I sorted out the closet in her room. It was in a bit of a pickle . . ."

All sympathy for Meg vanished, and I trembled with a sudden, blistering fury at her interference. I opened my mouth to say, "It was none of your business," but exhaustion got in the way. "Oh, go and get Chloe."

I was sorting the jams on the shelf and had my back to Meg when she returned. "Fanny . . ." she said. "I think Chloe's ill. She's very hot."

I whirled around and took the stairs two at a time. Chloe was lying on her back. She was flushed and her cheeks were bright red. When I picked her up, she cried and ducked her head in an unfamiliar way.

"I'll hold her while you drive to the doctor," Meg said.

"I'll ring Will for you."

We were standing by the cot in a hospital ward, looking down on Chloe, so small and ill.

I could hardly speak for trembling.

"I know what you're thinking," said Meg, more or

less calmly. "All sorts of dire thoughts, but she'll be fine. The doctor said they just wanted to keep an eye on her overnight. She's picked up a chest infection with a stomach bug, that's all, and they have it under control."

"But it happened so fast."

"That's babies. Believe me." Her voice became very gentle. "Do you understand, Fanny? All you have to do is get a grip."

I grabbed her arm and steadied myself. "I can't."

"Yes, you can," she said patiently. She went to ring Will and came back to say that he was on his way.

The nurses showed me where to fetch water and how to sponge Chloe down. They checked her pulse, wrote up her notes, spoke in professional terms. Meg was right, it was probably nothing serious, but I sat through the night beside the cot, my eyes fixed on my baby daughter, not daring to look away.

As instructed, every fifteen minutes or so I dipped a sponge into warm water and squeezed it out. I lifted one tiny arm, bathed and patted it dry, then the other. After that, I began on the pink clad assembly of minute bones that were her feet, then her little legs.

I sat down and, again, took up the vigil.

The nurse, fair hair twisted up into a tight pleat under her cap, checked on Chloe and the thermometer quivered a little when she snapped it back into its holder. She sent me a grave smile, and I could not be sure whether it offered pity or reassurance.

Babies don't die, do they? I wanted to say. *Not now, not these days, especially if they're as round and strong as Chloe.*

She must have sensed my panic. "Shall I bring you a cup of tea, Mrs. Savage?"

Around midnight, Will arrived. He was unshaven and looked awful. I refused to look at him as I spelled out the details. "They say the antibiotics will start working within twenty-four hours."

He bent over the cot and touched Chloe's cheek. "Little one," he said. "You'll be better now." He straightened up. "I'll stay here with you."

I fetched another chair and we sat, side by side, for the rest of the night only speaking to each other when it was necessary.

In the morning, it was clear Chloe was on the mend, and I told Will to go back to London.

Four days later, Meg and I regarded each other pretty lifelessly over the kitchen table. Neither of us had had much sleep since Chloe had come back from the hospital for she still required a lot of nursing.

Meg twisted a strand of hair round her finger. "We can relax now."

I am not so sure, I thought. I am not sure that I will ever take anything for granted again.

I looked down at my hands, which appeared so white and thin that I hardly recognized them.

"Babies do this," Meg said. "It's to test us."

I managed a weak smile. "I am grateful, Meg, for the support."

She seemed pleased. "For the moment."

We sat and drank coffee. Upstairs, for the first time in days, Chloe slept a tranquil sleep—which, at that

160

moment, I considered the height of my ambitions. The phone rang and Meg answered it and I sat and stared out of the kitchen window across the fields.

"Will is on his way." Meg put down the receiver.

To both our surprise, I dropped my head into my hands and cried. Meg came over and touched my shoulders. "Leave Will to me. You concentrate on Chloe."

This was too much. I peeled my damp face away from my hands. "Meg. Thank you for everything that you have done, but you must leave Will and me alone."

"Fanny . . ." Meg had on her caring expression, and I was never quite sure how much to trust it. "I've looked after him in the past. I know how to handle him."

"No. It's fine."

She shrugged. "As you wish. But I suggest you have a rest before he gets here."

I was deeply asleep when Will shook me awake. "It's six o'clock, Fanny." I managed to drag open my eyes. "Good girl." He placed a cup of tea beside me and sat down on the edge of the bed. "Meg has seen to everything downstairs, so we thought it best to leave you as long as possible."

I lay quite still.

"Can I talk to you?"

"What is there to say?"

He looked marginally more groomed than in the hospital. At any rate, he had shaved. He looked down at the floor as he spoke. "I have been a terrible fool. Liz is nothing to me. I am nothing to her. You are the person I love and with whom I wish to spend my life. I can't explain it further, without sounding beyond contempt."

I tried to explain what I felt, and did it badly. "Will, what we had was private and not to be shared. God knows, you share everything else with the world. Don't you see? That was the one thing that belonged only to us."

He hunched over his clasped hands. "I know, but—"

"I can hear Chloe, Will."

"I'll get her."

He reappeared with a pale, sleepy baby. "Here." He put her down in the middle of the bed and lay in his accustomed place.

Chloe gave a pallid chuckle. Will propped himself up and offered her a finger. "Poor sweetie. Better now." Chloe kidnapped his finger, pressed it into her mouth and bit. "Ouch . . ."

He extracted his finger. "Fanny, I know how bad it is, how bad it looks but, I beg you, don't make it more important than it was."

"Will, what am I supposed to make of it?"

"I don't know," he said, in a hopeless way. "It was a terrible mistake. I will regret it to my dying day. I didn't stop to think, I didn't make comparisons. It was just for the moment, and I took it. I am sorry. I am so sorry."

Deprived of the attention, Chloe shrieked, sounding much more like her old self. Will hauled her into his arms and pressed his cheek against hers. "Precious."

Chloe now bit his nose and Will yelped. "When did she start doing that?"

"She's probably teething."

I took a deep breath. "I don't know if we can be married any more."

Will reached out for me but I flinched. "Don't touch me."

"What can I say, Fanny? What can I do?"

I glanced at the clock. Six-thirty. I swung my legs out of the bed. "Get moving, Will, it's the Rotary Club supper. We won't stay late."

His mouth dropped open. "We're going?"

"Do we have a choice?" I opened the wardrobe door and dragged out the dress that I had earmarked. "Can't let the Rotary Club down."

"But what are you going to do?"

"I don't know, Will. Go to the Rotary Club supper."

I pulled off my sweater and T-shirt and transcribed a slow, provocative circle in front of my husband. He swallowed and went pale. My body was still a little slack, breasts not quite settled back to their normal size; it was the body of a girl . . . no, not a girl, a woman, who had given birth, and I wanted him to see it.

That night, I glittered, or so Will told me later. But perhaps he was filtering a vision of a new, rather terrible me, through a guilty prism.

Oddly, along with my outrage, along with the wound he had dealt me, I had gathered a peculiar confidence, and a determination not to be beaten. I wanted to face this challenge.

Will watched my every move as I donned the pink dress with full skirt and a pair of high heels. I brushed my hair until it crackled and let it hang down over my shoulders.

We left Chloe with Meg. I got into the driver's seat,

kicked off my shoes and piloted us into town. I parked in the hotel car park and ran through a briefing. "Pearl will be there. There will be an auction of books and things. A raffle. The usual. The fund-raising is for the neonatal unit in the hospital. Got it?"

"Fanny. Stop this."

"No," I said. I gathered up my bag and shoved my feet into the high heels.

"If you want me to leave," he said in a low voice. "Tell me."

"I don't know," I said. "I will think about it. Let's go in."

Attired in a green dress shot through with silver, Pearl exuded a certain magnificence. "Your father's here," she said. I looked around. He was with a blonde woman in black and pearls. When he saw me, he raised his hand.

A glass of indifferent champagne was pressed into my hand—I could tell by its color and general look. "A good turn-out," said Pearl, and I could have sworn her eyes flickered down to my legs to check if I was wearing tights.

By now, I knew the form. We drank the champagne in a reception room with lots of gilt trimmings. From there, we progressed to dinner and were served chicken, followed by a rubbery lemon mousse. Afterward, there was coffee and mints wrapped in silver paper. I ate what I could. The man on my right turned out to be a professor of semantics at the local university and we discussed the idea of being "good" and being "truthful." He argued that to tell the truth was not, necessarily, to be good. "For example," he said. "Are you being good if you are asked

164

by the huntsmen which way the fox went, and you tell him?"

I lifted the coffee cup to my lips and encountered Pearl's shrewd gaze. Afterward, as the guests prepared to take their leave, she sought me out. "Are you feeling all right, Fanny?"

"Chloe's been ill, and I've been up for the last few nights."

"I wanted to have a little chat and encourage you to do a little bit more in the constituency. The Evergreen Club could do with a bit more attention . . ."

I said through stiff lips, "I do what I can, Pearl, but I have been away visiting my mother."

By some miracle, Mannochie appeared at my elbow. "Do you mind, Pearl, there is someone I wish Fanny to meet."

He led me away to an empty anteroom. "Thought you could do with rescuing; Pearl can be a bit overbearing at times. Sit here for a minute and, with a bit of luck, she'll bugger off home."

I sank gratefully onto a spindly gilt chair. "That was nice of you. I think she feels I don't do enough."

"It's not always easy," he said.

"What isn't?" asked my father, gate-crashing into this tête à tête.

"Being a political wife," said Mannochie. "I was going to reassure Fanny that she was doing a good job."

"So she is," said my father.

Mannochie excused himself, and I watched him walk through the lobby. "Do you know, I still don't know his Christian name. No one ever calls him anything but Mannochie."

"Really?" My father sat down beside me. "Some people don't like their names, I suppose. How's Chloe?"

When I told him, he said, "I'm sorry. Poor little Chloe," and looked at me, sharp and watchful. "And what about you?"

"I'm fine. No, I'm not. It scared me to death."

His eyes did not leave my face. "Look at it this way: Babies have to get ill sometimes. Nature has to build up the immune system."

I almost choked. "At the expense of mine."

He changed the subject. "I thought you might like to know I've got a new shipment coming over from the Margaret River. I think you'll approve. My bet is on the Semillon and Sauvignon Blanc. Come over and try them."

"I will." I promised and, to my horror, felt tears spring to my eyes.

He searched my face. "I think something is wrong. Can you tell me?"

But there was no chance to talk.

"There you are . . ." interrupted Will from the doorway. "I've been looking for you everywhere. I thought you might like to know that I've rung Meg to check on Chloe. She is fine, and I want to take you home."

Chapter 15

IN THE CAR, WILL asked me, "Were you talking to your father about us?"

166

"Would it make a difference if I had?"

"Yes," he said shortly. "It would."

I disliked driving in the dark and I gripped the wheel like a vise. "Actually, we were discussing wine."

"But you do talk to him about most things?"

"He *is* my father."

The road curved to the right and the white line was difficult to follow. My hands were slippery on the wheel. "You talk to Meg all the time." In the semidark, my voice sounded bitter and hostile.

"Yes, I do," he replied. "But I never had a father. Nor did she."

Eventually, I turned the car into our lane and drove between the fields. "This evening was a farce," I said.

"Possibly," Will replied. "But it was your choice."

I parked in the drive, jerked on the brake, switched off the ignition and the interior of the car was plunged into total darkness. "Choice didn't enter into it."

"So now what do we do?" he asked.

"I don't know."

He sighed heavily.

I struggled to control my panic and, with panic came doubt. "What I don't understand, Will, is that we hadn't had time to get bored with each other." I removed the key from the ignition. "Which means something was lacking. If it was, you should have told me."

This situation was my fault.

As was his habit, Will sat upright in the passenger seat. "You mustn't blame yourself, Fanny . . ." Silence. "I can't possibly ask for more than we have and share." Another silence. "I'm not good at this, Fanny." He twisted to look toward the laurel hedge. "Nothing was wrong. It was a moment when I was offered temptation, and instead of refusing it I took it. How stupid was that?"

"That is one way of explaining it, I suppose."

"Fanny—" he began.

I cut him off. "The bed is made up in the spare room." I pulled on my shoes, got out of the car and left Will to lock up.

I lay awake, stomach unsettled, eyes wet, in mourning for a marriage as I had envisaged it. I was frightened by the violence of my feelings and by how savagely I had been thrown off course by an event so commonplace, so everywhere, so discussed.

And no less intense was my primitive, visceral desire to hurt Will—to slash his treacherous flesh, to drive a knife as deep into his heart as he had done into mine.

I twisted and turned in the half-occupied bed.

At four o'clock, I got up and slipped into Chloe's room to check on her. I hovered in the doorway but could not hear anything and, with a shudder of apprehension, put my ear close to her lips and listened for the faint breath of my sleeping baby.

On the landing, I paused by the Gothic window. Darkness. Nothing else. During the last few days my waistline had shrunk and I retied my dressing-gown cord so tightly that it bit into my flesh.

The spare-room door was open and I looked in. The night-light in the passage softly illuminated Will, who was hunched on his side. As I watched, he muttered and flung out his hand—just like Chloe. Drawn like a magnet, I went into the room and knelt by the bed. This side of Will, this sleeping, vulnerable, dreaming side, was private; it belonged to me, and I would not share it.

His eyes flicked open. "You were watching me."

"You *betrayed* me, Will."

"I know. And I betrayed myself, too. Double whammy, Fanny."

"I don't know you one bit," I said.

"But you're wrong. You do know me." He held out a hand. "Come."

I slid in beside him, cold flesh beside his tousled warmth. He did not try to touch me, and we lay side by side, like marble effigies.

His confession did not come easily. "You had a baby, and it was different."

"I did my best. I came back as soon as I could."

"Yes, but half your mind was elsewhere. And so was mine."

"You mean you felt jealous."

"No, not jealous precisely. A bit sidelined." He rolled over toward me. "A little."

How could I deny it? The small-print department on motherhood had been careless, too, as to precisely what would happen, which meant that Will no longer took full possession of me—as once he had.

"I miss the old you," he said, and added miserably, "I felt safe when you had only me to think about."

That was as close as Will had ever come to admitting that his upbringing had laid a finger across his soul.

"I love Chloe beyond words," he said, "but it is different."

169

I thought of the rooms of the spirit, and of how I had moved from a familiar one into another, as yet strange and unexplored. "We change," I said, for I was beginning to understand better. "We can't escape it."

I must have slipped into a doze, for I started when Will asked, "Is it the not knowing me or what I did that's worse?"

"I think . . . I think it's that you didn't understand what *I* meant by us. Or if you did . . . it didn't stop you bringing Liz home. Into *our* home."

"I'm sorry, Fanny. Do you believe me? Please . . . *believe* me."

"Does it matter what I believe?"

"And I'm sorry, too, for making you cynical. Cynicism's the politician's line." His hand journeyed over the space between us and came to rest on my thigh. "I imagined it would be different but it isn't, and you get caught up in the Westminster round," he said. "That's the trouble, and I know it's affected me. That's been a shock, Fanny. Finding out just how deep the cynicism is." The hand on my thigh grew heavy. "I've been wanting to tell you for some time."

He shifted closer, wooing me with his own disappointments and frailties. I fought the impulse to cling to him and to weep until there were no tears left.

"I need to know what you're going to do. I'm not sure I can live with the suspicion that, every time you leave home, you might happen on another woman up in London."

"But you won't have to."

We must have slept for I awoke, stiff and feeling

slightly sick. Chloe was practicing her version of the dawn chorus and I stumbled out of bed and pulled on some clothes.

Sleepy and beautifully rosy, she cuddled against me and I carried her downstairs and fed her pureed banana and cereal. Frantic for some resolution, almost mad with exhaustion, I strapped her into the car and drove over to Ember House.

"You have circles under your eyes, you've lost weight and the atmosphere between you and Will can be cut with a knife. Would you like to tell me? You can, you know." My father swung Chloe up into his arms.

"I'd like some fresh air, Dad. Could we go out into the garden?"

We walked across the lawn toward Madame Mop, a bad statue of a woman holding what looked like a bucket but my father was fond of her. I narrated the bare facts and set Chloe down to see if she could take a few rudimentary steps.

"Bastard," he said, and that shocked me more than anything, for my father never swore.

Between us we balanced the tottering Chloe, who shrieked with delight at the novelty. "You'll need a strong nerve, Francesca, and cleverness. You've been badly hurt and I dislike Will for that. Very much. But you're not the first . . . or the last in such a situation."

I listened to his beloved voice, which had seen me through childhood.

"At the moment, you imagine it is the only thing. Indeed, it is the only thing you can think about. But it isn't the only thing. The family matters, Francesca, very much." He paused. "It is a shock to discover that no one can expect serene and perfect happiness for always."

"How can I manage knowing it might happen again?" I said.

"It may. Or it may not. We can never know."

Chloe's knees buckled and I bent down to pick her up. She crowed with delight and offered me a small dirty hand.

It was quiet in the garden, damp and cool. English weather. It was possible to think here.

Chloe was kidnapped onto her grandfather's knee and they played this little piggy. They both shrieked with laughter.

"You enjoy that more than she does," I accused him fondly.

He kissed the fair little head. "You must hold the family, if you can. I tried but I . . . I consider it a stain on me that I failed. You must do what you think best, of course, but that's my advice."

We walked around the garden several times and showed Chloe the tree house, the old rabbit hutch and the potting shed. Then it began to drizzle and we went inside.

My father sat me down in the kitchen and made me drink a milky coffee and eat an apple. "Think of your situation, and think about what sort of person Will is. You must try and forgive, and then when you are sorted out, you must give up working for me because I think you need to concentrate your energies on your life with Will. I will employ someone else. It's easy. Raoul can step in for a while perhaps. . . . Whoever, there are plenty of others. Don't look so horrified—if you wish you could keep your hand in, in a minor way, until Chloe is older. Then you can come back. You can keep up with the research and the learning. You are lucky, you can still think and study at home. When you have a moment. Some women never even have that."

"That's not fair, Dad."

"Who said things were going to be fair?"

"Why should I give up my life?"

"Quid pro quo," he said. "You make a choice. Also you must be kind to yourself. Women aren't generally. At least, not anymore. They flog themselves into the grave because they think they have to do everything. In marrying Will you took on another job. How would you manage with the traveling and seeing to the clients and all the other things you have to do? I couldn't rely on you, and the business can't take that. You need to be with Will, not detached. You need to be up in London and there at weekends."

I let myself back into the house. The hall smelled of bacon. Light filtered through the window and picked out the fleck of the stair carpet. There were letters for posting on the hall table, umbrellas stuffed into a blue pot that I had bought for spring bulbs. Will's navy blue coat hung beside mine on the pegs. A radio played in Meg's part of the house.

I took off Chloe's jacket and hefted her onto my hip. Will emerged from the kitchen. He was dressed in a suit and tie. He avoided my eyes. "I might have known you'd

173

run off to your father."

Chloe tried to bite my nose and I tussled with her. "What's that supposed to mean?"

He stuffed his hands into his pockets and leaned against the door. "I've been thinking since you've gone. We might as well acknowledge it, Fanny, this is not going to work. I've been a fool and you have every right to call it a day and start again. I'll make sure that Chloe and you are all right."

"It is my call, I think."

The tenuous contact of last night had vanished.

He braced himself. "OK? Is that what you want?"

"I have to change Chloe." I pushed past him and, with knees that felt like water, carried Chloe up the stairs to her room.

I laid her on the changing mat, which was patterned with yellow teddy bears and, for some reason, bells. She was tired from the outing.

I cleaned and wiped and patted and put her into her cot and turned on the musical mobile. The wretched tune tinkled away, and the ducks embarked on their stately, circular dance.

Chloe's eyelids drooped. I leaned over the cot and watched the changes in her face as she slipped into sleep. What was the truth of all this upset? The truth was that, now that Chloe was here and well and safe, the luxury of choice had vanished. That was the deal. I *knew* about the chill of a child's lonely incompleteness. I knew inside out the bewilderment and the corrosion of unanswered questions.

"I won't leave your father," I promised my sleeping

baby. "I can't do that to you."

Neither, I realized, could I do that to myself, for I loved Will. I hated what he'd done, but I loved him. I loved his passionate devotion to the idea of a better world; I loved the possibilities that beckoned in our future. I was not willing to give them up without a fight.

I moved noiselessly round the room, restoring it to order. I folded towels, checked on the nappies, screwed the top onto the baby lotion. "Weeping Eros is the builder of cities . . ."

The phrase slipped into my mind. Where had I read that? Never mind, I got the point. It was as important to help myself as much as others.

I would weep at times, but build my city, too. I would rule it, and grow strong.

I went downstairs and found Will in the kitchen, hunched over the remnants of his breakfast. At my entrance, he looked up, so tired and beaten that my heart contracted with pity.

"Fanny?"

"I've decided to give up working for my father full time," I told him. "I'll just do the odd bit of paper work and stuff. He's going to take someone on, someone else."

I crossed over to the dresser and picked up the diary, which shed an avalanche of invitations and reminders. I opened it up. "Let's go through this; we have a busy month."

A few days later, I was lying in the bath. Will was brushing his hair in the mirror—he was a little nervous about losing it, but since it was as thick as ever there was no chance of that. He moved his head and caught my eye. "What made you stay in the end?"

"The fact that it isn't the end. I love you. I love Chloe."

He abandoned the beauty parade and hunkered down beside me. He kidnapped the sponge and took over the task. "I promise I will never, ever do it again." His arm rested on the side of the bath. It was brushed with golden hairs that lay flat and silky against his skin. Underneath, the muscles were hard, quite different from my softer body. I reached up and took his hand. He stared down at me and I returned his scrutiny more boldly than I would have done in the past.

Here was the deal, one worthy of the Members' tea room where Will so often huddled with his cronies. I would do my best. I would stitch up my wounds. I would stay and demand his loyalty. Exact the energy, subtlety and commitment that this marriage was owed. In return, I would put on my tights, canvas the streets and run his house. I would smile, entertain and support.

Yet in the future I would be watchful.

I would reserve the right to inner immigration. My father had told me once that when faced with the intractable, or the intolerable, people fled inside themselves. They studied, they dreamed, they learned. He said he was sure that was how his mother and her family survived in Fiertino during the worst moments of the war. My situation was hardly intolerable—I was neither oppressed nor abused—but my spirit was dented. Nothing so terrible there, either.

176

Every girl . . . and every woman, the woman into which I was growing, required an insurance. That was mine.

Will said, "Do you think you can forget? Do you think we can put it behind us?"

My eye caught the postcard lying on the chair beside the bath, which had arrived in the post that morning. It was from Benedetta and showed a view of the church and the colonnaded piazza filled with flowers. The red varnish on my toenails matched the scarlet of the geraniums. A bright, optimistic red.

After a second or two, I replied. "Yes."

As the professor had argued so cogently, being good and being truthful were not necessarily the same. But that was my secret.

Chapter 16

THE YEARS OF CHILDREN, politics and of a marriage slipped by.

There was no more talk of a house in Brunton Street. Instead we bought a mansion flat in a utilitarian-looking block in Westminster and it did us fine.

Mannochie helped us to move in, earmarking a tiny room off the hallway for his office. I said no offense, but I wasn't sure that I wanted him let loose in our home and he smiled and said in his wry way, "I won't bother you. If you give me a key . . . I am housetrained and I will behave myself."

So, the soft-voiced, soft-footed Mannochie would lie quietly in his basket until called? I was stacking china at the time and he helped me to lift the box onto the kitchen table. "Don't you ever get sick of this, Mannochie? Do you ever stop and think what this kind of life does to you? Does to us all?"

He unwrapped a stack of saucers and stuffed the newspaper into a black bag. "I'm too busy to think. You could say I'm wedded to the business."

It was astonishing, really, how willing Mannochie was to subsume his life into ours. Perhaps not thinking too hard was the answer, an effective weapon. Like the orphaned lamb draped in the hide of a dead one and presented to a new mother, Mannochie would take on our taste and smell. I shoved a box under the kitchen table. "Enough. Why don't I show you what I plan to do?"

There was a good view over the rooftops to Westminster Cathedral and Mannochie surprised me by declaring out of the blue, "That's what our politics are about. To stop the poor from being segregated in attics and basements."

"Do you know, Mannochie, I've never heard you utter anything political before. It's usually all tactics and statistics."

He turned his head and looked at me. "Always a first time."

To punish me—just a little—he sat me down and ran over the forthcoming commitments. "State Opening. The usual Christmas engagements at Stanwinton. Recess."

"And what," I asked, "is the role of the wife in all this?"

He ticked off the points on his fingers. "An adjunct. A

perfect, smiling, willing adjunct who wears tights."
When I grimaced, he added. "Not so bad, Fanny."

I wagged my finger at him. "Bit like childbirth, Mannochie. You read about it, go to classes, practice the breathing but the minute labor happens you say to yourself: Hey, there has been some mistake."

When Will came home, Mannochie and I were holed up in a comfortable way in the kitchen, drinking our way through a second pot of tea which was so strong that my teeth felt grainy. He flashed me a provocative look. "What, not finished the unpacking?"

With a foot, I pushed a box full of Chloe's plastic toys in his direction. "Help yourself."

"I'm just off." Mannochie took his mug over to the sink and washed it. He winked at me. *See how house trained I am.* "Will, I will need to talk to you about the traffic scheme. Small shopkeepers are organizing a protest. They want you in on it."

Will looked blank. "Yes. Sure. I'll listen, but I won't take sides."

"Shouldn't you?" I asked, after Mannochie had departed.

"Course not." Will ran his fingers through his hair, which made it stand up. The effect was of a bewildered schoolboy. "You know we should not take a view on local issues. It's death by a thousand cuts. Stick to the national ones."

We settled into the flat and into our routines. Will came and went—to his chosen arena of deals and alliances, ambitions and objectives. I noticed that there was less talk of ideas and ideals and more descriptions of personalities and who had done or said what, and perhaps it was not entirely coincidental that his career flourished. There are episodes in any marriage when something becomes crystal clear. I knew Will had arrived when I caught him gazing into the mirror and squaring his shoulders. "Practicing for the leadership of the party," I teased, and he flushed deep scarlet. He hated it when I reminded him of it. Which I did, frequently. But what I did not tell him was that I hated having caught him doing that, too.

And I? I patrolled and marshaled a different world, in some respects as crisscrossed with alliances and deals as Will's. Like his, my world sucked me in, like the deep intimacy of the double bed—warm, smothering, sleepy making—but I joined him as often as possible. I watched over my daughter as she grew, changed, and changed again. I watched her fiercely, tenderly and always determined to keep her safe. Every week, I sat down and did the paperwork for my father. Meg lived with us. Once or twice a man appeared on the scene, but he did not last. At odd intervals, she got herself a job, but they did not last either. And, in the later years, her drinking was not so bad. Months would go by without incident.

Not long after he had turned sixteen, Sacha arrived at our front door with two tartan suitcases, and announced: "I would like to live with my Mum." I don't suppose I'll ever witness the same expression of pure joy that I saw on Meg's face when she heard those words.

More often than not, the rooms in the house were full, there *was* the rustle and mutter of a family sounding under its eaves. Our marriage grew and deepened, went through troughs, blossomed, withered a little, blossomed again but it was never stagnant, and we were happy.

Before I had had time to catch my breath, Chloe had been gone for a week.

Elaine rang. "How do you feel?"

"Like my arm's been chopped off. You?"

"I'm going to tackle Neil tonight. I'll let you know."

I felt Chloe's presence in every room. If I loaded clothes into the washing machine, there was her favorite pink blouse. Her hipster jeans sat on top of the clean laundry and I ironed them into shape. I picked up her sponge from the bathroom floor. An abandoned copy of *Harry Potter*—"Comfort reading, Mum"—was wedged between her bed and the wall. I rescued it and placed it beside my own bed. The insurance-loss adjuster, I recorded her absence in socks and a mute mobile phone, in silence where there had been words, in the hairs snagged in a hairbrush.

"Mum," she cried down the phone when she rang from Sydney. "You never told me how exciting it would be."

I put down the phone in the hall, where I had taken the call, and caught a glimpse of myself in the mirror above the table. Like Will, I made sure that I had a good haircut, but I was lucky enough to be able to deploy an added armory of the correct lipstick for my coloring, plus a pretty blue sweater. On the checklist, the hair was still dark, mouth still full(ish), skin still glossy . . . Nothing new, nothing remarkable either, and yet, with

Chloe's going, I felt that I had changed. To what, I was not sure.

This time round, Meg had got herself a part-time job in a bookshop, and during the day we did not see each other. But in the evenings, if I was at home, she sought me out and we found a certain solace in each other's company. The work was dull, she said, but she valued dull. In a bookshop you could escape the front line of illness, anger and disagreements. If there was too much drama and unpleasantness in a book, you could always put it down. Her descriptions of book buyers were funny and sharp. She also said she was surprised how many men sneaked out of the fiction section novels that were about relationships and read them surreptitiously beside the crime books.

I cooked light, nourishing suppers—risottos, grilled salmon, chicken in soy sauce—and made a point of sharing them with her.

"Will you congratulate me, Fanny?" she said over one such meal. "I haven't touched a drop . . . since your anniversary." She gave me one of her mischievous looks. "I know you don't understand what it's like; how can you?" She speared a piece of fish onto her fork. "But if this delicious fish pie was whiskey or brandy I'd be the happiest woman alive. The terrible truth is, alcohol is so reliable; much more reliable than a husband, or love."

I found myself laughing.

After we had finished, we moved into the sitting room and I opened the French windows. A moth flew in and attempted suttee on the lamp. I got up and coaxed it out into the night.

A tiny dusting from its wing had left a mark on the cream silk of the shade. I brushed it away, flicked the switch, and we sat in the summer's dark, watching a bat swoop over the garden. Meg was very quiet. "I will mourn Sacha when he goes."

"I know."

"I missed such a lot of him. The law took him away, Fanny. I used to watch you with Chloe and envy you so much."

"You were wonderful to Chloe." I could not see her expression. "I was worried when you first moved in that I could not trust you with her."

"Do you think I didn't know?"

It was Meg who had helped me with Chloe's first meals. "Scrape a bit of banana onto a spoon," she advised. It was Meg who showed me the trick of preventing nappy rash (use mouth-ulcer ointment) and coaxed Chloe to say her first word. On weekends, when Sacha came to stay, Meg made a point of sweeping up both children for a couple of hours so that Will and I could have a little time together—and, yes, I had been grateful. Later, it was Meg, who, when I was busy, went over and over the spellings, times tables, history dates, physics problems.

A second moth flew into the room. "Why don't we shut the door?" said Meg. "It's getting cold."

I did so, and switched the light back on.

"What a mess I made of myself," she said in her ironic way, and laughed. Then she hid her face in her hands.

I drove over to Ember House and found my father in his office, dispatching the day's business. I bent over and gave him a hug. "Chloe called from Sydney. Says she loves it."

The Fiertino expedition was first on the agenda. We discussed timetables, car hire, health insurance and where Benedetta had arranged for us to stay.

"I instructed her to choose carefully," said my father. "It had to be just the right place for your first time there."

I sensed a great excitement in my careful father. He laughed and joked and whistled a snatch of Puccini under his breath. "Look, I found this the other day. Do you remember?" He produced a framed photograph from his desk.

I took it from him. "I remember that. . . . You used to have it on your desk. For years."

The photograph was of a stone funerary monument to an Etruscan couple lying on a couch.

"We must visit the Etruscan museum," I said and put the photograph on a shelf.

"Good idea."

Outside, the rain dribbled halfheartedly and my father shut the window. "I'm sorry Will isn't coming."

"There's too much going on, and it's touch and go with this scheme he is so wrapped up in."

"Your husband," he said, "is very shrewd. He knows he can't let up and, if you are in the game, you have to stay in the ring. I admire that in him, and this is his chance to prove himself."

"I get very tired of some subjects," I could not help saying.

My father tapped his papers. "He could be selling arms."

It struck me that my father was looking especially tired. "The doctor is keeping an eye on everything, isn't he?"

"Of course."

"Blood pressure OK?"

"Stop it."

I was about to insist that he make another appointment before we went, when I glanced at my watch. "Must go, Dad. I'm standing in for Will. Can't be late."

I kissed him good-bye and sped off to the opening ceremony of Stanwinton's spanking new sewage works, ten years in the making. Will and I had made jokes about the reams of paperwork required to get it under way.

During the night, the telephone rang. I fumbled to turn on the bedside light and looked at the clock. Two o'clock. My first thought was: *Chloe.* The second: *Will.* The third: *Mr. Tucker.*

I snatched it up. "Look," I muttered into it, "if that's you, Mr. Tucker, I'm going to—"

"This is the hospital, Mrs. Savage," a voice said. "Your father has had a minor heart attack . . . he's comfortable at the moment, but we think you should come."

I woke up Meg. "Dad's in the hospital. I'm going right away."

Looking rather frail, she pulled herself upright. "Wait, I'm coming too."

Like a mad thing, I drove through the night with Meg shivering in the passenger seat. Please, please, don't let it be serious, I prayed silently, and pressed my foot down on the accelerator.

But we were too late.

The night sister materialized as we came into Intensive Care. Cool, slender and neat, she took us aside. It had been a massive second heart attack, she said, with an air of having rehearsed these words many times. Fifteen minutes ago. He would not have known very much about it.

Meg gasped and began to cry. I fiddled with the strap on my bag, which was slippery with sweat, though I was cold all over. My first reaction was: I should have gone with him to the doctor. My second was: I'll have to ring Benedetta and cancel the trip. Then I thought . . . but I don't remember much, except that I was grasping at inconsequential things. "Why didn't he wait until we got here?" I said in a stupefied way. "He would not have liked not to have said good-bye."

The night sister put an arm around my shoulder, led us into the relatives' room and sat us down. She fetched cups of tea, and I sat on a torn plastic chair and stared at an overflowing ashtray.

Meg tried to pull herself together. "I'm so very, very sorry. But better quick, Fanny, don't you think?"

"No," I said. "No."

The night sister's professional expression indicated that Meg made sense and, in the end, I would come to agree with this point of view. "Try to drink the tea, Mrs. Savage."

The tea tasted of leather and tannin. Anyway, I was trembling too hard and it was slopping into my lap. Meg took it away and put it down on the table.

I asked the night sister, "Did he say anything? Did

186

you talk to him? Was he . . . frightened? Did he know?"

"He knew enough to ask me to say that he loved you. And he was thinking of you."

"But he didn't wait," I cried out, in agony. "He didn't wait for me to say good-bye."

"He couldn't," she explained, quietly. "But we told him you were on your way. We talked to him, even when he was unconscious. Hearing is the last sense to go, you know." She laid a hand on my arm. "I'm sure your father knew you'd get here if you could." She looked from me to Meg, who was sobbing by the window. "He would not have known much about it."

"But he was alone . . . he didn't have any of us."

"I don't know if this makes it any better, but I held his hand," the night sister said.

When we got home, it was dawn. I rang Will at the flat, but the answer-machine clicked on.

"Darling, it was an all-night sitting," he explained, when I finally got hold of him. "I'm coming down now. I'm just going to order the car and fling a few things into a bag. I'll ring Chloe and tell her and, if you agree, I will persuade her not to rush home. I'll tell her Alfredo would not have wanted that."

I rang my mother. "Oh," she said. Then, "I must sit down." After a pause, "Could you tell me again?" A clink of china sounded in the background, and radio music, and other voices that belonged in my mother's life.

"It was a heart attack."

"I won't come to the funeral, Fanny. I don't think I could. I will think of him, though."

At this, I wept down the phone. "Listen to me," Sally said. "You must remember that Alfredo considered you the best thing that ever happened to him. Remember that."

It was the first real motherly thing I could remember Sally ever saying to me, and I wrote it down on the notepad by the phone, with the date scrawled on the bottom because I wanted to remember it. *"Alfredo . . . considered you the best thing that . . ."*

Death was a joker, but his timing was awful, or perhaps that was the best joke of all? It would not have hurt him to have spared my father until after the Fiertino trip. There were plenty of other subjects to harvest, and one fewer would not have mattered.

The day after my father died, I wrote to Benedetta.

He was so looking forward to seeing you and Fiertino. Although he had not "been" there in the strict sense for years, it was, in many ways, the most important thing about him. . . .

She wrote back by return post.

My dearest Fanny,
Your father saw the world through his eyes, true, but he was careful to think about other people, too, and you were more important than Fiertino. I knew he was so happy that you were settled and he rejoiced in Chloe. Please come and visit me whenever you wish, . . .

It was Benedetta who decreed on my tenth birthday that there should be no more bath times with my father. That puzzled me. Perhaps ten was a magic number? Perhaps it was secret, like my mother was a secret? But, if I had questions, I had not yet learned *how* to question. On my tenth birthday then, washed and brushed within an inch of my life, and tied into a thick, old-fashioned dressing gown with a cord belt, I was escorted downstairs by Benedetta to the door of my father's study.

He was at his desk, surrounded by wine books, writing up the day's business. Conscious that "ten" hung over me, I went to stand beside him and when he patted his knee, I shook my head.

"I was forgetting," he said sadly. "You are a big girl now and we must talk about grown-up things."

He pulled a book from a pile on the floor and showed me the picture of a vineyard in France. "I know the family who owns it," he said. "They are called Villeneuve and we are good friends. One day, I will employ one of their sons, Raoul, perhaps, or Pierre, to work here and, if you wish, you can go over there to learn. They managed to survive the war and build up a new business." He flicked through the pages. "It was very strange, Fanny, that the year the war ended the vines produced the best, most glorious vintage ever."

War again. I nodded politely.

I was more interested by the framed photograph on my father's desk. It was of a man and a woman carved in stone, lying together on an ornate couch draped in material. He had a square face and a beard, she had curls falling down her back and dangling earrings. He had his arm around her, and she leaned back against him.

I remember asking my father what it was about. He took a little time before he answered. "I think it is about constancy, Francesca."

I swiveled around to look at my father. Greatly daring, I asked, "Is it Mummy?"

There was a short, tense silence. No, it was not, he answered and, if my question hurt him, he did not betray it by so much as a flicker. No, the picture was of an Etruscan funerary couch. Late sixth century B.C.

"Was that when I was eight?" I asked, for time had no meaning.

My father laughed. "The Etruscans were a people who, long, long ago, used to live in the Fiertino area where the Battistas come from. They made such a lot of things that people are always digging up bits and pieces and putting them in museums. I like this one particularly because he and she will never be . . . parted."

"Is that good?" I asked.

"Yes, I think so." My father stroked my cheek. "Would you like to hear again about my home?"

I nodded.

"A day's journey from Rome, there is a valley called the Val del Fiertino. On one slope of the valley grow chestnuts and beeches. On the other, wheat, olives and vines . . ."

I knew it by heart.

My head grew heavy and I leaned back against the chair. "Try to remember all this," he said. "One day you and I will go there. We will go home." He tugged gently at one of my plaits. "That's a promise."

"Why did you leave it, Daddy?"

"The war came and a lot of things were destroyed and it was dangerous. My mother wrapped me up in a coat and do you know what she did? She tucked a bar of soap into my pocket, and took me away and we came to England."

I did not know what war meant but I knew it was bad and, once or twice after that story, I woke up in the night sobbing. "What is it little one?" asked Benedetta, who swooped to my rescue and bore me away to her room and showed me a picture of a lady with a blue cloak sprinkled with stars.

He was clever, my father. He knew how to plant a footprint in a child's mind. Images crept into mine and put down long, tough, fibrous roots—just like the vine.

Chapter 17

MANNOCHIE CAME TO THE rescue. Organizing. Planning. Canceling appointments . . . and helped to calm an anxious, tearful Chloe on the phone.

Where did I want the funeral? Burial or cremation? Which hymns? What music? I tried to think. Good wives were trained to make things take shape, to make events happen well, to smooth and soothe, and a good daughter followed suit.

Anyway, I had to keep Meg stable for she had taken my father's death badly. *"I loved him, too,"* she said.

"If you let us down now," I told her, tight lipped and hollow eyed, "then . . ." I did not finish the sentence but it was not necessary. Meg understood well enough.

The funeral came and went. My father had left written instructions as to what he wished. With Will at my side, I sang "Lead Kindly Light," listened to the readings and shook hands with a great many people. "Such a tragedy," murmured one. "So sorry," another.

"Sorry . . . ?" It was such a small word for what I felt.

After the funeral, Will dashed back to London for a couple of days. Meg went back to work, and Sacha rejoined the band.

My father had left instructions that he wished to be cremated but I should bury his ashes where I thought fit.

Where was "fit?"

In the evening, Meg came home and dumped the shopping on the floor. I had ensconced myself at the kitchen table, trying—and failing—to get my brain around a list of things that needed doing. I felt peculiar, distanced, almost weightless. I needed silence, and I needed to think. My father had been alone in that hospital. *That* was the image now in my mind. No sun, no joyous harmony of color and scent there. Just coldness.

She cocked a sharp eye at me. "Have you eaten today?"

"No . . . yes, I had some breakfast."

"I'll make you a sandwich." She cut the bread and reached for the butter dish. "I suppose you'll have to sell Ember House."

"I don't want to."

She placed a neat cucumber sandwich in front of me. "Eat."

I took a mouthful and started to chew. The wet, floppy texture of the cucumber made me feel faintly sick.

"Will you be able to afford to keep it on?"

"I don't know. I'll have to talk to the lawyers and the bank."

"What does Will think?"

"It's not his decision," I said, more sharply than I intended.

"Have it your own way, darling." She put cups and saucers back into the cupboard. "By the way, since you've been so busy, I bought the socks for Will."

"What socks?"

"He mentioned he needed some. I've put them on your bed. I thought it would help you."

I stared at her. "You needn't have bothered." I could barely articulate the words.

"No." She smiled brightly. "But I did."

I gathered up the plates in silence.

"I can see I've been naughty. Sock buying is a sin," Meg said, and added sadly, "Fanny, did you know that your back can be so disapproving?"

"Can it?" I whirled around, a plate in my hand, and Meg shrank away. "In the name of pity, can't you see you have Will, more than you should? Is that not *enough?*"

She held out her hand. "I didn't mean—"

"Oh, yes, you did, Meg." Then I heard myself say, "Anything to keep your thumbprint on him." And I wondered who this person was that I was turning into.

Meg gave a little gasp. "Wrong, Fanny, so wrong. It's because it makes me feel useful. It makes me feel

I have a place."

The plate slid from between my hands. The sound as it smashed onto the tiled floor cracked through the kitchen. I crouched down to retrieve the pieces . . . and so did Meg. Our faces were so close and our fingers almost touched as we reached for the same shard of china. "You're upset," she said.

"For God's sake, leave me in peace," I whispered.

Meg straightened up. There was an awkward, terrible pause. "I think I need a drink," she said. "Want some?"

"There isn't any in the house."

"Oh no?"

I looked up at her. "I don't want a drink. And neither do you."

Again, the ghastly suspension of sound. "Don't worry. I told you, I've got it under control. I can manage a little one, now and again. I'm lucky that way . . ."

The sharp edge of the broken plate bit into my flesh. "Meg. Stop. Think. You've been doing so well . . ."

"Precisely." Meg went in search of her contraband whiskey bottle—her lover, brother, friend and child—and I did nothing to stop her.

I crouched on the kitchen floor and wept.

When the storm had subsided, I fetched a dustpan and brush and swept up the mess. I lifted Meg's shopping bag onto the table and looked inside it. There was a paperback book, a self-help manual written by an American author whom I did not know, and I flicked through it. A phrase caught my eye. "Feel the fear, but do it anyway."

I closed the book, put it back in the bag and made myself go upstairs to Meg's bedroom. She was sitting on the bed, staring at a photograph of Sacha. There was a full glass in her hand.

She offered no resistance when I pried it away. "Where have you been hiding this, Meg? How much have you had?"

They were always so crass, these questions. She looked up at me. "Only a mouthful. I had a bottle in the wardrobe. My safety net."

I set the glass down on the bedside table and sat down beside her. "Don't drink any more. I'll help you, I promise."

"Why on earth should you?" She shrugged despairingly. "Anyway, it isn't like that. It's bigger than people saying they want to help."

"Alfredo always said that even as we laugh we should take life seriously, for it's the only one we have."

"Um," said Meg, and tears fell down her cheeks.

"He was right," I said, feeling my loss stretch coldly into the future. I gave a sob. "Alfredo was right."

Meg's hand crept toward mine. "Oh, Fanny," she said, "and there I was thinking that it was all just a huge and awful joke."

Will rearranged the ministerial diary, and we drove over to Ember House. When it came to the point, I could not bring myself to walk through the front door.

Will put his arm around my shoulders. "Come on, we'll walk around for a bit."

The grass was damp from recent rain, and everything

had the half-drowned look of the English summer garden. I stopped to anchor a rogue spray of clematis by the wall, and water showered down on me. Will brushed it off.

The rain soon came down in earnest and he said, "We can't put this off any longer," and led me into the house. "Give me your hand, Fanny," he said, and held it fast.

Even in the short period since my father's death, the house felt different. Less familiar, less comforting.

Will made coffee and I produced sandwiches. Will ate his hungrily but I only pecked at mine. I was thinking about the house, and how I could not bear to let it go.

"Will, what do you think about living here?"

He looked thoroughly startled. "Live here? It hadn't crossed my mind." He helped himself to an egg sandwich. "Fanny, are you serious?"

I knew it was mad and totally illogical, but I whispered, "It's my home."

Will put down the sandwich. Too late, I realized the implication of my words. "But it's not mine," he said. "And I rather thought our house was our home."

"I don't want to sell Ember House."

He held me by my shoulders and searched my face. He seemed puzzled by what he saw, which irritated me. Was it so puzzling to be grieving for my father? "If you want me to think about it, of course I will. It's just not what we planned."

"Oh, the *plan.*" I shrugged him off, and witless with misery, slammed the coffee mugs into the sink.

"Fanny, what *is* it?"

I stared out of the window and bit down on my

knuckle. "I can't get over the fact that Dad did not have me there when he died. It haunts me and I won't forgive myself."

Will stood behind me and put his arms around me. "Hush, Fanny, hush."

His mobile rang in the hall. Bullying and impolite. Instinctively, he tensed and dropped his arms but I hissed at him, "You're *not* answering it, Will. Just this once."

He cocked his head as the ringing continued but he stayed where he was. All the same, I knew that I'd lost him. "Might have been Robert," he said quietly. "The deal is if I back the government on the National Health Bill, then my name is definitely on the list for the Exchequer."

"But as a minister you *have* to support the government. It doesn't matter what you think."

"There's support, and there's *support,*" he said.

Once or twice, Elaine and I had discussed power. What was it? In what sort of shape did it come? How did a wife fit around it? *Very snary,* we agreed. Power wraps a person up as tight as a knot. *Very snary* are the courtiers, the adulation, the chauffeured cars and the handing over of ideals in return for the commodity called power. Ideals are so much more uncomfortable than sitting warm and snug in the back of the limousine.

And power was what Will was really concerned with. That much was now clear.

"I can't bear to think about any of it," I said and fled to my father's study.

His fountain pen was still on the desk where he had last put it down. The red light winked on the answering machine. I reached over and switched it off. I picked up a book from a pile by the window, *A Disquisition on the Grand Wines of Bordeaux*, and replaced it, unread.

I grasped the edge of the curtain. Years ago, I had got it wrong. Grief was not a blade slicing into the flesh. No, grief was dull and heavy: It made your limbs drag and your head ache. Grief enjoyed playing with its victims, for I could swear I could hear my father in the study.

"After 1963," he was saying, "and we are talking Bordeaux here, of course, with its vintage of rain and rot and worthless wines, came 1964, badly undervalued because of the previous year. Nature, having taken away with one hand, now gave us lovely rich, rounded, elegant wines with the other . . ."

A tiny movement alerted me to Will's presence. "Fanny, darling, we had better look at the papers."

I heard a voice saying—and it sounded strange and distant—"Will, there are so few people to whom one is joined, cell for cell, understanding for understanding. Far too few to lose or betray," and I realized it was mine.

We bundled up the papers and took them back home. Among them was a file with "Francesca" written on it.

I opened it when I was alone in the bedroom. I was not sure what I expected—legal or financial instructions—but I was unprepared for the small treasure trove it contained. There was a child's drawing of a house, with a path leading to the front door, with a stick man and woman holding between them a stick child with a bow in her hair.

It was one of my drawings from nursery school.

There was an essay entitled: "Show effects of America's isolationist stance during the 1930s, giving two examples." The mark had been C. And a poem, handwritten on expensive paper. "Your absence grates on my skin/Which breaks into scarlet rubies/Until a red river slides toward the sea of my grief."

I pressed fingers to cheeks that had grown hot. The poem, a relic from a failed love affair—all right, *the* failed love affair, with Raoul—was unutterably bad, but my father had not only found it somewhere but chosen to keep it.

There was also a wedding photograph of Will and me, an invitation to the Chevalier du Tastevin dinner which, once upon a time, I had coveted above all else, and a curl of baby hair taped onto the back of Chloe's christening photograph.

Tenderly, I shuffled them back into order—those small, telling fragments of our past that had been so carefully hoarded by my father, my watchful, beloved father. As I replaced them in the file, I noticed yet another fold of paper. It was a rough pencil sketch, amateur and impatient. But the subject was obvious enough; a house planned around a central courtyard with a loggia at one end. Underneath the sketch were the words: "Il Fattoria. Val del Fiertino."

I found Will watching the news on television and I sat down beside him. "Will, I've made a decision. I've decided to take my father's ashes to Fiertino. I know that's where he would want to be, where he needs to be . . . and I'm going to book the next flight because *I* need to do it as soon as possible."

The newscaster, unmoved by my statement, continued smoothly to recount the day's events.

"Without me?"

"Without you."

"And . . ."

"And nothing. I would like to go away. It is as simple as that."

"Of course you must, Fanny." He did not look at me. "If that's what you want."

Chapter 18

EARLY ON THE MONDAY morning, I was almost ready.

I was saying good-bye to Will. A plumber banged away at a dripping pipe in our bathroom. Maleeka's cleaning materials littered the hallway. The radio in the kitchen was at full blast. Will's car was in the driveway and the driver had kept the engine running. Will had lost his wallet and was rampaging upstairs in the search. In short, everything was perfectly normal—except that the following day I would be driven to the airport to catch a plane, and the scent of an unusual freedom in my nostrils was almost unbearable.

Will clattered downstairs. "Got it. What time are you flying, did you say?"

I tucked a copy of my schedule into his briefcase. My husband's mouth was set, but not in anger. It was something deeper. He was bracing himself against my going. I kissed him tenderly, but with a palpable sense of relief that I know he sensed. He kissed me back, almost perfunctorily. "Take care."

"Do your best." I brushed my fingers over the set mouth.

He snapped his briefcase shut. "You know what? I've started to wonder, sometimes, if it's all worth it."

"Go," I said hastily. "You'll be late."

I watched him trudge over to the car, fling his briefcase into the back and get in.

They sped off down the drive and almost immediately the phone rang, which it had done incessantly with friends and acquaintances ringing to console. This time it was Raoul.

"I'm sorry, Fanny, that I did not make the funeral, but you knew why."

"You were in Australia. Did it go well?"

"I've got a nice deal shaping up that I will tell you about at a better time."

"How is the family?"

"Larger and much more expensive. Thérèse says she feels a hundred but she doesn't look it." His laugh was full of energy and conveyed deep admiration. "My wife is a beautiful woman."

"If I was very nice to her do you think she would tell me her secret?"

"Living with me, clearly. We are going to Rome for a couple of years. Did I tell you?" Like the Rothschilds of old, the Villeneuves frequently dispatched their family members all around the wine world to consolidate business contacts.

"Wonderful."

He cleared his throat. "I need not ask if you miss your

201

father. I want to tell you that I will very much. For all sorts of reasons. He was a good friend and I valued him the . . . more because he was from an older generation. One does not have many such friends, and I am grateful for the trouble he took with me." He added, "And with you, Fanny."

There was a startled silence. The manner in which he said the last breached our unwritten code for there was tenderness there. I said hastily, "Actually, tomorrow I'm taking his ashes back to Fiertino. I think that is where he would wish to be."

To my surprise, Raoul did not endorse the plan—and, in the scheme of things, only Raoul, because of his friendship with my father, had the right to question my decision. "Are you quite sure? Alfredo was a great romantic in many ways, Fanny, but his life was in Stanwinton. Perhaps . . . you are right. It will give you time. Give yourself a moment to investigate the wine. I would like your thoughts on the super Tuscans." He paused. "I would like to talk to you about the business. Will you contact me when you feel better?"

I promised I would.

The plumber called me, and I went upstairs to find out the worst, which was nothing much, but he charged royally for it. I wrote him a check and ushered him out of the house.

"If you want to be a real friend," I said to Elaine, who had driven over the day before to console me over my father, "help me clean out Chloe's room. I couldn't face it after she left."

Elaine was still wrestling with her own problems with Neil. "We're waving flags at each other from opposite trenches," she reported. "He doesn't want me to go. He tells me that I'm his rock and I tell him that, even if I didn't have good enough grounds, his unoriginality would ensure that most right-thinking women packed their cases . . ."

"And?" I queried.

"I have not quite got there, yet," she said.

Even so, Elaine still had time for me and had understood perfectly when I explained that, with my father's dying, I felt as though I had been ordered up to the front line of battle without a suitable weapon.

"Quite natural," she said. "It means we are on our own. In every sense of the word."

After lunch we went upstairs. As a pile of discarded clothes hindered complete access, I had to push hard on Chloe's bedroom door. Elaine surveyed the mess. "Seen it before," she said. "It's probably radioactive. Can't Maleeka do it?"

"She could. But she wouldn't emerge for at least a year."

Elaine picked up one of the Barbies that had migrated into a Barbie gene pool on a shelf stuffed with childhood objects that Chloe refused to relinquish. This one had long blonde hair, cone breasts, a wasp waist and nothing on. Elaine manipulated one leg up above the head. "I could sort of do that once," she said wistfully.

I laughed. "Chloe cherished great hopes of the Barbies, but they let her down. She never got over the fact that their legs would not bend into ballet positions."

Elaine regarded the doll gravely.

She leaned against the window and looked out across the sunny lawn and the border in which a few opportunistic delphiniums raised their plumes. "I am nearly forty-seven," she murmured, "and I keep asking myself 'what else is there?' Is this . . . me as I am now, is this *all* there is to life?"

I was searching in the hall chest for my passport and came across a bundle of out-of-date ones. I loved Chloe's old passports. They recorded her journey from tiny minx in plaits, to teenager who chose to sulk at the camera. The up-to-date model, of course, was with her in Australia.

I stroked the photos of Chloe and felt the grain of those years beneath my finger, soft and sentimental memories which, like pieces of mosaic, assemble into well-loved pictures. Chloe singing in her cot. Chloe winning the egg and spoon race. My father holding up a glass of wine to the light and asking: "What do you think, Francesca?" Will lying with his head in my lap, drowsy and at peace. Sacha putting down his tartan suitcases in the hall and asking: "Can I come and live here?"

Meg's voice cut into my reverie. "Fanny, any chance of me coming too?"

I took a deep breath and kept my back to her. "If you don't mind, Meg, I think not."

"I'd love to see the place we have all heard about for so long. I wouldn't be any bother."

I shoved my passport into my pocket, and turned. "No," I said flatly. "I have to do this on my own."

"Well, that's quite clear, then." She pulled at a finger until the joint cracked. Her eyes narrowed and darkened.

To my astonishment, Will turned up at the airport. "I didn't think we'd said good-bye properly."

Weak with relief that I had got this far, I leaned against him. "Must be a first."

"I've run away from school and the diary secretary was not amused."

He felt warm, firm and, despite everything, reliable. The uncertainty had vanished and he was under control. Here was the embodiment of a successful politician who had come to see off his wife at the airport; the well-cut suit symbolized the fusion between his energy and achievements. It was Will at his most attractive and I never failed to respond.

"Go carefully with the car tax, won't you? Don't lose patience and make mistakes," I said, then added, "If that's what you want. If that's what you still believe."

"I do." His gaze fixed on the bookshop behind me. "Why *are* you going, Fanny? Truthfully."

"My father . . . I would like some breathing space. I want to get away."

He frowned. "Oh, well, then," he said.

A family group, pushing two trolleys stacked high with suitcases shot past us. We stepped apart, and his mobile phone shrilled.

He dived for it, "Sorry about this . . ." and talked into it.

I picked up my hand luggage. Inside, cocooned in bubble wrap and one of my father's sweaters, was the urn containing his ashes. "Bye," I mouthed and moved off towards the departure gate.

He clicked off the phone and caught me by the arm. "Fanny, don't go without me. Wait until I can come with you."

"No," I said, panic stricken that I might be persuaded to stay, and guilty that I did not wish to. "Please . . . let me go."

And I shook him off and fled in a manner that clearly shocked him.

I was too tired to read on the plane and for the first slice of the journey I dozed and woke with a start from a dream where dank grass and gray mud clotted my shoes. I waded into a river of dead leaves, fighting for breath as the level went over my head. A little later, I found myself wreathed in a white river mist and its cold slid deep into my bones. In that dream, I cried out for the sun.

The Mediterranean coastline, vividly colored and fringed by a bright blue sea, came into view and I breathed in deeply with relief. The stewardess dumped a tray of food in front of me. "Enjoy," she said.

I inspected a plastic lump, a roll attached to some dubious cold meat, drank the orange juice and found myself thinking of Caro. Her final words to me—her wedding present, which had been so crude and hurtful at the time—made better sense with experience. Nails screeching against the surface, wincing at the sound, Caro had attempted to wipe the blackboard clean of my father to begin again.

I could have explained how I felt to Will. I could have

said: "When I married you and I was swept up by the tempestuous emotions of early passion, of coming together in love, it was irrelevant who belonged to which sex. It was a meeting of souls and minds. But once the marriage was made, the duties allocated, it mattered very much to which sex I belonged."

What was more, when he had taken Liz into our bed Will taught me that to be a wife was separate and distinct from being a woman.

I glanced at my watch. About now, Stanwinton would be busy with afternoon traffic, swirling in complicated movements around the gyratory system, composed largely of school children being bussed about. Afternoons provided the window to visit the dentist, slot in the extra music lesson and pour emollient on childish ruptures that had occurred in the school battleground by laying out fruit juice and frying heroic amounts of fish fingers. . . . Later there would be homework to supervise, clothes to sort out and an adult meal to produce. And I would be busy with Meg or Will.

I looked down from the plane window at the green and brown of the Italian peninsula. I wanted a rest from that part of my life.

As the plane began its descent, I uttered a silent thank-you to my father.

"Fanny . . . *Fanny!*" Benedetta, who had insisted on taking a train from Fiertino to meet me, carved a swath through the clump of spectators waiting in the arrivals hall. She gathered me into a plump, garlicky embrace.

"Let me look at you," she demanded, and did so, long

and hard, then pinched my cheeks and kissed me all over again. Her English had deteriorated. My Italian was by no means perfect, but as I drove the rental car, we managed to discuss her arthritis, her son who lived in Milan but did not contact his mother as often as she would like, and exclaim at the horror of the Fiertino hillside, which had always been open and free, but had now been carved up for summer homes by city dwellers. "You never know, these days, who you will bump into," she said.

We drove out of Rome, past dusty oleanders and fields of mass-produced tomatoes and zucchini. Anxious in the unfamiliar traffic, I strained to absorb the most significant facts. Casa Rosa, where I was going to stay, had been bought by an *inglese* couple, who, having failed to raise enough money to do it up, had retreated back to England. Now, it was abandoned, except for an odd letting or two. Not that the agent knew her job. "*Santa Patata,* she was born with no brain."

Eventually, Benedetta instructed me to turn off the main road into a valley that ran north-south, and we drove between vineyards and fields of corn—small, immaculate and clearly cherished.

Olive trees shimmered silver white in the heat. The road wound lazily through the valley and disappeared up the slopes and into the horizon. The hilltops were dusty brown—*crete sensesi,* as my father had described them, "The color of old leather that has done good service." The river ran down from the steepest side of the valley, then turned into a twisted ribbon of smoothed, burning rocks.

"Slow down, Fanny, we are nearly there."

My stomach contracted. What would it be like? What would I think of Fiertino, after all those years of talking? Like the pilgrims in the Stanwinton church, I had been marching toward a vision of Paradise, and now it was in sight.

And . . . yes, there was the church and the piazza, hemmed by dusty plane trees, and the cobweb of narrow streets radiating out from the town center.

And . . . no. The Fiertino that my father described had not much traffic, no garish adverts, no squat, modern housing that pressed up against the older, sepia villas.

As we drove past the church and skirted the piazza, Benedetta did not draw breath. The builders had cheated the *inglese*—anyone could have told them. The walls they built cracked, and the plants and vegetables died during a scorching summer. Her worst scorn was reserved for the sin of failing to ask for help before "they ran back home."

Set back from the road down a track, Casa Rosa was a quarter of a mile or so from the town. I was so busy negotiating the potholes that I missed the first sight of it. This I regretted, for I would have known five seconds earlier what I knew the minute I got out of the car and walked to the front door.

Painted in pinkish orange, which had weathered in streaks, Casa Rosa was a flat-fronted, two-story house. Nothing magnificent, nothing special—but it spoke to me. It said, *I should be yours*.

OK, I thought. At least that's clear. It's a little inconvenient, since I live somewhere else, but it is quite clear.

It had long, shuttered windows on the ground floor

and smaller ones upstairs. The tiled roof had weathered as subtly as the stucco, and they matched each other for disrepair. There were ugly holes in the stonework, tell-tale scars from damp and missing tiles and a plant grew out of the masonry by the chimney. Even the kindest eye could not ignore the raw, unfinished look, its air of desperation and need.

Benedetta shrugged. "You need *la passione* to make it good." The front door needed persuasion to yield. "*Allora,* it is the pig." Bendetta threw her weight against it.

Our arrival into the hallway was the cue for a rustling of insects and the raising of a great deal of dust. Benedetta looked horrified and took it as a personal affront. "It's worse than I thought; I shall help you clean."

"No, you won't." I slipped my arm around her shoulders.

The kitchen was in frightful condition, but the battered stove was usable and water issued from the fur-encrusted taps. A wooden table had been liberally splashed with wax from a sequence of candles that had been stuck into the neck of a large Chianti bottle standing at its center.

Upstairs, there were three bedrooms and a bathroom consisting of little more than a basin and an open drain in the floor. But the window was long and elegant, the sort of window that looked perfect with white muslin hanging from it. The two smaller rooms had beds, but were stuffed with empty suitcases and cardboard boxes.

The main bedroom overlooked the valley.

I gazed hungrily upon a blazing sky, at the line of full-bosomed hills melting from green and brown into purple, at the gray-green swath of olive trees and, to the west, the vines, which marched in immaculate parallel lines across the slope.

I carried my suitcases upstairs and put my hand luggage carefully onto the bed. "Benedetta, I will need your help," I said, as I extracted the urn with my father's ashes. "I must find the right place."

"Ah . . ." She touched the lid. "Alfredo. Yes, we shall think. It is important." Her fingers lingered a second or two longer. "Perhaps the priest . . . but I think Alfredo would prefer to be out on the hillside."

"Perhaps," I said. "But we must get it right."

Benedetta laughed, a deep belly laugh. "Ah, Fanny, but I think you will."

Chapter 19

"POOR YOU," SAID MEG.

I had rung to report my arrival and thrown in a few details about the state of the house. There was no point in explaining to Meg that the state of the house was the point. Its quasi-dereliction and the suggestion of redemption suited my mood. No point telling Meg that Casa Rosa was the perfect outward setting for the curious inner landscape in which I found myself.

Anyway, there is nothing quite like running away. No marks out of ten for this wife. *Not* a trouper. But I did not care. I tossed and turned in a strange bed, and yet I was perfectly, gloriously happy. Later, a hard, un-English light from the unshuttered window nudged me awake just after dawn and I uttered aloud into the cool air: *"Yes?"*

"Chloe rang," Meg informed me, finally. "She'd forgotten you'd done a runner. We talked and she's fine. Sacha had a long talk with her, too. Actually, Sacha's thinking of joining her for a while." When I failed to rise to the bait, Meg plunged in the needle as only she knew how. "You know, Fanny, there *was* no need to hide the left-over bottles of wine from your lunch with Elaine. It just shows you don't trust me an inch."

Weeping Eros might have goaded me into building a city, but when it came to the question of Meg, I suspected I had never got past digging out the foundations. I glanced up. Through the doorway into the sitting room, light and sun pooled across the floor, and I thought, I am here and she is there.

"Enjoy yourself, Fanny," she said, an admonition designed to make me feel worse.

I kept my eyes fixed on the sun and the light.

The phone was tucked into a niche by the front door, surrounded by an audience of dead insects. I brushed them onto the floor and rang Will. Our initial conversation was strained and difficult. Will was hurt by the manner in which I had shaken him off, and I was sorry— but not sorry enough to lie. "I *love* it here," I told him, but failed to add, "I wish you were here."

"That's what I was afraid of." He sounded distracted and uncharacteristically low. "Fanny, I've been asked onto television to talk about future plans. I'm of two minds. What do you think?"

"Any news on progress?"

"The wheels grind on. The car lobby is raging out of control. So, it's a case of I'm damned if I do appear and damned if I don't."

We reflected on this for a second or two.

"The balance has shifted, as it does. I have an awful feeling that this one is going . . . wrong."

My body was irradiated with warmth, right down to the tips of my painted toenails, and Will's distress was powerless to touch me. I felt almost insane with the novelty of stepping back. Should I tell the truth and say, "Will, I'm off the case," and confess a great, burdensome distaste for the ins and outs, the double-dealing and the stratagems, the straitjacket of politics into which Will and I had been laced?

"Be honest," Will begged. "Tell me what you think I should do."

I wheeled out the old tactics. "What's happened to the man who said that a project should be fought over because it meant it had been tried and tested?"

"Perhaps I'm tired. Perhaps I've had enough."

I wasn't fooled. Will's doubts and fears might be black, but he hadn't given up. He was still in there, sharp on the scent. "Don't go on the program," I said. "You'll be a hostage to fortune."

"You think that's best?"

"I do," I said—guiltily, for I did not care what he did.

The house's outer walls were built of thick stone. I kicked off my sandals and, leaving a trail of damp prints on the *cotto,* padded into the sitting room, which smelled faintly of ash and sandalwood. Its window had a similar view to the one from my bedroom, sweeping across the valley to the hills beyond.

A couple of elderly armchairs stood on either side of the fireplace and I imagined that the English had sat in them and mulled over their plans—*Let's take a wall down here, replaster there; can we afford central heating?*

Ash and cigarette ends were stacked up in the fire-place and on the table there was a jam jar stuffed with dried flowers. I touched one, and brittle petals floated to the floor.

The kitchen was no better. The whitewashed wall was stained and, in places, rubbed down to the original lime wash. The ceiling was greasy, and the beams blackened. A bunch of dead herbs still hung from a clumsily inserted hook. I dragged up a chair and took it down, then stood back with folded arms and took stock.

If this were my kitchen, I would love it so tenderly. (Was this really me, thinking this?) I would make it glow in creams and yellows and whites. I would scrub and bleach the table, place blue and white china plates on a dresser and hang fresh bouquets of herbs.

In return, on cold evenings, it would invite me to make Benedetta's mushroom risotto, lashed into perfection with Parmesan and butter. On hot ones, when the sun slithered down the sky and the air was pungent with the aroma of herbs and citrus, it would hint, perhaps, at grilled chicken with lemon. I knew a place, too, where Mrs. Scott's beaded cover would come into its own, on a jug of fresh lemonade.

If the Casa Rosa were my house, I would make up the beds with old linen sheets and polish the floors with beeswax, as the women in the family must have done when its fortunes had been high. I would plant spinach and chard and beans in the plot behind the house and arrange books on the shelf beside the fire.

I went outside to the loggia. Covered with a vine, it was shaded from the sun, and I sat down in a chair. Here I faced away from Fiertino, and, apart from the concrete olive store at the crook of the valley, had a view of open, unimpeded country.

Sweat gathered at the base of my spine. An ant roamed over my foot. The heat shimmered over road, houses, fields and trees. I felt it warm my bones, my veins, my spirit. I raised a finger and flicked it against the chair arm and told myself that that was all the movement I need make.

Benedetta's bungalow was squeezed alongside ten others, on the slope above the bridge in the southern quarter of the town. There was no garden, just a rectangular plot that contained a row of tomatoes that had been trained up stakes, a couple of olive trees and a bright green plastic oil tank. She told me that the houses had been on the site of the old school, which, like so much in the valley, had been destroyed by the big guns when the Allies chased the Germans north.

I was introduced to Signora Berto, her dead husband's sister, a large woman a few years older with false teeth and hair dyed raven black. Benedetta's brother, Silvio, also put in an appearance; he sat and fixed me with an unfaltering, gimlet stare, but it was impossible to take offense.

Signora Berto's accent was difficult and at first I struggled to follow what she was saying. "Your grandmother was fine looking. She was brave too. She worked in the fields, even when the guns were going, to bring in the harvest when there was no one else to do this."

I felt a glow of pride. "My grandmother did that? My father never mentioned it."

"He was only a small boy. Children did not know everything. We took good care to hide some things from them."

My grandmother. I rolled the words over my tongue. Dodging mines, driving oxen, diving for cover when the shelling was bad. Hold the family, I whispered to my father's shade—which was as much to do with holding memory as anything else.

Benedetta's kitchen was tiny and cluttered with religious pictures, church magazines, papers and tomatoes piled on plates. Big and red and fat. A Formica-topped table occupied most of the space but we squeezed around it and ate Benedetta's famed *spaghetti con vedura* and veal fried in sage and butter.

The valley was changing, they told me. For one thing, the olives were now big business and everyone was hurrying to put in for subsidies. For another, the English had invaded, snapping up barns and houses like there was no tomorrow. "No matter," said Silvio, who was working on several conversions. "The English have the problems and pay the bills. We have the jobs."

I told them that I planned to walk on the hills in the early mornings, and Signora Berto looked alarmed. "Be sure to wrap up warmly," she said. "You might catch cold."

The temperature in that tiny kitchen must have been eighty degrees at least. I tried to catch Benedetta's eye but she agreed with her sister-in-law. "You can borrow my scarf." She patted my arm. "Tomorrow I will show you everything."

She was as good as her word. Talking nonstop, she piloted me knowledgeably between the church with its fifteenth-century frescoes, the piazza with its carved stone colonnade and fountain and the tethering stone where the merchant trains used to stop and secure their horses. Benedetta introduced me to the signora who ran the shop she favored, which sold rosaries and prayer cards, and to the mini-supermarket, which was stocked with local olive oil, tubes of garlic pesto, dried tomatoes and out-of-date boxes of Baci chocolates, and to the delicatessen, which sold bottled artichoke hearts and mortadella sausage the size of a side plate.

Afterward, we drove along the valley in bright, hot sun. "There," she said eventually, as I guided the car down an avenue of chestnuts. "There is the *fattoria* where the Battistas used to live."

The heat slapped at my flesh as I got out of the car. *"The* fattoria *was old, very old,"* my father had told me, *"and the brick was the softest color you can imagine. It had a garden with a statue and a box maze. I thought it the most beautiful place on earth."*

"I don't understand, Benedetta," I said, as I took in an ill-proportioned, mean-spirited, concrete building. Grimy net curtains hung out of the windows; there was no garden, and the outbuildings were of the same prefabricated material.

She avoided my eye. "Didn't your father mention that the old house was destroyed in the war?"

"No, he didn't."

"Santa Patata," she said awkwardly. "How stupid of him."

"I suppose he preferred to remember it as it was."

The sun reddened my skin as I walked around the house, considering the gap between what I had imagined and what was actually there.

"We shouldn't have come . . ." Benedetta said.

In one way, perhaps, she was right. But in others, I needed to find out what was true, and what was not. As I retraced my steps, my eye was caught by traces of a stone arch that had been incorporated into the concrete wall—a graceful echo of what had been lost.

I pointed it out to Benedetta who fanned herself vigorously. "The guns," she said. "Very bad."

We got back in the car and headed back to Fiertino. After a while, I asked Benedetta, "Do you think it would be possible to stay on in Casa Rosa? Could I take it for the month?"

Benedetta smiled broadly. "We make the telephone calls now."

I tried to explain to Will that I had fallen in love with the Casa Rosa and tried to point out—gently—that some time off would be good, perhaps for both of us.

"You're probably right," he conceded, "but . . . Fanny . . . is there something I don't know, something we should talk about?"

"I'm sorry. I know it will be a bit inconvenient."

"I don't really get it."

"Try."

"Why now? You can go back any time."

I felt as though we were at opposite ends of a large room, straining to make ourselves heard, but I was not going to move.

"What's this house got that's so marvelous?"

"I'll bring you back photos and show you."

"I've checked with Mannochie. There are a couple of things that you really should be at."

"Does Mannochie ever give up? Get Meg to stand in for me. She would like that."

He sounded doubtful. "It's not ideal."

"It's the first time, Will."

There was an uneasy silence. "Fanny, am I losing you?"

Then I felt guilty, and guilt generally succeeded in making me lose my temper. "Will," I hissed down the phone, "I have looked after Chloe, run your house and . . . put up with Meg. I have smiled my way through endless charity functions, thousands of suppers, teas, meetings and endless bloody surgeries. I gave up a job I loved to do, not to mention my time, my weekends and great chunks of my life. All I'm asking for is a few weeks off-duty. My father has died and I want to think about him. I need to think about him. I am tired and sad.

I am missing our daughter."

I heard the snap of the cigarette lighter. "I didn't know you felt like that."

"Well, you do now."

When I was fourteen, the dentist had removed the braces from my teeth. For years, it seemed, my mouth had been weighed down with metal and every day the sharp edges had nagged another area of tender gum into an ulcer. Smiling had been painful and never for one minute did I forget that I was ugly and awkward. The moment of release from their torture was to experience a miraculous airborne quality in my mouth.

I put down the phone, only to relive that miraculous airborne quality of pure release.

Of course I was sad, but the sadness was twisted up into other strands—and to feel sadness was a part of being intensely alive. I sat on the stairs in the Casa Rosa and propped up my chin in my hands and considered. How often do we have time to seek out our secret selves and bring them into the light? To examine and say, with delighted recognition, so this is what I am? This is what I might be? This is where I will go?

I remained on the stairs for a long time, breathing in the house, breathing in peace, quiet . . . me.

I had brought my wine books and embarked on a program of study. I immersed myself in local history. I read about Punic wars, and of the chestnut woods that had supplied the timber for Roman galleys. Of Popes passing through, of civil wars, and of the pilgrim road—the *via francigena*—which connected

Fiertino with the whole of Europe.

In the cool of the early morning, I walked the hills until I knew that Benedetta would be waiting to give me breakfast. In the evenings, I strolled along the road still pulsing with the day's heat, with the cicadas at full cry, and ate at Angelo's in the piazza.

Afterward, I explored the town, plunging into the noise-filled network of streets and houses where past and present muddled agreeably along side by side. In the church, modern stained glass sat uncomfortably in the fifteenth-century stonework and I headed for the frescoes on the north wall, which were famous and squabbled over by art historians.

But if I had expected the glowing, gentle Christ of Bellini, or a massively reassuring Massaccio Divinity, I could not have been more wrong. The paintings depicted the erring human at the mercy of violent passions. A cauldron boiled a rich man and his wife. A stern angel speared a man in an obvious state of lust. Naked, screaming women clustered in the foreground. The corpses of children and babies were strewn upon the earth. A second angel bore down, sword in hand, upon a fleeing priest. Behind the scenes of retribution, this landscape of terror, an unforgiving desert stretched into infinity.

A notice on the wall informed the reader that the frescoes, painted at the time of a plague visitation, "depict God's displeasure for man's eternal state of sin."

I went out into the sunlight, in no hurry to return.

Greedy for every nuance, every detail, I absorbed the shapes and feel of this landscape. It was strange to me, yet it took only a trick of the light, a glimpse of a building out of the corner of my eye, or a snatch of a song, and a shutter in my mind folded back . . . and I was in bed at Ember House, slipping deeper into the sleep folding over me to the sound of my father's voice.

In the old days, Benedetta told me, the women beat their washing on the flat stone by the bridge. On St. Anthony's day, the men brought in hay to the church and asked the statue of the saint to make their crops yield, and perpetual Tuscan rose, *le rose d'ogni mese,* flourished unimpeded everywhere. "It not like that now," she said. "Obviously."

Up in the churchyard, surrounded by the cypresses, lay generations of the Battista family, my family. They had names like Giovanni, Maria Theresa, Carolina, Bruno and I wrote them down in my notebook.

The week slipped by.

One morning I sat down to rest on the slope above Casa Rosa. The sun made me drowsy. I closed my eyes and heard my father. *Once upon a time, there was a family who lived in a big farmhouse.*

I opened my eyes. For the first time, I noticed a line of pylons, which marched through the farms and fanned out across the valley, then on into the distance. The heat haze shimmered above the house, giving it a trembling, insubstantial quality. I was afraid that, if I reached out to touch it, it would disappear.

It was going to be another scorching day.

I rubbed a sprig of thyme between my fingers and sniffed. I saw a car drive slowly along the road and come to a halt outside Casa Rosa.

Chapter 20

WHEN I GAVE BIRTH to Chloe, Elaine gave me her old baby clothes. *A good quantity, to start you off,* she said. They were a little worn and stiffened from constant washing. The hem of one tiny dress needed mending, a button from a pair of dungarees was missing. But I loved that testimony to their previous life. In giving them, Elaine had welcomed me into the domestic pilgrim train. In time, I passed them on again.

It struck me then that, one way or another, the past has a way of keeping pace. Or, rather, it keeps its hooks pretty firmly dug into the present.

Raoul, presenting himself at my front door, was definitely from the past. He did not offer any detailed explanations, saying only that he and Thérèse had been house hunting in Rome. Thérèse had returned to France and he had stayed on. "So here I am, Fanny."

He had changed very little over the years, except to become—naturally—more assured; he fitted, as the French say, into his skin. More sophisticated, more knowing. He had always dressed well and taken care of his appearance but never at the cost of the important things.

"I'm so pleased to see you." I kissed him on the cheek.

"I'm taking you to lunch," he said. "We are eating in a hotel owned by a friend of mine."

We drove north toward Montepulciano. Raoul talked knowledgeably about the wine, its history and, more importantly, its future. The hotel was a modest house tucked away in the village of Chianciano. "Don't be fooled by the paper tablecloths," Raoul said, as we were ushered into a room filled with diners. "This place is a local legend."

We fussed pleasurably over the menu but there was no debate about the choice of wine. We ordered a Prosecco with the arugula salad and plumped for a 1993 ruby Brunello di Montalcino to accompany our onion tart. It was complex and almost flawless. "The fruit of a perfectionist," I said, after the first mouthful.

"But of course," Raoul said. "He dares everything; waits until the very last moment of ripeness before harvesting."

Noses in our wine glasses, we paused. I breathed in summer and fruit, sun and mist—a voluptuous, lazy exchange—and searched for the words with which to describe it precisely.

There was a familiar concern in Raoul's eye. "You haven't lost your zest for the business."

I shook my head and grinned. "I'm my father's daughter."

"It's impossible to predict what the elements and man can make between them. Sometimes . . . the worst. Sometimes magic."

I put down my glass. "I don't think we always seek magic," I said.

He gave the smallest of frowns.

"I think it's change we crave . . . diversion. A different way of looking at things." I found myself telling him about Meg and some of the more difficult moments at

Stanwinton. The sun, the wine were loosening my tongue and it was not unpleasant. "She once said she hated me for knowing when to stop . . ."

"Lucky you. Knowing when to stop is one of the secrets of survival, Fanny. And knowing when not to. Speaking of which, tell me about Battista's Fine Wines. What are your plans?"

"I haven't talked to Will yet. Dad's assistant is holding the fort for the time being, but when I get back . . ." I looked across at Raoul. "I couldn't let his business go."

"Are you feeling better?" he asked, carefully.

I took a moment or two to answer. "You were right in one sense, Raoul; there is not as much of my father in Fiertino as I had imagined. I had all of him back home. But I find there is a great deal of me. I am beginning to feel much more happy and peaceful."

"Not everyone can say that when they go abroad. Most of them discover bed bugs, bad stomachs and an extra dose of bad temper. You know, Fanny, I have often thought . . ."

"What?"

"Your father? . . ." He leaned toward me. "Forgive me if I am trespassing, but did he really want to come back to Fiertino? After all, he could have done so many times." Raoul shrugged. "He had such strong ideas . . . and places change. They do not stand still, and your father was a clever man, he knew. It wasn't realistic to come back and to expect it to be the same."

"Perhaps," I said. "Perhaps you are right." I changed the subject. "How is your family?"

Raoul took the hint. "Getting older, but there is nothing startling about that."

"And Thérèse?"

He frowned. "She has no idea that I am seeing you. It is not a good position, but there it is. I did not mean to come here, in fact, but . . . well, as you can see, I am here."

He gave the impression of having crossed some kind of mental Rubicon. I looked down at my glass. "You mustn't lie for me."

"That sounds very English."

"And what does being English mean?"

"Never forgetting your manners."

I started to laugh. "I've always been perfectly behaved?"

"All right. Not admitting that there is more to say. And we've had a long time to consider."

The blood stormed into my cheeks and seeing this, Raoul took my hand. "I am not going to take advantage, Fanny. We know each other too well for that."

Now I was trembling—with surprise at being so propositioned, and delight as well.

I let my hand continue to rest in his. "I have been faithful to Will."

"I suspected that would be so. And I to Thérèse." He poured the final glass of the Brunello. "Some of my friends consider their . . . episodes . . . to be a little like wine tasting. You sample, you savor, but you don't take the bottle home." He pushed the glass toward me. "It was not my way."

The waiter removed our plates and replaced them with

fresh ricotta, a bowl of cherries, and a dish of tiny almond cakes designed to breach the sternest of defenses.

"I have always been ashamed of how badly I . . . how badly I handled things when . . ."

I chose a cake and bit into it. "I wasn't very kind to you."

The dish had a border of faded blue and white— exactly what I would have chosen for the kitchen in Casa Rosa.

"I was only a girl," I said, trying to put this part of the past into its proper place. "I didn't understand. I was curious and, when it came to it, I was offended, because I did not understand. I hope you have forgiven me."

"I know. Of course, I know."

I traced the blue and white pattern with my finger. "Raoul, what do you consider to be most vital when judging"—I raised my eyes and smiled—"a wine?"

"You tell me."

I mulled it over. "You need independence. You need the courage, of course, to assess the bottle rather than the provenance or the pedigree. Maybe that's it; you just need courage."

"Experience helps, I promise you."

I swallowed the last piece of almond cake and raised my eyes again to his.

I saw Liz only once, at a children's party held in the House. I looked up from dabbing Chloe's chocolate-engraved face with a paper napkin and there she was. I knew it must be her because someone called out her name.

She was unaware of my presence, which gave me the advantage and allowed me to recover my equilibrium and from my surprise. For Liz had nothing special in the way of beauty. She was dressed in a green corduroy skirt and black sweater, with her hair pulled back into a ponytail. Her figure was excellent, though, with a round curving haunch that must have been attractive to men. She was talking to a couple of the other wives and hugged a sheaf of notes to her chest.

"You're hurting me, Mummy." Chloe wriggled free and promptly fell over.

I bent down to soothe her. Chloe snuggled into me and I lifted her onto my hip. As I did so, Liz turned and caught sight of me. She went pale and, within a few seconds, left the room.

Chloe begged for a kiss and I gave her one, with more love than I can describe.

I have no idea what Liz made of that encounter, but I could imagine a little of her feelings. She would *never* guess my reaction. I did not hate her, nor did I despise her for taking Will (after all, I had taken him, just like that). Those emotions were redundant. No, what intrigued me was the realization that Liz had been instrumental in pushing Will and me further on. She had shown me that, for good or ill, I had left the fellowship of the single girls to which she belonged. My curved haunch was no longer an invitation to other men, for now a child sat snugly on it. A new set of templates had replaced the old ones. Unlike Liz, if I left a room, it was no longer an isolated gesture. Anything, *anything,* I did was connected to Will and Chloe.

. . .

Raoul had business in Pienza so he dropped me back at the Casa Rosa and we agreed to meet the following day.

I sat down to write up my wine notes. "The Brunello . . ." My pen stopped, mid-sentence.

If I had not pushed Raoul away all those years ago, who knew what my life might have been? If I had not been so miserably confused and embarrassed, aghast, at that episode in the tree house, then . . . might I have been Thérèse, coiffured and immaculate, sheltered and protected by the exquisite framework of the Villeneuve existence?

"Why haven't you been in contact?" Will asked abruptly when he rang.

This was the moment to say: *Guess who turned up? Raoul. He happened to be in the area.*

"I've been rather busy."

"Doing what?"

"Walking, dreaming. You know . . ."

"Fanny, you gave me no warning . . . what I mean is, it is as if I've just woken up and discovered I've been living with someone I didn't know."

"Will, I've calculated that I have spent approximately five thousand seven hundred and forty-five days of my life working for you. This was predicated on the assumption of one commitment per day of our marriage, minus two hundred and sixty-six days for childbirth and holidays."

"As much as that?" he said. "Doesn't time fly when you're enjoying yourself?"

I gave a burst of laughter.

"That's better," he said.

Benedetta seemed tired and low at breakfast. Was I becoming a burden? She would have none of that. "No, no. Fanny. It's my son in Milan. I worry that he spends too much. Never saves. I tell him to come home. I tell him he needs his mama." She spread out her hands. "He agrees he should come home to his mama. But how to do it?"

I sat at her table, drank her coffee and ate bread and apricot jam. The sun blazed through the window and flooded across the picture of the Madonna on the wall and the array of well-used saucepans on the shelf.

"Benedetta, how was the *fattoria* destroyed?"

She folded her hands on the table. "You don't want to know."

"Tell me."

She heaved herself to her feet. "I must see to the tomatoes."

I followed her into the tiny garden. It was nine o'clock, but the sun was already a power drill. Benedetta attended to the tomato trusses and nipped out the leaders. "Lucilla . . ."

"Lucilla?"

"Lucilla was your grandmother's sister," she explained.

"Ah," I said. "Dad mentioned her once, but didn't explain when I asked who she was."

"Perhaps he wouldn't. It was . . . it is difficult." She fussed over a tomato, which had a touch of scale disease.

"When she was nineteen, Lucilla married a Fascist and went to live in Rome. I was still small, but I knew people did not like it. . . . The Fascists made people volunteer to fight, and they sent out enforcers from Rome. They beat men up if they refused and put them in prison. Lucilla arrived one day with her husband, and we children were forbidden to go anywhere near her. I remember running down the road with my brother, and I saw Lucilla standing outside the *fattoria,* crying and crying. Eventually, her husband put her back into the car and drove away."

She harvested two plump tomatoes and handed me one. "Try."

It tasted of sun and spice. "Did they ever come back?"

"They did. Toward the end. Your grandmother and father had already made it to England. The Germans were blowing up the roads to make it difficult for the Allies, and they set ambushes everywhere. Many houses were damaged. Lucilla and her husband came back; I don't think she knew what else to do. This time, she drove the car. He sat in the back, very pale, very fat, hugging a bottle of brandy. She helped him out and took him into the *fattoria* to beg for help from your grandmother. She did not know that your grandmother had already gone." Benedetta fanned her neck where sweat was glistening in the folds. "In the evenings, we all gathered in a safe house, but it was never the same place twice."

My father had told me some of these stories. He'd described how the women piled prams with hoarded provisions and trundled them to the safe houses. How they hid hams, cheese, chickens and oil. How everyone

231

became used to secrets. Carrying them. Hoarding them. Using them as currency for survival. "No one was willing to tell Lucilla where the safe house was."

Benedetta picked up the bowl of her harvested tomatoes. She looked distressed and agitated and I hastened to tell her there was no need to continue if she did not wish.

She ignored me. "In the end, it wasn't the Germans. It was . . . the Partisans came down from the hills and demanded to know where Lucilla's husband was. Everyone was silent because, whatever her sin, Lucilla was still one of us."

"And?"

Benedetta's face gleamed with sweat. "The *fattoria*. It wasn't the guns," she said, her eyes wide with the anguish of confession. "It was me. I heard the Partisan leader ask, 'Where is this man?' and I ran up to him. 'I know, I know,' I shrieked, *'in the fattoria.'*"

Back in the kitchen, Benedetta stood in front of the picture of the Madonna and crossed herself. "I had been taught always to tell the truth. The next time we looked, the *fattoria* was ablaze . . . and they must already have been . . ." The pause seemed like an hour. "Lucilla was a good wife, faithful unto death."

I walked up to the cemetery on the hillside outside the town. The headstones and sarcophagi were a garish mix of colored marble, white stone and plastic flowers. It took me a while to locate Lucilla's grave. She was not buried with the rest of the Battistas. She had been laid to rest at the extreme edge of the cemetery, in the north corner. Her stone was a meager one, its inscription terse:

LUCILLA BATTISTA. BORN 1919. DIED 1944. There was no mention of her married name, or that of her fat, pale husband, and no sign of his final resting place.

I took the car and drove to Tarquinia in the heat of the day and bought a ticket and a guide book to the fifteenth-century palazzo where the Etruscan artifacts were kept. Inside, I wandered up and down the gallery. The palazzo was well maintained. Harpsichord music played in the rooms. The marble floors of the palazzo exuded cool, and the rooms were shaded by green silk blinds. I admired a pair of winged terra-cotta horses, a fine bronze mirror held up by Aphrodite and a statue of Heracles subduing the horses of Diomedes.

Then I saw it, and I recognized it at once.

Behind the final glass showcase, and expertly lit, was a funerary carving from an Etruscan tomb. It was composed of a couch, over which a tasseled cloth had been thrown. Stretched out on it were two figures, a man and a woman. She was young; her huge eyes had once been painted, and the trace of a smile hovered enigmatically on her stone lips. He had a curled beard and his arm around her shoulders. He was smiling, too. The inscription read, MARRIED COUPLE, FIFTH CENTURY B.C.

But I knew that already from my father's photograph.

I consulted my guidebook. "The Etruscans lived and cultivated the *opulenta arva Etruriae,* the fertile fields in which they grew wheat and vines. It is thought that, in the end, plenty made them decadent."

I put out my hand and touched a marble sill under the window.

"Etruscan women," continued the guidebook, "enjoyed the freedom to go out, to share feasts and to drink wine. The Etruscans honored their wives and sought out their company."

I raised my head from the text. The last phrase had already imprinted itself on my mind. "Nor did they share them."

Chapter 21

"DON'T DO THAT, JAKE," said Elaine.

Her seven-year-old son pursed out his bottom lip and continued to ignore the pile of paper I had provided and to scribble instead all over my plastic tablecloth with a purple felt pen.

"Can't think what's got into him, today," said his mother, wresting the pen out of his hand.

Taken by surprise, Jake opened his mouth and bawled. Elaine ordered him to stop—sharpish—otherwise he would have no chocolate biscuits for tea. Jake dropped to the floor, thrashed about and gave such a loud roar that even Sophie, who had chosen to retreat from the adults into splendid isolation, was forced to look up.

Elaine gave Jake a light tap on the bottom. "Stop it. *Now.*"

Jake took this as the signal to commence battle royal. Five minutes later the roaring and rollings puttered to a stop because he had—temporarily—exhausted himself. Elaine picked him up and plonked him on her knee.

"Sorry about that. Sorry about the tablecloth."

I inspected the damage. "To quote my darling father:

'Look at it this way, it's washable.' "

A great deal of shrieking was now heard from the garden. Six-year-old Chloe was being chased around the paths by Gordon, Jake's older brother. Whereas Sophie, Elaine's eldest, who had reached the heights of teenagerdom, remained hunched over a pile of magazines and flicked up the volume control of her tape player. Sophie was not keen on conversing. On arrival, she had immediately clamped on her headphones and retreated into them.

Jake whined and Elaine lectured him in an undertone. "You must not do that to Fanny's tablecloth." His bottom lip quivered.

"Go and play with Chloe, Jake." Elaine pushed him off her knee and Jake did not wait for second instructions. He took off like a rocket.

I poured Elaine more coffee. "You're doing a magnificent job, my girl."

She cradled the cup in her hands. "Each day, I am reminded by my own children that human beings are, at bottom, uncivilized, raging animals, and how fortunate it is for them and the world at large that the likes of you and me accepted the post of lion taming. Ask yourself, Fanny, how would anything function without us?"

I glanced out of the window. Jake was now tearing across the lawn after Chloe, closely followed by Gordon, who was wielding a plastic sword and yelling.

This was followed by the sound of a body smacking into something solid—possibly the garden shed—followed by a cry. "You or me?" I asked Elaine. "Me." She went out the back door and could now be heard scolding

Gordon for deliberately obstructing his brother.

I turned to Sophie. "Are you reading something interesting?"

She put her finger down to mark her place in an article entitled: "How to Make the Boys Sit Up and Take Notice." "Yeah," she replied.

"Would you like to help me get the lunch ready?"

She closed the magazine with a look of how-trying-adults-are. "What would you like me to do?"

"Could you open the tin of tuna while I make the salad for lunch?"

I removed a couple of hard-boiled eggs from a bowl of cold water and cracked them. They had not been as fresh as they might have been, for the shells were obstinate and tiny fragments clung to my fingers.

Sophie half opened the tin, and stopped. "Aunt Fanny, is this tuna caught in dolphin-friendly nets?"

"I'm not sure, Sophie. I haven't checked."

She put down the can opener. "Do you mind if I don't touch it, then? It's against my principles."

I was curious. "Are you always so careful about what type of food you eat?"

She shrugged. "We are so cruel to animals and the grown-ups don't care." Her little face was pinched with anger.

"Have you talked to your father about this?"

She shrugged. "What father?" For a moment, I thought she was going to cry.

I related this conversation to Elaine whose face darkened. "That man . . ." I assumed that she meant Neil, "didn't come home last weekend. He said he had meet-

236

ings." She paused. "I don't know what he gets up to. I reckon it's best not to ask." She sighed. "Didn't I warn you? We're on our own, Fanny."

After feeding the children lunch—Sophie made a point of leaving the tuna on the side of the plate—we shooed the children into the garden, and Elaine and I sat on the bench and talked. In the distance, the rooks wheeled in and out of the trees. "At least it's peaceful here," she said. "You're lucky."

I pointed to the north fields where the builders were already marking out foundations for the development of new houses. "Not for long."

After a late tea, Elaine rounded up the children and loaded them into the car.

As she climbed into the driver's seat, she said. "I still love the old boy, all right, but if I'm truthful, it's immensely disruptive when he *does* come home. All the routines go haywire. Still . . ." she glanced at Sophie, "I'll have to have words about him shaping up a bit more to his responsibilities to his daughter."

I waved her good-bye, and scooped up a tired and distinctly scratchy Chloe. I bathed her and read her a good chunk from *The Little House on the Prairie.* We had got to the bit where Laura and her parents have bidden farewell to their relatives and said good-bye to their home and are setting out at great risk to journey west and make a better life.

Chloe's eyes filled with tears when she thought about the cats and dogs that were being left behind. I assured her that when the family did find their new home, they would gather up lots of new cats and dogs.

We played the game of trying to guess what names these cats and dogs would be given. "If there was a Daddy dog," she said, "I would call him Will."

"Of course, you would, darling," I said. "It's absolutely the best name for a Daddy dog."

I went downstairs and into the garden. It was the guinea pig's—Chloe's birthday present—bedtime, too. Cocoa had other ideas and scuttled busily about her run until I cornered her. I picked her up, and she sat quietly. I stroked her furry nose and talked to her. Her bright eyes regarded me as both enemy and friend.

Back in the kitchen, I scrubbed angrily at the table-cloth. "Damn you," I said to it.

I ran water into the sink and washed up the day's detritus, before tackling the sitting room where Chloe, Gordon and Jake had fought the battle of the Klingons, which might not have been so bad if they had not had such muddy feet. I knelt down and picked up clumps of mud, which broke into fragments in my hand.

I checked the clock on the mantelpiece. Will had promised to be home by now.

I switched on the radio, to hear the news and check if there had been any crisis, or emergency debate. But the battery was low, and I had forgotten to buy a new one. The radio snapped and crackled. "Damn you, damn you, too," I shouted at it.

I finished brushing up the mud, plumped up cushions, drew the curtains. They were my normal tasks, a very ordinary banishment of the day's turbulence and disruption.

I checked my watch.

I decided to take a bath. I went upstairs, pausing on the landing to look out of the window. Soon new houses would emerge out of what had been a reliable, if dull, vista of plow and crop.

Will arrived home way after he promised. I listened to the car draw into the drive and a hard, ugly feeling sat in my chest. It was so late, I had eaten my supper in front of the television and scrapped his into the bin. The top of the news showed the Prime Minister going into Downing Street, flanked by an entourage that included two beautiful girls.

I felt cold and sick.

He burst into the room, importing into the quiet house the bracing echoes from a busier, more important place.

"Hallo," I said.

"Darling." He kissed me soundly. "How are you?"

He flung himself down in a chair, and then bounced up immediately. "I could do with some exercise. I've been sitting about too much. It's been a long slog, this one . . . endless amendments and fiddling . . . you would bloody well think that a bill trying to protect children would go through without a murmur but, no, someone always has to object."

He rattled on and then stopped. "You are very quiet. Is there anything wrong?"

I said furiously, "I got a final demand in the post this morning for the telephone bill. I gave it to you, and you were going to pay it."

"Is that all? Sorry darling, I promise to do it tomorrow."

"How many other bills are unpaid?"

He looked bewildered. "None that I know of."

"I bet. I bet that there's a festering heap somewhere, which you cannot be *bothered* to deal with because you are too busy with the important things like ruling the world."

"Let me know," he said, "if you find it."

I shoved a coffee and a cheese sandwich under his nose, which he wolfed down. I moved around the kitchen, doing the final tasks for the day. He talked to my back. "There's a lot going on at the moment . . . and poor old Ted has had a heart attack, did I tell you?"

"No, you didn't. I'm sorry."

"Apparently, he will recover, but he will have to take care."

I did not reply.

Will tried again. "Robert is all het up over the Treasury's bid to put up VAT. He says it will penalize the elderly and poor. He's right of course, but the mandarins are not listening . . ."

I dried up a couple of plates and put them into the cupboard. Then I screwed the top on the jam and said, "Don't be late up, will you?"

He stood up and came over to me. "What is it, Fanny? I don't imagine for a minute that you're cross because I haven't paid a wretched bill."

My fists balled into my hands, and I turned away.

"Fanny . . ." Will gave me a little shake. "I insist you tell me."

I took a deep breath. "Will, this is the third time in a

row that you have been late. Am I to make anything of it?"

He clicked his tongue. "Fanny . . . you are . . . silly!"

"Each time, you tell me you will be home at a certain time, and each time I end up throwing food away because you're not. What am I supposed to make of it?"

He took a step back. "So that's it." He sat down heavily in a chair. "So, that's what you're thinking."

I picked up a pile of ironed laundry and hugged it to my chest. "How do you know what I am thinking? I could be thinking any manner of things, including . . . I don't know."

"We patched all that up, a long time ago, Fanny. You promised you would forget all about it. I don't do anything, *anything,* with anybody but you."

"I wouldn't have brought it up again, I don't *want* to bring it up again . . . only."

"Oh, for God's sake."

I went upstairs to the bedroom and got undressed. The face that now regarded me in the mirror was apprehensive, and worn out.

I put up my hand and pushed my hair this way and that. With all the many others things on my plate, I had not been paying sufficient attention to my appearance, and I had allowed my hair to grow too long. If sophistication was my aim, it was no longer sufficient to rely on the good luck of possessing glossy skin, a (more or less) slender figure and the smug assurance of being a younger woman.

I was lying in bed with the light off when Will came upstairs and blundered about in the dark. Eventually, after spending time in the bathroom, he got into bed, and I smelled a strong blast of toothpaste.

Before I went to sleep, I heard Will say, "I hope you remember that I'm here for a long weekend, and we planned to take Chloe to the Stanwinton fair."

Chloe hovered between choosing the bumper cars or the more sedate pleasures of the merry-go-round. I urged the latter. "Darling, look at those lovely prancing horses, just like at Granny's. Daddy and I will watch you."

But Chloe plumped for the throat-clenching delights of sitting with her father in a spinning bumper car.

Will lifted her into the car and got in beside her and grasped the wheel with the expression of *I am going to win* on his face. "Hold tight," he advised his daughter.

I wandered around the fair ground. It had rained so much lately that the pitch was sticky with mud and the crowd was forced to pick its way gingerly from attraction to attraction. In the background, a hurdy-gurdy ground out tunes, the cotton candy stall was doing big business and the terrifying rocket ride had a queue that snaked around the helter-skelter.

A glowing Chloe, followed by Will, demanded cotton candy and to have a go at the hoopla because she wanted to win a sweet goldfish. "We don't want a 'sweet' goldfish," I muttered to Will. "OK?"

Later we ate hot dogs and bought a bag of nuts and divided them among all three of us. Will choked on a peanut and Chloe howled at the sight of his crimson face.

When we got home, Meg had left a cake on the

kitchen table. "Thought I'd make myself useful," went the note. "I'm out for the evening."

Will helped me to put Chloe to bed and read her the next installment of *The Little House on the Prairie.* "I have a feeling," he remarked when he came downstairs, "that it is going to take years for Laura and family to reach the West."

"It does," I said, curtly.

Will began to lay up our supper, and arranged the knives and forks in position in a thoughtful way. "Fanny . . ."

"Could you fill the water jug, please?"

He placed it on the table. "If that's the way you want to play it."

We ate in silence and, afterwards, I shut myself up in the sitting room and did some work for Battista Fine Wines. Will went into his study and the door closed.

I was wrestling with the nonappearance of a delivery from Chile which I had to trace, otherwise money would be lost. There were a fair number of possibilities—customs, breakage, misaddressing—but I found it impossible to grapple with any of them.

Was I being unreasonable? I had stitched up my wounds, built my city and there were long, long periods when I forgot about Liz entirely.

I looked up to see Will's shadow in the doorway. "Are we going to sort this out or not?"

I put down my pen and waited. He came and sat down and made sure that he was facing me. "First off, there is no one conveniently tucked up in London. OK? Second, I don't believe that is the problem. I think it is more to

243

do with the fact that you are feeling hemmed in. Chloe is only six, and there is a lot asked of you here."

My first thought was: *Will is right*. But my second thought was to tell myself that a variant of those words had probably been used, in one way or another, by thousands of men who had come home to face an eruption of suspicion, fueled by fatigue, or boredom, or powerlessness.

I put up my hand and rubbed my temple. "I don't know. I don't know what to think."

Will sighed.

That made me furious. "It is all very well you huffing and puffing as if I was some neurotic female. Why do you think I am feeling like this in the first place? Who broke the faith?"

And at *that*, he was furious. "Oh for God's sake," he said. "It is over and done with. Finished. Gone."

We took Chloe for a walk in Stanwinton wood before Sunday lunch. The wood was mainly deciduous but with patches here and there of dark green fir, which cast pools of infertile darkness over the woodland floor. Progress was not rapid, but neither was it the painful slow creep that was forced on adults by a toddler. Chloe was in a singing mood, and snatches of television jingles dropped from her lips as she ran around, jumping over puddles and sticks, and insisting that a fallen trunk was her den.

I helped Chloe to walk its length. Her balancing was erratic and I was forced to hold on tight. Then I lifted her down, and she bounced to the ground and was off.

Hands in pockets, Will slouched along.

"My father said he would drop in for tea as he would like to see you," I broke the silence. "You've missed each other lately."

He shrugged. "That's good of him."

We continued onward and Chloe darted in and out between us and wove excited circles around our figures. "Mum . . . Dad . . . look at me . . ."

"Fanny," Will said, at last, "What can I do to make you feel better . . . ? Do you need a holiday? Or, to go and talk to someone . . ."

I stared at him. A holiday? A session pouring out words into a therapist's ear? I was about to say something angry when I realized that these were not bad ideas, they simply came nowhere close to measuring up to what was required.

"I'll think about it," I said.

"It's time to go home," he said abruptly. "What a wasted, bloody weekend."

We collared Chloe and drove back to the house. Will parked the car and jerked on the hand brake. "How long before lunch?" he asked.

I wrenched open the door and said, "Get your own lunch." I threw myself out of the car and fled across the lawn to the far end of the garden. But such was my haste and confusion that I did not notice the tricycle that Jake had taken out of the shed and abandoned. I tripped over it, lost my balance and down I went, crashing heavily onto my hands and knees.

The world spun. I leaped to my feet and tried to continue, but a hammer was (apparently) smashing into my knee caps. I gasped with shock and limped instead over to the sanctuary of the garden bench.

Will came racing over. "Anything broken . . . ?"

Tears of pain and humiliation streamed down my face. "Go away. Leave me alone."

He hunkered down. "You've ripped your trousers. Let me look at your hands." He turned them over. There was a big cut, already welling blood, on the right hand.

Chloe picked up the tricycle and told it off. "Naughty Jake," she said. "Naughty tricycle."

"Put your arm around my shoulders." Will gently hefted me to my feet and we hobbled indoors and Will rolled up my trousers and exposed impressive wounds on my knees. They hurt, too.

"Poor Mummy," said Chloe and rushed to fetch the dish cloth.

Will said, "Chloe. I think we need the Elastoplast for Mummy's knees. Let's go and get it."

While they were upstairs, ferreting around in the first-aid box, I sat in the chair, trying not to cry, trying not to laugh. In a curious way, the blow to my knees had shaken off my black feelings. In fact, the smart of my wounds made me feel alive, adventurous, open to what might happen next.

I was still crying with pain, but not from suspicion or from the hard and choking grip of distrust.

Will and Chloe returned. "You hold the Elastoplast, Chloe, and when I'm ready you can give it to me." He fetched hot water, bathed my cuts and dabbed disinfectant onto my knees and hand. Chloe handed him the strips of Elastoplast.

"Good girl," he said. "We're a team."

I emitted little, shuddering sighs. "I share you with so many, Will."

"No, you don't," he said. "Not really."

His hands were gentle. "Careful Daddy," Chloe said. "Don't hurt Mummy."

To the accompaniment of Chloe's fingers fluttering like butterflies over my legs, Will knelt down beside me and patched me up. Chloe sang a little song. "Mummy's hurt, Mummy's hurt" to the tune of "London's Burning."

"Better now?"

"Yes," I said.

He looked up. "Truthfully?"

"Better now," I said.

The following day, I rang up the hairdresser and booked the first appointment available.

Chapter 22

WILL ONCE SHOCKED CHLOE and me by suggesting that some MPs often had no idea what they were voting for: They just headed for the side of the lobby where their whips stood guard.

"That's disgusting, Dad," she said. "Such sad old men. Have they forgotten what they're there for?"

"My sentiments exactly," I said.

Will looked pained. "Neither of you could possibly understand."

"I know enough to have a sodding opinion," said our (then) sixteen-year-old daughter.

"Don't swear, darling," I said automatically.

She shot me a look that suggested that if I wasn't careful, I'd be joining the ranks of the sad old men. "You don't understand, Mum. Our generation doesn't think of it as swearing. It's just words we use."

"Could you just not use them then?"

"Actually," said Will, "I have a little problem coming up."

He explained to us that a vote on the banning of fishing and shooting was struggling through the House. The party line was to vote for the ban, but Will wasn't happy about it. "I would never fish or shoot but to ban them makes me uneasy. It's an attack on personal freedom."

"Dad . . . either you're one way, or the other. You can't fudge it." Chloe bit a cuticle.

"If you vote against the party, won't you be given a smacked wrist?" I asked.

Will hesitated. "I doubt if they'd leave it at that. Then there'd be the wrath of the animal rights people . . ."

"Oh good," said Chloe, "a real battle."

"You can't then, Will. They might threaten Chloe. The mad ones do that sort of thing."

"Don't mind me," said our daughter.

"If I vote against," said her father, "I will be sent into exile, and handed the black spot."

"How about doing what's right?" asked Chloe implacably. "Isn't that what you always say we should do?"

I exchanged a meaningful look with Will. "Yes," he said. "But sometimes . . . it is not always practical."

Chloe stood up from the floor where she had been

flicking through magazines, and tossed back her hair. "Dad, I absolutely forbid you to let the party bullies decide. You must vote for what you feel. If you don't, I will never believe anything you say again."

"Chloe, darling, you will see, as you get older, that everything is not quite that straightforward. Sometimes, in order to achieve some good, one has to be a little flexible . . ."

"Oh rubbish," she said.

In bed that night, Will asked, "So what do you think I should do?"

I grasped the edge of the sheet and felt its nap on my fingertips. "You are making your way, and that is what you want and what I want for you. And there is Chloe. I *have* to think of Chloe. So do you."

"And conviction and principle?"

I wanted to say that the question was bigger than I was. I wanted to be a coward and to pretend that I was confined to the business of stacking sheets and moving food from the oven to the table, and that some questions were impossible for a single person to answer.

Why?

I could say that the merest hint of a threat to Chloe was enough to make me abandon every shred of conviction I ever held.

I could say that I minded passionately about the fish and the birds, which I do, and I did. I would never, ever have told the huntsman which way the fox went.

But I should say that I had grown used to the trappings of life with the up-and-coming politician, and knew how difficult it would be to relinquish the idea of him.

And so it was.

I was getting ready in the Casa Rosa to meet Raoul.

Things were certainly far from straightforward and, of course, I knew what I was doing.

I stood in the bathroom and sponged cold water over my shoulders. The towel rasped against my skin, which was tender from the sun. I rubbed cream into my legs and arms and cut my finger nails. The cuticles were white against my brown skin.

Outside the cicadas were almost deafening.

At eight o'clock precisely, Raoul knocked on the door. "May I come in?" Tonight, he had changed into a formal linen suit and his hair was still damp.

I stood aside and let him in.

He did not waste words but took me in his arms, and I let him.

"Don't look so worried," he murmured.

"How can I not?"

He touched a finger to my lips. "Shush . . . I know."

He twined his fingers through my hair and tugged gently and my scalp prickled. "I have wanted to do that for a long time. Never cut your hair, will you Fanny?"

"I shall have to when I am old."

He bent over and kissed me. His lips were soft, a little dry, and questioning. There was the faintest trace of wine on his breath and he smelled of expensive aftershave—a hint of unspoken and mysterious pleasures. I placed my hand on his chest and felt the texture of the linen under my hand and the suggestion of warmth from his body beneath. Then I pushed him gently away.

"Where are we going?"

"To my friends who live at a house called La Foce. They are expecting us for dinner. I think you will enjoy them. They are very powerful in the wine world and I thought it would be good for you to meet."

"Thank you." I picked up my bag.

"To be honest, Fanny, and I want to be honest, I am also hoping this evening will lead to other . . . more than those sort of connections."

We dined lavishly at La Foce and sampled wines from the golden year of 1970. We discussed new methods, new theories of production, the use of oak casks . . . The Italian was slipping from me easily and fluently now, as was the language of wine.

We ate melon perfumed with summer. The meat was so tender that it fell apart at the touch of my fork. The grapes accompanying the cheese were dark and bloomy and bursting with juice.

Raoul shone. The elegant rooms and furniture provided a setting that suited him. Every so often he sent me a look, or touched my arm, or deferred to my opinion. Look, he was saying, at how seductive I can make seduction. I can do it well, and you can enjoy it. *Please* enjoy it. This, here, tonight, is a taste of what we can share. Light, joyous, civilized, and full of sensual pleasures.

Relaxed and happy, I talked and laughed, relished the feel of my dress against my skin, the fall of my hair on my shoulders.

I described my father's interests and the business to my hosts, and imagined being woken by Raoul. I would be naked, warm, lazy, protesting that I needed my sleep, and I would allow him to do what he wished. It would be an interlude filled with mutual gratitude and delicate sensation: to be tasted, savored and noted. *Exquisite. Complex. Flawless.*

Our hostess served coffee, and I told her about my daughter. She was clever, she would be beautiful. . . . She murmured how proud I must be . . . and suddenly, I was gripped by the terror at how easy it would be to destroy Chloe's optimism and trust. As easy as it would be to drop and break one of those delicate cups.

We drove back to Casa Rosa. Bright, intense moonlight spread over a silver landscape and the cypresses pointed their dark fingers into the sky. Raoul parked the car outside the house.

"Are you going to let me come in, Fanny?" He brushed back the hair from my hot face.

Again he kissed me, and I was startled by how different it was from Will. With Raoul there were no accustomed pathways that had been followed across the years, no previous knowledge, except for what I now saw was an imperfect memory of what happened in the tree house.

"I have always loved you," he said.

"And Thérèse?"

"I love her, too, and I would never harm her. Am I making sense?"

I touched his cheek. "Perfect, lovely sense."

It was an extraordinarily intimate moment.

It was very hot inside the car. I opened the door and got out, conscious of every movement, of the arrangement of my arms and legs, of the texture of my clothes, the feel of my damp skin.

Raoul came around the car and drew me close and we looked up into a sky sprayed with a million stars. "I can't get over the difference a few hundred miles makes," I said in a low voice. "If only we had night skies like this."

"Has it been worth it?"

"Yes, it has. I've had my bad times, but very good ones, too . . ."

We were silent.

"Fanny, it took me quite awhile to get over the tree house. It was a good lesson, how sex can destroy something very quickly if it is wrong."

I let my hand rest on his arm. "As I said before, I knew nothing about sex, or not much, and I was frightened by the experience." I smiled. "But I got over it. It took a little while, and by then you had gone back to France. Life went on in a different way. It was bad timing."

Raoul disengaged himself and took my hand. We wandered toward the house, for there was no reason to hurry. The moonlight made it appear larger than it was, and very mysterious, with the glass glinting darkly in the windows.

"*Are* you unhappy, Fanny? Is that why you are here?"

"I came to bury Alfredo's ashes. I can't quite decide where yet, but I don't think he minds waiting. I think he would want me to take my time. And . . . I suppose . . . I came here to escape for a bit, and to think.

I have been unhappy."

We reached the wooden column by the door. I touched it experimentally, feeling its heat. "Anyway," I said, "unhappiness passes. It's not such a bad thing to remind oneself."

"Are you going to answer my question?"

"Yes, I must."

Raoul pushed me up against the column. I felt beautiful, mysterious and elated. I felt like a bird climbing into flight. And why not? Once, Will had betrayed me. Why not I? Uncertainty, mystery, playfulness . . . could be mine. I could take them and bundle them up into an area marked "Private," and Will would never know.

Raoul placed a hand on my waist and smoothed his fingers across the curve of my back.

I arched, and stretched out my neck, and waited for my surrender.

But I had forgotten about the past and its hooks.

I remembered driving away in the car, fleeing from Will. *I almost persuaded myself that if I'd worked where Will did, and watched the prowling men, I, too, might have listened to a serpent and eaten of the fruit.*

Raoul was propelling me in the direction of the door. It would only require a couple more steps, the tiniest surge of energy, and I would step over the threshold.

"Will, what we had was private and not to be shared."

Had I said that?

And then I thought of Will, clearly and properly. I knew that if Raoul and I went into the Casa Rosa together, that would be the moment my marriage would die. And what would remain? A man and a woman living under a roof, and the many rooms under that roof would be empty, and echoing, and desolate.

"No," I said sharply. "Raoul, I've made a mistake."

"Fanny . . ."

"I wish I hadn't, but I have. I can't get away with it."

"Yes, you can."

"Not in that way. *I* can't get away with it. With what's in my head."

"Could I point out, Fanny, that at this moment I'm not interested in what is going on in your head?" Raoul's hand tightened on my flesh and fell away.

"I'm very sorry. I don't expect you to understand."

"That is beside the point," he said, and moved away.

The moon slid through the sky, and its light threw the shrubs and vines into relief. It seemed to me that it lit up, too, those fragments of myself, those lost in a marriage, for which I had been searching.

"I think I'll go," said Raoul, and I did not blame him for this flash of anger.

"That would be best."

I reached up and held his head gently between my hands and kissed him for a third and final time, feeling his mouth and smelling his expensive smell. Then I stepped back and, as I did so, a figure came around the side of Casa Rosa.

It was a woman, dressed in a full blue skirt that adapted itself smoothly to the lines of her body as she moved.

"Hallo," said Meg. "I thought I heard voices."

She walked toward us, confident and inquisitive. "I've been waiting for you to return, Fanny. One could

255

imagine all sorts of things, but the car was here so I did not imagine you had gone far. At first, I wasn't sure that the taxi had dumped me in the right place. My Italian is dreadful and I couldn't get the directions straight. Then I spotted a wine book on the kitchen table."

The moonlight glinted on her fair hair as she kissed me on the cheek. "Surprise."

"Surprise," I said.

"Hallo, Raoul. I haven't seen you for a long time. Fanny always keeps you to herself whenever you come over, but she brings me up to speed on your news. How is Thérèse, and the children of course? And that gorgeous château?"

Raoul did not miss a beat. He took her hand and held it. "Fanny did not mention . . ."

"Fanny wasn't expecting me. But now that we are all here . . ." Meg looked up at him. "You know, we should meet more often when you are in England. I'm sure Will would love that . . ."

Raoul looked over his shoulder toward the car. "Well, I have a lot to do tomorrow. But I might be around for a little longer. If so, perhaps we can all have dinner."

All three of us knew that this would not happen.

"Oh yes," said Meg. "That would be cozy."

Chapter 23

"Just what are you doing here?" I demanded after Raoul had driven away.

"Arriving in the nick of time, it would seem," she said dryly.

There was no answer to that.

Meg followed me into the kitchen and dropped her suitcase onto the floor.

"If I said, Fanny, that it seemed a little greedy of you to have all this space in a lovely house in Italy and not to share it . . . or I could say, that I missed you. So does Will. He does love you, you know. And . . ." She bit her lip, but spoke with her usual mockery, "I love whomever Will loves . . ."

Her eyes shifted away, and I knew she was frightened of my reaction.

"Have you been sent out as spy or missionary?"

"Neither as it happens."

Meg commandeered the single chair in the kitchen, leaving me to stand. "He was nice. My darling brother is always nice to me. But he made it plain that he didn't wish me to appear at his side. He said . . ." She grimaced. "He said it was your place, not mine. But before you go all dewy, he had probably calculated that if I stood in for you people would talk."

"Meg—"

"Will never gives up. When he dies you'll find 'percentage swing' engraved on his heart."

"Who taught him to be like that in the first place?"

"I suppose it might have had something to do with me." Meg nudged her suitcase with a foot. "I'm sorry to have surprised you, Fanny. It was not nice of me, but you can make room. We've lived together long enough."

My energy had returned and I knew I had to confront Meg. The compromises were over. "Go home," I said. "I

257

won't have you here. This is *my* breathing space."

Meg's lip quivered. "Don't be nasty, Fanny. I'm not sure I can bear it."

"Try."

"I have tried, and I need you."

It was close to midnight. It was hot, I was bone tired, the airport was miles away and, as usual, Meg had brought her baggage of the funny, the sad and the monstrous with her, and there was nothing much to be done.

I made us tea, and we drank it.

Before we went to bed, we went out for some fresh air and walked down the track toward the road.

"What about the job?"

Again Meg shrugged. "They're easy come, easy go. I can go back when I wish. Anyway, the book trade isn't exactly booming in Stanwinton."

Our feet stirred up a wake of white dust as we walked. Cicadas sang in the undergrowth. The darkness was scented—basil and marjoram, a hint of lemon—and far, far removed from the cool, rain-laden, sodden air of Stanwinton.

"What will you do with me in the morning?" she asked.

"I don't know." I let a silence fall and then asked, "So, what is the news from home?"

"The polls show support for the government is slipping. Will is getting fussed, but I say to him: What can you expect? Everyone needs a change. People get fed up with continuity and the same good intentions, however well meant."

We turned into the road and walked past olive trees

and the vines and, where the road divided, we halted. One fork led down to Fiertino whose lights, even at this hour, still shone like a necklace of brilliants. The other, the road to Rome, snaked up over the hill and disappeared over the crest.

Meg wiped her face. "It's so hot. How can you bear it?"

"That's the point of here. It's hot. It's mysterious. It's beautiful." I spoke more passionately than I intended.

"Poor you, you've got it bad."

I laughed. "I suppose I have." We turned to walk back. "I've discovered a bit about my family and had time to think. Sorted out a few things."

Meg kept her eyes on the road ahead. "If you call Raoul sorting out?"

"Raoul and I have been friends for a long time, long before I met Will."

But Meg had lost interest in my affairs. "I have been a good girl while you've been away." She held up a finger. "Clean as a whistle."

We turned up the track toward the house.

"I wish I had been different," she said, suddenly. "I wish I coped with my life better. I would never have ended up so . . . wanting, so under the spell of a substance. Once on board, it never goes away. Every day is defined by whether I have or I have not had a drink. You are never, ever free of it."

I sighed, for I did not want to think about Meg and her problems and take up her burdens. I wanted my peace and my lovely liberty that I had found here—my happy mornings and gentle evenings.

"Drink takes away husbands, lovers and friends. And my son has grown up and gone away."

"So's Chloe."

"We can be two old lags, then, together."

"Less of the old." I noticed that Meg's face looked very odd. "What's the matter?"

"I'm trying to frown, but I've had Botox. I reckoned if I couldn't frown, life wouldn't seem so dreadful."

I found myself standing on a dusty, moonlit road with the dawn stealing across the sky, helpless with laughter.

"You should try it, Fanny," said Meg when she could get a word in edgewise. "You're getting a few lines."

We found some extra sheets in the chest of drawers on the landing and made up a bed in the second bedroom. The sheets smelled of camphor and moths balls and, curiously enough, were embroidered with the initials "MS."

During the night, I heard Meg call out. I threw back my sheet and crept into her bedroom. Meg was hunched over on her side, and the sheets were twisted and bunched. I bent over her, and she muttered something unintelligible—a troubled, sad sound. Inadequate to console, and guilty that I did not want her here, I straightened the sheets and pulled the curtains closer.

"I'm frightened of not winning my particular battle," she had admitted as we made up the bed with the monogrammed sheets. *"For the rest of my life, I will be on twenty-four-hour watch. But the demon will try and slip under my defenses, in the dark, when I am sleepy or sad. It will try and outwit me in the sunshine, and the*

boredom of the day when nobody minds whether I am there or not."

Her eyes flicked open for a second, but she looked through me, and beyond. Her eyes closed.

After I was satisfied that she had quietened, I slipped downstairs and extracted two bottles of Vigna L'Apparita, which had been a present from my hosts at La Foce, from the shelf in the kitchen and hid them under a cache of sacking and cardboard in the scullery off the kitchen. I was not going to sacrifice those.

I was tired and my head ached and I upended the contents of my bag on the table, looking for aspirins. My mobile phone registered a new text message. "I LV U Mum. Cxxx"

I sat down and cradled my aching head and wept tears for my father and Chloe's absence. Tears of confusion and—more than a little—of regret.

Somewhere, I must have picked up a flea for when I woke in the morning, there were bites on my legs and arms.

I grabbed my bag and left Meg still asleep at the Casa Rosa.

It was market day in Fiertino, and the square was choked with vans and stalls selling cut-price kitchenware, raffia baskets, china, and every conceivable type of vegetable and fruit—a lush display of reds and imperial purples, acid and mossy greens, ochers and pale pinks. The waxy yellow of new potatoes.

I purchased a bucket and rubber gloves from a stall; a broom, disinfectant, cream cleanser, descaler from the mini-supermarket.

"Signora." The glossy haired woman who tallied up my purchases at the till, spotted insect bites on my arm and tossed a tube into my basket. *"Per i morsi,"* she said, with a smile. *"Gratis."*

I thanked her and drove back to Casa Rosa in the now broiling sun. I tied a scarf around my head, boiled water and began operations.

I scrubbed the wax-encrusted table. Next, I tackled the kitchen floor. Then the bathroom. I brushed every nook and cranny of the house. I cleaned the windows, chipped away at the fur-encrusted taps, washed down the walls, erasing with chemical and scourer the stain of doubt on myself.

Perhaps one regrets more the things that one did not do, rather than the ones you did?

What would my father have thought? Look at it like this, he would say . . . Surely what was important was to feel, and to resolve never to have an empty heart?

The tips of my fingers puckered into corrugations, my back ached from stooping, and I was soaked with sweat from head to foot. My bites itched and stung. To clean Casa Rosa properly was a hopeless task, but I was going to do it.

Meg eventually appeared as I was still hard at it. "Looks to me like a bad conscience, Fanny. A scrubbing away of sins. Don't ask me to join in." She had a red mark on her cheek from sleeping on it and her hair was tousled. "Any hot water?"

"I've used it up."

Meg looked thoughtful. "It's very frontier," she

remarked. "Still, if that's what is required, Fanny, I'll wash in cold and join you in spirit."

I was on my hands and knees, my hands in the bucket. "Ring up the airport, Meg, and book your flight home."

Swiftly, she knelt down beside me. "*Please* Fanny. Let me stay."

"Why is *she* here?" whispered Benedetta when I took Meg over to see her. "To make trouble?"

"Of course not."

Benedetta looked at me as much to say: *Don't be a fool.* She opened her eyes wide and I caught a glimpse of how lustrous and large they once had been and why my father had once loved them. "Big nuisance, Fanny."

Meg, however, was on her best behavior. Even so, she was not offered a fresh tomato from Benedetta's crop, and I took the hint.

Which was why, on the following morning, we walked down to Fiertino and had breakfast in Angelo's café, where Maria, his mother, was serving behind the bar.

"You will ring the airport today," I said, as we settled at a table on the pavement. "But you can stay for a few days."

"Yes," she said.

"*Amore . . .*" Maria called out, busy at the coffee machine.

"That's what mothers call their sons in Italy," I explained.

"A mummy's boy." Meg smiled winningly at Angelo who blushed, and she watched his well-covered form as

Angelo hastened inside to answer his mother's bidding.

"No more than Sacha."

Meg tried to frown. "Sacha does not always obey his mummy."

She had reduced her brioche to crumbs. "Eat up. You should breakfast like a king . . ."

Meg was struck by the allusion. "I used to say that to Will. He was always being bullied at school and I could never get him to eat breakfast. Sometimes, he was sick with nerves."

"Will? Bullied?"

"Didn't he tell you? No, well, I suppose he would want to forget. Anyway, he would probably die rather than admit he spent the first three years at big school frightened witless."

It was a peculiar sensation—making discoveries about someone whom you imagined that you knew inside out. But, not unpleasant. Not unwelcome, either.

I was intrigued. "Go on, Meg."

Meg ate a morsel of the brioche. "There were lots of things. I was frightened of my grandparents. Or at least frightened of them dying on me. They were so old and boring, and found us difficult to deal with. I got this idea into my head . . . I was terrified that I would go home and find them dead. That's why Will always waited for me after school. And he got bullied for loving his sis."

"And the others?"

Meg sounded impatient. "There were so many."

"Why didn't you tell me this before?"

"How often do you talk about your school days?"

A horn tooted. It was Raoul. He parked under a tree

and strolled across the piazza. "I've come to say good-bye. As it turns out, I can't stay."

Meg searched in her bag and produced a lipstick, and applied it. Its dark pink glistened on her mouth.

Raoul's departure did not surprise me. There was no point in his staying. We both needed a polite gap and to make the readjustments. I thought with a flash of bitterness of how I would miss our conversations.

He accepted coffee and we talked of nothing very much. Eventually, he got up to go. His eyes encountered mine briefly. "I will be in the UK later on in the year, Fanny. I will give you a ring."

"Have you any idea where you are going to bury Alfredo?" Meg watched Raoul's car vanish down the street.

"Not yet."

"I thought that was the whole point of this little trip." I drank my coffee and did not bother to reply. Meg focused on a van unloading pallets of spinach and melons. Several cantaloupes tumbled to the ground, there was a commotion to retrieve them, and she said, "Are you planning more changes, Fanny? I didn't *quite* buy the burying-of-Alfredo's-ashes story. Especially when I saw that Raoul had put in his appearance. This little escape is more of a not-waving-but-drowning gesture, which means it must be to do with my brother." She paused, and then suggested with obvious distress, "Perhaps you are thinking that the marriage has run its course? Marriages do. You start out full of good intentions, the *best* intentions, and they go wrong. And you

265

think, how did I get myself into this situation?"

I took a packet of sugar from the bowl and unwrapped it.

"You don't take sugar," Meg pointed out.

It was no use arguing. The dead weight of our shared history, and Meg's cleverness saw to that.

"I remember . . ." *What? . . . taking Chloe to her first party in London, held in one of those large, expensive houses in South London. The hostess, whose name was Bridget, served tea and celery and carrot sticks. The babies were propped up in the center of the room and, every so often, one or another fell over. Concerted conversation was impossible. So we drank our tea and ate carrot sticks and reassured each other that we were not fat. Bridget was good natured and up front. "I can't believe I've ended up like this," she cried. "A wife! I thought I was going to rule the world."*

"So? What do you remember?" asked Meg.

I shook my head. "Nothing."

"You are well rid of Raoul." She decided to be direct. "If you don't mind me saying."

"I do mind you saying. It's not your business, Meg."

"What's it worth for my silence?"

"I'll tell Will. Of course."

"I wouldn't if I were you," she said.

I discarded the packet of sugar. "I bought myself some time."

"I'm sorry I cramped your style."

"No, you're not." I gave Angelo the money for the bill. "Go home, Meg, and don't interfere."

"Consider me warned." Meg got to her feet. "Other

people's lives are just that. Other people's lives. And a complete mystery."

Meg did not go home after a few days. Of course, she didn't. Initially, there were difficulties in changing her ticket. Then it appeared there were no available seats to London for at least a fortnight. Then she said, "Look, I might as well stay on until you leave. It's only one more week."

Meg had a habit of sleeping later than I did. I refused to waste one moment of my time at the Casa Rosa, thus I got up early, drank my coffee on the loggia behind the house and studied.

When Meg woke, we walked into the town, commandeered our table at Angelo's and breakfasted. I wrote many postcards, including one to Elaine. "No more biding, Love Fanny."

Sometimes the piazza was almost deserted. Or, summoned by a mysterious force, there was an influx of the puttering vans the Italians favored, and their fumes mixed with the odors of coffee and vegetables from the supermarket next door.

We lingered into the morning. Our only major expenditure of energy was to shift our chairs into the shade as the sun moved around.

Every day, we shopped for our lunch, selecting a different vegetable as the main ingredient. Tomato or aubergine? Zucchini or big, fat mushrooms? I chopped and arranged. Meg confected the dressings. (She had a knack of mixing balsamic vinegar, olive oil and mustard just right.)

In the late afternoons, we braced ourselves to climb into the hot car. More often than not, we drove to a nearby village and town and drank iced coffee and bought postcards.

That week slipped away, too.

"Will would like this," Meg said. She favored Angelo, who was serving us with large and delicious cups of breakfast coffee, with one of her dazzling smiles.

"Will?"

"Your husband, Fanny. You remember him? Don't you see? He's never had a chance to sit and do nothing. He's always been so driven." She cupped her chin in her hands and watched two little boys arguing with their mother. "I think Will is very brave, and it's not his fault that the world is so difficult and awful. And the system makes it impossible to get things done." The two boys now turned on each other. Meg's eyes narrowed. "Still, if I know my brother, he won't let it get the better of him."

I phoned Battista Fine Wine a couple of times and discussed progress with Marion, who had been left in charge. Concerned for Elaine, I rang her, too.

"I'm in real crisis," she said. "I'll tell you when you come back. But I'm holding up."

"Do you want to come out here? Could you? I would look after you."

"No. That's perfectly darling. But I can't."

"It's wonderful here, and I'm very happy."

"Bet Will isn't."

When we first did up the house in Stanwinton, we made

268

the mistake of employing cowboy plumbers. We wrestled with the results for years. Everytime there was a leak, the water forced the crack behind the basin even wider. In much the same way, the peaceful existence in the Casa Rosa was working to detach me from the jangled woman who had arrived there, clutching an urn.

Each day that I spent in the valley, I grew more detached from my former life. I looked back at it, dim and blurred, through the glass, without nostalgia, only half remembered, imperfect in detail. An inner sleepiness folded around me, almost smothering, and I was happy to sit and do nothing as the light deepened, turned brassy and the heat set in.

I thought about Chloe, the thick rope of feeling that bound me to her, and how, after she was born, I was no longer a separate person. I thought of Raoul, my first lover, from whom I had fled—for a second time. Of Will, my great love. The shapes of our lives and the spaces between them.

I took Meg to see the frescoes in the church. She stared at them for a long time. Finally, she turned and walked back over the striped marble floor and out onto the piazza. "Too hellfire for me," was her only comment.

I also insisted on taking her to the museum in Tarquinia and asked her if she recognized the funerary carving. "Oh yes," she replied, "I recognized them at once. The happy couple." She read the inscription. "Obviously, they died so young that there wasn't time for boredom or hatred."

After that, by mutual agreement, we dropped the cultural trips.

Chapter 24

INSTEAD, MEG AND I were perfectly happy to shop. When the sun dropped behind the hill, and it grew cooler, we browsed through boutiques and markets, tried on neat Italian sweaters, discussed handbags. We bought pretty straw baskets and silk scarves for Meg.

Maria tipped us off about a shoe shop tucked behind the church. "All the shoes from Rome fetch up there." She winked. "But not the prices."

Meg said she was more than happy to help shore up the local economy.

The shop behind the church was in the medieval quarter where the streets were even narrower. It was dark and womb-like and smelled pleasingly of leather and varnish. Racks of shoes stretched from floor to ceiling.

Meg was enraptured. She held up a pair. "Could be Manolos." Ignoring the utilitarian black slip-ons that had "Stanwinton" written all over them, I pounced on some red high heels that didn't.

Meg slotted her feet into the shoes and turned full circle. She was excited, absorbed, almost like a young girl, and I could see exactly why Rob would have fallen in love with her. She examined her feet in a tiny, almost useless, mirror. "Will bought me my first pair of shoes. He took a job in the supermarket, stacking the trolleys, and saved up. I kept them for years." She twisted around to consider her back view. "It was his way of saying thank you."

I replaced the red shoes on the shelf. "It's too hot in

here. Another time."

"More fool you," said Meg, and paid for hers.

Will rang late on Thursday morning. "Fantastic news, Fanny. Chloe's got her results. Two As and a B. I've phoned her, and she's incoherent with excitement."

A lump sprang into my throat. "Clever, wonderful Chloe."

We discussed her university plans and which of her friends had got what. While we were talking, I entertained a vision of Chloe, now properly grown up, graduating in a black gown, getting married, coming home with a trio of grandchildren. Time was slipping this way and that so quickly, and I had to catch up with it.

"Did you send her my love?"

"Of course. How are you both?"

"Practically comatose."

"Good." He cleared his throat. "The house seems very empty. But I have been in London quite a lot. The flat's a bit of a mess, I'm afraid. I'm sorry you were invaded by Meg. I know you wanted a bit of a breathing space. But these last few weeks have been hell." He continued in the same vein. Dreadful weather. Tedious boxes. Finally he said, wistfully, "You seem a long way away."

I brushed a dead fly onto the floor. Did I miss it in my cleaning frenzy? "Guess who turned up? Raoul. We went out for a marvelous dinner with his friends and talked vineyards and vintages."

"How nice," he said guardedly. "By the way, there's a stack of papers from the lawyer waiting for you here."

"Yes, I know." I made an effort. "Tell me what's happening."

"The polls are gloomy," he said, "but perhaps that's to be expected . . ."

While Will talked, I stared out of the window at an olive tree that grew precariously but defiantly on the slope above the house. The undersides of its leaves appeared white in the sun.

I heard the rustle of a cigarette packet. "Fanny . . . as I feared, the second-car tax is to be dropped. It's too sensitive. With an election coming up . . . so, very politely, I've been told to bugger off, keep my head down and someone will fling me a bone if I am very good. End of story. I suppose, after all this, I don't care very much."

This would not be true. "Then we needn't waste any more time on it, Will."

"I thought you'd be a bit more sympathetic."

"I am sympathetic. Very. I'm sorry you've been disappointed, but it's over."

In the hall of the Casa Rosa, I turned myself around; the telephone cord twisted across my leg but I wanted to look at the vines on the other side of the road. How curious. Why had I failed to notice that the pylons had invaded up to here, and one of them sat precisely between two cypresses on the hilltop?

"Fanny, when are you coming home?"

I heard myself say "I don't want to come back. I feel at home here."

I fancied that I heard the shock register audibly. And then I thought: Will minds, he really minds, and the terrible thing was I felt a creep of satisfaction, of power stirring.

"Fanny," he said, "you know once you told me that

you did not know me . . ."

Now, it was my shock that he should allude to the dark, locked room in our marriage that held the silence suspended between us.

"You said you did not know me," he repeated. "But it's me that doesn't know you anymore . . ."

I don't know you anymore . . .

I *had* wounded him.

I had put out a hand and rocked the boat, hard, and the certainties had suddenly vanished and Will was hurting.

Meg was not stupid and it had not taken her long to cotton to the fact that Benedetta did not like her. "Look," she said, later that evening, as we prepared to walk over for supper, "on second thought, I'll leave you two to talk over old times. She will want to know all about Chloe. I'll eat at Angelo's."

Dressed in her best print frock, over which she had tied her best lace apron in my honor, Benedetta was in a cheerful mood. In the kitchen, Radio Vatican provided a background commentary and various things were cooking on the stove. From her vantage point on the wall, the Madonna smiled down on us.

"My son . . ." Benedetta handed me a knife, "cut the tomatoes for me, please. . . . My son's phoned to say that he is coming in the winter."

Red, luscious slices fell away from my knife and I snatched up one and crammed it into my mouth. As always, it tasted of sun and earth. I arranged the salad on a plate and scattered basil over it. We ate on the back porch and talked about my father.

"He never forgave himself, that your mother left."

I dared to ask the question. "Why do you think he never married again?"

"And give you a stepmother? Alfredo told me he *never* wanted that for you."

Best not to pursue the subject further.

Back in the bedroom at Casa Rosa, I addressed the casket that held his ashes. "Where shall I put you, Dad? Where would you like to be? Will you tell me?"

An hour or so later Meg returned, and I sat on the stairs in my nightdress while she chatted away to me from the kitchen.

"Tea?" There was a clatter of water as she filled the kettle. "I had a good meal." The gas popped and she appeared in the kitchen doorway. There was a faint color in her cheeks and her hair looked soft and shiny. "Sure you don't want some tea? Angelo's is fun at night, full of young bloods who make a lot of noise. I enjoyed it, even picked up a word or two of Italian, so you don't have to worry about me."

Would I go home. Or would I not?

Will I?

Won't I?

Will he ask: "Have you grown tired of me?"

Will she reply: "I can't explain. I have no excuse but, in a strange way, it is nothing to do with you."

Then I thought of my daughter and my wilder longings dulled, cohered, settled. My daughter was owed it that I went home.

The sun was rising and the heat whispered over my

face. Who was I now? This girl . . . no, this woman, who smelled faintly of sweat? Fresh sloughed of dull skin that had grown over me, still grieving for my father who should be here, but filled, too, with a new curiosity and impatience.

I was me, Fanny Savage.

I was still dreaming over my first cup of coffee on the loggia, when Benedetta puffed around the side of the house. I sat her down and fetched a glass of iced water. "Fanny, you must know that foreigners are noticed. And there are many eyes in Fiertino."

"I'm not a foreigner," I protested. "Not exactly."

"*Santa Patata.* I lived for ten years in England and I was still a foreigner."

I inhaled sharply and picked up her hand. "You were my mother."

She rubbed my wrist. "I was and I wasn't."

"How have I sinned?"

"Not you. Meg. She was seen by Angelo in the Bacchus with a couple of men. Bacchus is not a good place. She doesn't know. The women don't go there. You must tell her."

By the time Meg woke up Benedetta had long gone. I tackled her at once. "You've been spotted."

"Oh, for God's sake." Meg slapped at an ant on her arm. She was pale and groggy with sleep, and her hair straggled sweatily over her shoulders. "It's none of your business where *I* go. But for your information, I had a peach juice, that's all. I just wanted some company. Is that so dreadful?"

"No. But why didn't you mention it?"

She gave me one of her looks. "Think about it."

My own hair felt hot and heavy and I scraped it back. "Angelo's concerned. He just wanted to warn you. It's probably nothing much but they know things that we can't. We are, as Benedetta has just reminded me, foreigners."

Meg's ravaged morning face was unreadable. "Angelo thinks I'm worth bothering about?"

"Obviously."

"It's just a bar with a few chairs, and a naughty picture stuck up on the wall." Her mouth tightened belligerently. "Who cares?"

I was cross and rattled, and more than a little exasperated. I knew she wanted me to say: "I care." But I could not bring myself to do so.

The curious, hopeful expression that sprang into Meg's eyes faded. "Perhaps your behavior doesn't bear too much examination, either, Fanny."

Perhaps it didn't. There was no answer to that.

"OK. Point taken," she said. "But I'm not promising anything." She glanced down the valley. "I suppose it *is* a very small town. Very Dark Ages."

We patched things up and decided to go to Siena. We swept the floors, brought in the washing from the garden and went around the house closing the shutters.

Meg was wearing a red skirt and a white blouse and huge sunglasses. I put on the dress that I had worn to the dinner in La Foce. She linked her arm in mine. "We do credit to each other."

In the car, she asked me, "Did I really interrupt some-thing with Raoul?"

"I had already sent him away."

"But why?"

I glanced at her. Her hands were folded in her lap and she was looking straight ahead. "I don't need a lover."

"You don't *need* a husband."

"Ah," I replied, "but I have one."

She turned away abruptly but not before I spotted tears running down behind the large sunglasses.

When I married Will, I thought only of him—my hunger to know him, my yearning for completeness, my delight and pride in his ideas and ambition to help and my excitement that we had chosen to be together. He felt the same. Only later did I understand that I was required to pick up other lives and carry them as well as my own.

We spent the afternoon exploring the city, and wan-dering the streets to no great purpose. We bought salami, olive oil and raffia mats, and Meg insisted on presenting me with a blue and white plate for the kitchen at home. "A corner of a foreign field," she said, "for Stanwinton."

We agreed that the cathedral looked like a black and white peppermint and decided to give it a miss, heading instead for a café on the edge of the piazza where we ordered pistachio ice cream and coffee.

"This is nice." We were in the shade and Meg removed her sunglasses. "Pity Will isn't here." I made no comment. "You know what I think? I suspect a bit of mid-life crisis with my brother. It happens, and Will would never say. He's not like that." She dug down into the frozen mixture—pale green, glossy and grainy with nuts. "I might tackle him."

At a stroke, the peacefulness and the accommodations that had grown between us over the past days were ruptured. I felt violently angry—and despairing—for I could no longer bear her prowling around my life.

Meg spooned ice cream into her mouth and swallowed. The sun had shifted again. Shadows lay over the famous shell-shaped piazza. Birds wheeled around the campanile, uttering shrill cries.

She flinched at my expression but I managed to say, quietly and without rancor, "Meg, I have to ask you again. When we get back to Stanwinton, will you look for somewhere else to live?"

Her spoon clattered against the metal goblet. "Oh hell," she said, and went pale under her tan.

"It would be best."

"I can't. I'm no good at just me."

"You don't have to go far away. Next door if you like . . . And you're better now."

She shook her head. "That's not the point."

"It is."

Meg stumbled to her feet. "I've just thought of something."

"Meg . . . come back."

She picked up her bag, swung the strap over her shoulder and disappeared into the nearest side street.

I counted out change and tipped the waiter, and set off in search of her. I combed the streets closest to the piazza and failed to find her. Finally, I turned into the via Duomo, which was lined with boutiques selling scarves, leather handbags, pearls of a size and whiteness that were startling in the comparative gloom. In one shop window, there was a particularly lustrous string, which I admired and, beside it, a large ruby and diamond ring in a leather case—definitive confirmation (as if I needed any) of the proposition that modesty and jewelry were wasted on each other.

On the opposite side of the street there was a shop whose long glass windows were thrown open to reveal shelving stacked with wine. I slipped inside, inhaling the familiar smell of wooden crates and the must that dusts the better bottles. The wine was arranged by continents and country: Chile, Italy, the United States . . . the reds racked in the green and brown bottles, the white reflecting a spectrum from palest yellow to deep amber.

I could see at once that an expert hand had made the selection: Château de Fonsalette Cuvée Syrah, Monte Antico Russo and, incredibly, a Beringer Private Reserve from the Napa Valley in California. It was a personal, idiosyncratic choice by a wine lover who had honed his or her discrimination to the finest pitch. My father would have enjoyed it.

I ran my hand along a shelf, touching the bottles with my fingertips. Years of thinking, tasting and making mistakes were on display here—a lifetime of inching forward toward true understanding, true knowledge and true feeling.

I wanted to do the same.

A movement behind made me turn and I saw a second room, which led off the main shop. It was dimly lit and windowless and a woman stood in its doorway, cradling a bottle.

It was Meg.

"A good one"—she held it out for my inspection—"but not outstanding. I think that is what your father would conclude."

I glanced at it. A 1988 Pomerol. "I disagree. This is outstanding."

"Oh, no," she said. "Trust me. I *know.*"

How can I trust you, I wanted to throw at her, when you step so carelessly on what is mine? My husband, my wine, even my daughter. How can you trust a trespasser?

Meg raised an eyebrow. Even *that* was Will's.

I turned away. In the street, the tourists plodded up and down, clutching plastic bags with interesting bulges. They were taking home olive oil and local pottery and, some of the better off, jewelry. They would take with them the scent and taste of Italy. Afterward they would go to a supermarket or shop, hunt out inferior oil or *sugo di pomodoro,* and carry them home, but it would not be the same.

Behind me, Meg was saying, "Your father was right about most things. Would he have advised me to find somewhere else to live?"

Chapter 25

ON THE WAY BACK to the Casa Rosa, Meg and I only spoke to each other when necessary.

Would my father have approved of my bid for change? When it came to Meg, I was not sure. Maybe he would have felt that you hang on to the bits and pieces of a family, whatever the cost.

I went to bed early, leaving Meg downstairs. I put out the light and settled down to sleep, feeling the relief of the patient who, after illness and incapacity, has taken a first step.

Later on, as I was dozing, a noise on the stairs, followed by a footfall on the path outside, made me sit up. I swung my legs out of bed and pushed open the shutters. "Meg?"

The moon had risen high and white and hard. Its light streamed into my bedroom and illuminated the thin and delicate figure below. The lights played tricks and set my heart pounding. From my vantage point, I thought for a second that I was looking at Chloe.

Meg had twisted up her hair into a sexy caramel knot, and she was wearing her new shoes. She looked young and pretty and hopeful. She raised an arm and the bracelets on her wrist gave a faint shiver of sound.

I leaned on the sill. "Don't go, Meg."

Her laugh held no joy. "Jealous?"

"I so am jealous." I mimicked Chloe's vernacular. She shook her head and I called out, "Wait. I'm coming down."

I ran out onto the path. Meg was searching for something in her bag and I grabbed its strap and tugged at it. "Meg, why don't you stay here? I'll make coffee. Or we can go for a walk."

She looked at me as if I was mad. "Why all the drama? I'm going out for a little diversion after a trying day during which I have been asked to leave my home. What's wrong with that?"

I dropped my hand. "I can't stop you, but think of Sacha. Think of Will."

"I am thinking of them. Very much. Go back to bed, Fanny."

I did not trust Meg's apparent calm. "Do you want me to go down on my knees? I will, you know, if that's what it takes."

Meg fiddled with her bracelets. "I must make you understand, Fanny. It's all right. I'm in control. But . . ." she seemed to be searching for an explanation, "I'm not the only woman to have fallen from grace, and to have inflicted these wounds upon myself. But, at times, I've felt so alone. That's what makes me so crabby and selfish, I guess." She nodded her head. "I appreciate the knees bit though, Fanny. I know what it would cost you, and I'm tempted to take you up on it."

I forced Meg back into the kitchen and made her sit down. "Talk to me. Come on. You can talk to me."

She seemed both surprised and gratified. "I've tried." Her mouth tightened and she fiddled with the bracelets. "OK. Confession time. I've tried very hard to absorb myself in other things. Clothes. Part-time work here and there. An occasional lover. Charity, or whatever those women do who have too much time on their hands. But apart from Sacha, and you and Will and Chloe, nothing burrowed very deep. My mind had been blown by drink . . . and lack of belief . . . in myself."

"I'm listening." I put on the kettle and the burner glowed and bubbled.

Meg seemed fixated by the glow. "But you are right, Fanny. It is time to make changes, and to think differently. When we go home, I will look for somewhere else to live."

"Close to us," I said.

Her eyebrow flicked up. "No need to go mad."

"All right, at a decent distance."

She smiled at me. A car drew up outside the house. Its engine revved, its door opened and shut. Meg gathered up her bag.

"You're not going?"

"Sure, I am," she said. She got up, put her hand on my shoulder and kissed my cheek, a light, cool touch. "We're quite good friends really, aren't we? In the end? I like to think so, Fanny."

I kissed her back. "Of course." Then I held her tight, and the breath of her forgiveness stole over me.

"That's straight, then. That's *something*. Go back to bed, my good and watchful Fanny."

"Shall I come with you? Why don't I? Give me five minutes."

"No, Fanny. I am on my own now. Remember?"

Defeated, I went back upstairs. I heard voices, doors banging, and the car accelerating down the road.

I opened the shutters wide to let in the night.

I'd intended to wait up until Meg returned but I was awakened some hours later by a light pulsing through the bedroom.

There was an exchange in Italian by the front door, followed by a knock. I reached for a T-shirt and pulled it on over my nightdress and went downstairs.

The policeman had a perfect crease ironed into his

shirt sleeve and an equally perfect one pressed into his trousers. The buckle on his belt gleamed and his hair was brushed and well cut. "So sorry, *Signora*," he said.

His female colleague had long blond hair and a tiny waist. She stepped forward and took my hand. Her expression told me that it was bad news. I found myself listening to . . . facts that I did not understand. Meg was dead . . . which I knew could not be true. But it was.

"Where did you find her?" I asked eventually.

"Outside the church." The policewoman was calm and detached. "We think she tripped and hit her head on the tethering stone by the fountain. But we are not sure yet. The doctor will tell us." She paused. "Did the *signora* have a history of illness?"

I bit my lip. "In a way, yes, she did."

When I had brought my knees under control and fought my way into some clothes, they escorted me into their car.

A hush accompanied our progress as I was led through the police station to the morgue. The policeman touched me on the arm. "Hold on to me if you want."

My nails dug into my palms.

At the policewoman's nod, the sheet draped over the shape on the gurney was pulled back.

I remembered thinking with relief, it's a false alarm; Meg's sleeping.

Her cheeks had a faint flush, and her hair fell back, concealing her wound. Her mouth was peaceful and there was not one line on the smooth, youthful forehead.

The policewoman knew, all too well, the many shades of bereavement, the most frequent being denial.

"The *signora* is dead," she said gently. "No doubt."

I sat down beside Meg. *"Don't bother to grieve,"* those peaceful lips might say. *"I've had enough. Battle over. Eh?"*

The policeman consulted his notes. "She had been drinking in the Bacchus. Too much, according to the report, and she was asked to leave at approximately half past two. She was seen walking toward the church and, apparently, knocked on its door. The witness states that he was worried because she seemed so unsteady and he went to offer help but, by the time he got to her, she had fallen." He added, "The tethering stone is a big block and it is perfectly possible that, on falling onto it, the *signora* wounded herself fatally."

I leaned over and touched the untroubled, line-free forehead. Then I picked up her hand and smoothed the beautiful fingers, one by one. Already they seemed waxen and doll-like. "Oh Meg . . ." Tears ran down my face. "I'm so sorry. I'm so, so sorry."

As I left, they handed me a plastic bag containing her things and a list and asked me to check it over. One ring, gold. The bracelets. One leather purse, empty. One cotton skirt. The new shoes. And, finally, one cross, gold. Surprised, I held it up between my finger and thumb. Caught in the electric light, the chain glimmered. "I can't stand religion," Meg had protested more than once. "So bossy. So pointless. So deceitful."

I returned to the Casa Rosa and made the first of many phone calls.

Some time later, I went into the kitchen to make tea, and

there was the chair in which Meg had been sitting only a few hours ago.

So many of the objects in kitchen—the coffee maker, the bottles of oil and balsamic vinegar, the blue and white plate on the table—had had direct, intimate connection with Meg. It was inconceivable that she would never come back to pick up the oil and shake it out. Never wear her new shoes. Never have a moment to pack up the blue and white plate and wedge it into a suitcase when the time came to go home.

Later, as the heat shimmered above the tarmac and even the geraniums on the piazza wilted in the heat, I walked past the café where Maria and Angelo nodded to me sorrowfully. I skirted the tethering stone, still roped off by police tape, and went into the church.

I swam through the gloom, toward the frescoes. I was convinced that Meg had been trying to get into the church to see them. I reckoned she felt that you knew where you were with them. Stupid with drink, she had forgotten that the church was locked at night to protect the very things she sought.

I looked up at them, and absorbed their harsh, unforgiving message. I unclenched my fist, felt pins and needles fizz up my arms and tried to make myself believe. Meg *was* dead.

Then I returned to the car and took the road to the airport, where I was meeting Will and Sacha on the afternoon flight.

Sacha was in Meg's room next door and I could hear him moving about restlessly. Will lay on my bed with his arm over his face.

I sat down and took his free hand and held it.

He dropped his arm. He had been crying. He was white with shock and fatigue and he had bitten his lip; it had left a rough, sore patch. "I suppose it was bound to happen, one day."

I climbed into the bed and took him in my arms and held him until he was calmer. Then I made him take some aspirin and stroked his hair.

"Do you want me to tell you what happened, or would you rather wait?"

He nodded almost imperceptibly. "Tell me."

Without camouflage, I described our visit to Siena, our conversation there, and the exchange back at the Casa Rosa. As I reached the end of the story, I felt myself grow hot and cold with shame and regret. "Until last night and our quarrel, she was under control."

"That was something." Will was eager to latch on to anything positive.

"I'm afraid it was my asking her to find somewhere else to live that set her off. I did try to stop her, Will. I promise you, but I feel responsible."

He took a while to absorb all the details. "Not even you could predict a fatal blow to the head on a tethering stone outside a church in an Italian town."

"Even so." I looked at the floor strewn with clothes in my haste to get dressed when the police arrived. "In the end we were friends. And she knew that you loved her, and Sacha." I bit my own lip. "I'm sure she knew."

The bedroom had grown very hot, and the bed was rumpled. I asked Will to get up and led him into the bathroom and made him take a shower.

I remade the bed, pulling the sheets tight and smooth. I threw open the shutter and let in the night air. I folded clothes and closed drawers.

I went downstairs and put the kettle on to boil. I poked at the tea bags in the mugs and the water turned from amber to brown—the brown that Meg had so despised.

Oh Meg, I thought, with a wild and terrible sense of loss. *Oh, Meg.*

Chapter 26

"SACHA?" I SHOOK HIM gently. "It's seven-thirty; things are done early here."

Sacha opened big, hot-looking eyes. I swooped down and felt his forehead. "You're ill."

Sacha was, clearly, running a fever and, having ordered him to remain where he was, I went down to report to Will, who was wrestling with the stove and trying to make coffee.

We drank it on the loggia. Unable to sit still, Will paced up and down. "I like it here, Fanny, and I like the house."

And I thought to myself: If I had waited for Will to join me and not insisted on coming on my own, Meg would never have followed. We would not have quarreled and she would not be dead.

Will and I went to the morgue without Sacha.

Will asked to see Meg's body alone, emerging shocked but reasonably composed. We negotiated with the police and struggled to shortcut any delays. The doctor signed the appropriate certificates, and we made arrangements for Meg to be flown home, pending the release of her body.

Will and I shared the endless phone calls. Mannochie. The funeral director. The vicar.

I phoned Chloe and told her the news. She was very sad and frightened. "Poor, poor Aunt Meg. Poor darling Sacha. I can't bear it for him. Tell him I love him." Her silence reverberated down the line. Then, "You won't die on me, Mum? Or Dad? *Promise?*" Then she added, "It can't be true."

Rob phoned up several times and Sacha staggered downstairs to speak to him. Will and I retreated out of earshot.

I asked Sacha afterwards whether Rob had any particular wishes, and he shook his head wearily. "He's left it all up to me. He doesn't feel he should interfere."

I urged him back to bed and dosed him up. "Your father is just trying to make it easier for you . . ."

I reported the conversation to Will who went straight upstairs and spent over an hour talking to Sacha. I went up eventually to find Will sitting on the bed and a red-eyed Sacha slumped on the pillows. I stood over them, fussed, and bullied them into drinking more tea.

In the morning, Sacha was better but feeling pretty weak. He did not need much persuading to stay in bed. I brushed his hair and sponged his face and brought him breakfast.

"Thanks," he said.

The police had promised that the formalities wouldn't

take more than a couple of days. But this was Italy and two stretched into three, then four. Meg would have liked the joke.

All Sacha wanted to do was to sit out on the loggia, and it was clear that he preferred to be alone. "I need to get my head straight, Fanny," and I judged it best that we left him to it.

Will, on the other hand, was restless. He had not eaten much and was sleeping badly. To give us something to do, I suggested we visit the Etruscan museum. He showed only a polite interest, but agreed to come.

We left Sacha well supplied with iced drinks and food. Armed with maps and guidebooks, I drove Will to Tarquinia. The car skidded on the dry road as I forced it up the slope and over the crest, past clumps of poppies and wild herbs, lavender bushes and olive trees, their bases plastered with dust.

Will leaned back in his seat and wiped his face. "Italy's too bloody hot."

"You get used to it."

"For God's sake," he said, and fell silent.

There was nobody much in the museum. We wandered down the marble passages where the green shades were drawn tightly against the sun. I showed Will the couple on the funerary couch. "Do you recognize it?"

At first he looked blank. "Oh yes," after a moment. "Your father had a copy on his desk."

"The real thing is much better."

"She's no beauty."

Perhaps Will saw only a dumpy woman with over-large earrings and a man with a ridiculous hairstyle. I nudged him. "He's nothing to write home about."

My attention was caught by an exquisite bronze candelabrum, worked with bunches of grapes and vine leaves. When I looked around, Will was still in front of the funeral couch. He was looking at the couple intently, eyes narrowed, his face a mask of distress.

We returned to the car and consulted the maps, for I was anxious to visit the Etruscan tombs. Chloe and I teased Will about maps but, truth be told, his skill had always got us places. Now I waited for him to say that women have no spatial awareness and for me to reply, "Women are better team players." But he didn't and I didn't.

We drove up into a *maquis* of rock and scrub. Here the landscape had a blind, bitter, cussed feel. Yet all those centuries ago, the Etruscans had made the place opulent and fertile. This had been their Paradise.

We parked close to the remains of an Etruscan town, which did not amount to much—a trace of mosaic pavement, the suggestion of a stone wall that ran up the steep hill. Drinks were being sold under a cluster of umbrellas, and an overflowing rubbish bin spilled its garish contents beneath an ancient arch.

We followed the track into the hills. The going became precipitous and it was very hot. In my sandals, my feet grew slippery with sweat, and Will was panting. An arrow indicated a steep incline and a second pointed yet farther up. The heat seared into our backs.

"Over there." I pointed to a dark opening, partly obscured by vegetation.

Will smiled grimly. "This had better be worth it."

He pushed back the vegetation to let me through, and we found ourselves in a large rock chamber lined with stone shelves on which the Etruscans had laid out their dead.

There was no mistaking an odor of semistagnant water and rock that never saw the sun. The smell was the essence of extinction. I laid a hand on a cold shelf. The ghosts of the Etruscan dead were locked into this place, far, far removed from the banqueting and harvesting, the wine, lovemaking and married love depicted in their painting and on their sculpture.

"I don't know why we make such a fuss about the afterlife," said Will. "Once you've gone, that's it. Meg has gone, so has your father. What's left?" He reached for my hand.

But I fled from the tomb and scrambled back down the path. I heard Will come after me and, by the time he caught up, I was breathless. I gasped for air and the heat whistled painfully into my lungs but I welcomed it. Far better to be here in the open, burning hot but alive.

I lifted my face to the sun. To emerge from the dark cave into the light was to know that I was free.

On the way back, Will asked, "Alfredo's ashes . . . have you decided?"

"No. Silly isn't it?"

"You can't put if off forever."

"I know."

Over a supper of grilled chicken and roasted peppers, Sacha told us that he planned to move on. "To Manchester, I think. I've got a couple of gigs lined up . . .

then I'll go and see Chloe in Oz. Hitch around and take a look."

"That would be nice." I kept my voice neutral.

"I miss her," he said simply.

"So do we." Instinctively, I glanced at Will and our eyes locked. *Don't* was the message in his. A mental nudge, I suppose.

After we had cleared up, Will said gently, "Fanny, go and get your father's ashes."

I carried the urn downstairs. "May I?" said Will and took it from me. "Now, we will find the place for Alfredo."

Holding the urn under one arm, he propelled me out of the house with the other.

We walked up the dust road, and the residual heat cradled our feet. "I should have paid more attention to the descriptions of Fiertino," Will said, in a conversational way. "Then I would know where I was. Where did your father's family live?"

The moon was as bright as burnished silver as I pointed down the road to the ugly replacement *fattoria*. "It was burned down at the end of the war," I explained.

"I see." Will considered. "I don't think that would be right. Nor, I think, is the churchyard. I think your father would prefer to be free."

I blinked back tears. "Yes, he would."

At the fork in the road, Will ignored the route into the village and we picked our way up the rise where the cypresses and chestnuts grew in clumps and the vines swept past them down into the valley. It was a mystery to me how anyone slept in the deep, perfumed Italian nights, and I said so to Will. He smiled.

"I don't believe you said that."

Down below, the lights of the village were tucked into the slope of the hillside under a starred palanquin. The moonlight worked its usual deceptions and Fiertino seemed to spring out of the landscape, untouched and complete. "I love this place," I confessed.

"I know you do. But, Fanny . . ." He was hesitant. "You do know you're only a visitor?"

It would have been so easy to say, *"No, I belong here."* But that would be to ignore many particulars and the evidence against. I *was* a visitor—a special one, but a visitor. I knew that now.

"Your father never liked me," Will remarked, in the same conversational tone. "I wish he had."

"He didn't say that," I replied. "You were different. You use politics to deal with difficult questions and difficult problems—how to conduct ourselves in society before death and . . . extinction. Dad thought it was a waste of time. He relied on himself."

"But I liked him."

"So did I," I said, with a half sob.

Will gestured toward the vines. "What's the grape?" he asked.

"Sangiovese."

"Was that a favorite?"

"He admired it."

"Why don't you settle him among the vines?" Will offered me the urn. "Don't you think he would like that?"

I knew he had got it right.

I picked my way between the swollen grape trusses and came to a halt. With a little painful thud of my heart, I upended the casket and watched my father's ashes drift toward the earth.

His *terroir.*

By the time I returned to where Will waited, I was shivering with emotion and he held me very close.

The following days were waiting days.

When it got too hot, we retreated to the loggia at the Casa Rosa and ate lunch of green bean and tomato salad from Benedetta's harvest and grew sleepy on a glass of the Chianti. At night we ate at Angelo's, and Sacha sometimes remained to drink coffee in the square. I was glad to see a little color returning to his face.

Naturally, Will was preoccupied, and very quiet. I waited until we were alone in our bedroom at the Casa Rosa before I finally coaxed him to talk.

"Meg's death has pulled everything into focus. What's so important as that? Nothing." He sat down on the bed. "I can only explain it as a loss of nerve," he said. "I find I'm not so sure anymore. There's an election coming up but facing things and fighting battles feels more difficult to me now than it did at the beginning. I used to be so certain about the things we needed to achieve. Now I wonder whether we do any good at all." He looked up me ruefully. "I don't know why I should feel that now, at the grand old, battle-hardened age of forty-eight."

I looked at him and saw for the first time that it is only after blazing desire has turned to tenderness and familiarity that true knowledge—the knowledge which I sought—was possible. And I thought with a little flutter of nerves of the degree of risk that I had taken. Not that I regretted it—but it was worth considering the destruction that might have been.

"Go on," I said. "What else?"

"You disappeared out here and seemed so absorbed in a quite different world, and I didn't think I could catch up. I thought you would vanish. Then I thought I kept you against your will. No, I don't mean against your will exactly, but caged, and when you had the first chance to fly away, you did." He gave a rueful laugh. "I suppose I was jealous of Fiertino, and of you in Fiertino."

I felt a pang that I had caused him any pain. "So the minute I go away you develop a first-class case of self-doubt?"

"I wouldn't put it like that exactly."

A little later, he said, "You really love this place . . . the Casa Rosa, and the town. Don't you?"

"Yes, I do. It's in my bloodstream. But that is not to say it is my father's Fiertino. That was different."

Will stood by the window and looked out across the valley. "I wish I didn't have to go back."

I did not have any illusions. I understood perfectly that once Will got back within sound and scent of the Westminster arena, his ears would prick up and his nose would twitch.

"Listen to me," I said and came and stood beside him and gave him the gentlest of nudges. "You are fine. Absolutely fine."

He bent over and kissed me.

The following day I visited the priest and arranged for a small stone with my father's name and dates to be placed among the Battistas.

I set about cleaning Casa Rosa for the last time. I swept floors, stacked china, dusted the bedrooms. Sacha and I packed up Meg's things and talked about her.

When evening arrived, and the shadows flooded the valley, I sat at the bedroom window and drank in every last moment, tracing every shape and fold until it was imprinted on my memory.

I loved the Casa Rosa, and never more than when I was saying good-bye to it. Yet, it was a dream, my dream, of fluttering white muslin at the windows, of marble floors and terra-cotta pots, of a life lived with perfection, that would nourish me very well on the black days. And even better on the good ones.

I went around the house fastening the shutters and made a lingering final inspection before we drove to Benedetta to return the keys.

She had a present for me. It was a small, blurred photograph of a house whose roof had fallen in, exposing a skeleton of blackened beams. I could just make out the shape of a fountain in the garden. I turned it over. Written on the back was "1799–1944."

"The *fattoria*," she explained. I put the photograph in my handbag and kissed her good-bye. *"Santa Patata,"* she said, and cried. "You will return."

I looked back only once as we took the road to Rome, and the view shimmered with the radiance of olive, grape and scarlet poppy. I thought of Meg.

How cross she would be that she was not here to climb into the hot car and say, "Typical, I've got the worst seat."

I pictured the vines pushing their roots deep into the *terroir* and the sun on the ripening fruit. . . . "You must dare to wait until the last possible moment before harvesting," as my father said, "to seduce it into such richness and flavor."

Chapter 27

WE BURIED MEG IN a peaceful and sunny spot beside the church at Stanwinton.

Then we all went back to work. Sacha to his group. Will to London and the increasing election rumors. Reclaimed by the charity suppers, the good works, and the regular journeys to London, I did my bit.

Mannochie had almost—but not quite—forgiven me for my defection. "Train tracks, Mrs. S.," he whispered into my ear at the glee club's annual fund-raising evening when I had the misfortune to laugh after an excruciating rendition of "London's Burning." The eyelash dye appointment was booked the next morning.

I was glad of it when, a couple of days later, and for different reasons, I blinked back tears as a group of clowns wooed the children in the cancer ward into laughter. "Look," said a mother who was standing beside me, pointing out her bald daughter. "She's laughing, she's really laughing." She pulled out a photograph from her bag and showed it to me. "Carla used to have the longest plaits," she said.

"So did my daughter," I replied—and I was the lucky one—the lucky, lucky mother.

It was necessary to hold several sessions with my father's lawyer and the accountant, but as soon as I had a spare moment, I went down to see Elaine.

She told me that she had decided, finally, to leave Neil and that was that. She was calmer and more settled than I had seen her for some time. "I'm going to set up that knitwear business," she said. "See if I don't. Will you wear my sweaters, Fanny?"

"Every day."

Probate for my father's estate came through, and it was clear there would be little money from it. If I was serious about continuing the business, Ember House had to be sold and any profit put back into Battista Fine Wines.

I explained to Will that I would have less time for his side of things but I would I do my best not to let him down.

He listened quietly. "I have no problem with that."

I touched his cheek. "I should think not."

He flashed his old grin at me. "It's your turn. And while you are at it, Fanny, do you think you could make us some money?"

I rang up Raoul and asked him if we were still in business. "Yes, we are," he said at once. "I look forward to hearing what you have in mind. And, Fanny . . ."

"Yes?"

"There's no point in being angry. We have too long a history. I'll see you soon."

"Yes."

Armed with cardboard boxes and cleaning equipment, Maleeka and I drove to Ember House and packed it up.

"Izt good mans," she said, as she cleared out the saucepan cupboard. "I know."

As always, Maleeka was oddly comforting. I touched her shoulder. "I know, too."

Together, Will and I chose what we wanted, and selected some pieces for Chloe. I kept my father's desk, the blue and white fruit bowl, several of his wine books and the photograph of the Etruscan tomb. And, of course, the file marked "Francesca." I went through my father's papers and sorted out the business files. The rest I burned—letters from my mother and Caro—tax returns going back twenty years . . . anything that I considered was not required in the future.

Ember House assumed the peeled, denuded aspect of a dwelling in which life had gone away somewhere else.

I rang Sally and asked her if she wanted anything sent over. "No," she said. "I left it all behind." She was coughing. "A cold. I've been quite sick with it."

It struck me that I could do more to breathe the mother-daughter relationship into existence, but there did not seem any real point. My mother had made that choice years ago. "Get better soon."

Sally protested. "A person could die of coughing here before they get any sympathy."

"Art not paying you enough attention?"

"Ouch," Sally exclaimed. "He's just pinched my butt."

300

After the final session at Ember House, I returned home exhausted and filthy. Sacha was home on a flying visit and insisted on making the supper. I watched him boil up the pasta and open a bottle of ready-made sauce. "Sach, I want you to know that you are wonderful."

He placed a heaped plate in front of me. "This looks disgusting."

It was disgusting. I ate a mouthful, and I was hit by such a longing for Benedetta's sauces, for wine, olives and sun, that I almost cried out. Sacha stared at his plate. "I wish Mum was here." Then he pushed it away and wept.

I waited for the storm to die down. "It will get better, I promise you."

"I hope so. Because it was awful, and Mum had an awful time and she's left behind such complicated feelings." I gave him a handkerchief and, after a little while, he stopped crying.

This was the closest Sacha would ever come to criticism of his mother and I loved him all the more for his loyalty. "It's not complicated for her any longer."

He turned his wet face and looked at me. "I sometimes feel as though she didn't love me enough to stick around."

I got up and took him in my arms. His hair was wild and—so unlike him—in need of a wash. "Sacha. Listen. Meg loved you more than anyone. You must get that in your head."

"Is life always so exhausting, Fanny?"

I tightened my grip. "You will have moments of great joy, I promise, and many, many small pleasures that will compensate."

"You think?"

I said, as steadily as I could, "It's taken me a bit of time, Sacha, but I do think."

He was quiet then. Then he got up and ran water over his hand and wiped his face. "You're not going to leave Will, are you?"

I went rigid with shock. "What makes you ask that?"

He shrugged. "It would kill Chloe."

"Chloe?"

"She said so."

Sacha asked me to sort out Meg's things. "Please Fanny, I trust you. Will you do it?"

The trust was a heavy one, but on a clear warm morning with just a hint of autumn, I braced myself and walked into Meg's side of the house.

Her bedroom smelled unused, but it was as chaotic as if she had walked out only a moment ago. Not surprisingly, her presence felt particularly strong and vivid in the bedroom. I picked up a bright pink silk scarf from the floor, one of her favorites, and pleated it between my fingers.

The cupboard door was partially open, revealing her clothes bunched up like anxious spectators. A photograph of Sacha in his leather jacket sat beside the bed, and a couple of books. I picked up one and rifled through it, and tucked into it was a postcard from Chloe. "It's cool," she wrote. "Hope you are well. Looking forward to seeing you."

I longed for my daughter. For her chaos, her occasional rudeness, the glimpses I caught of her private, interesting inner life. Her *"Oh, Mum, you're so sad."* I hated to think of her being so far away when the family had a crisis.

Sacha had owned up to the mess and muddle of his own feelings and I should do so, too. When it came to Meg, mine were as painful and as disturbing as his. They always would be. Yet, I must do my best not to remember her in a negative way. Nor should I for, in her own way, Meg had struggled so hard not to allow the negative to overwhelm her.

This much I could do for Meg—to remember her clearly and strongly. If I could accuse myself of not having been generous enough to her in life, then I must be generous to her in death.

Now, Meg's room was clean, airy and sterile. I twitched back the curtain, thinking of the many times we had irritated and displaced each other, kept each other company through the years and of how, in the end, we had arrived at a kind of benediction. I said aloud, "I'll miss you, Meg."

I was stowing the last of her clothes in the garage, ready for disposal, when I heard a car. I hurried out to see who it was. The ministerial sedan parked and Will got out, wearing his best suit and clutching the red box.

"Has there been a revolution?"

"Fanny . . . haven't you been listening to the news?"

"Election?"

We went into the house, and he dumped the box on the hall table. "Polls are suggesting that the party might lose seats. So it's battle stations."

I took a deep breath. "Come for a walk first. Before the balloon goes up."

The breeze was freshening on the ridge above the house and brushed the leaves on the trees with impatient strokes. Rabbit spore peppered the grass and, under the beeches, there was a faint imprint of deer. We walked along the ridge and came down by the hawthorn hedge where I discovered the tiny body of a fledgling. It had been dead for a long time, and had dried and stretched out of shape.

Will walked on ahead and I watched him.

I was trying to puzzle out, what in the end, I was doing here, with Will.

"Mama . . ." whined three-year-old Chloe, during a church service Will and I had been expected to attend, "Mama . . ." I was tired, so tired I thought I would not get through the day, let alone the service.

Will swooped down, picked up his daughter and held her close. Enchanted, Chloe ran her tiny hands over Will's face and poked at his eyes. And Will, gazing down with an expression that was shorn of ambition and striving that expressed only pure love, let her do so.

That was what it was about.

Will waited for me to catch up. "You will be able to spare time to climb on the battle bus?" he asked anxiously.

There was an edge to his tone—a reprise of the doubting Will of the Casa Rosa—and I knew, for certain, that they were all frightened that they would lose.

"I can manage without you," he said. "But I'd rather not."

"That's something, after all these years." I would like to have raised a smile, at least, if not a laugh. "It's that bad?"

His reply was dragged out of him. "It's that bad."

I braced myself mentally. "I'd better get going then, hadn't I?"

The tea-and-cake session for the party workers was, of course, well attended. There was nothing like an election for galvanizing the sheep and the goats, the supporters and the detractors, even if the press had already rushed to print its doubts about the party.

Mannochie came over. "Glad to see you back."

He was holding a mammoth sheaf of papers. I looked at them. "Are they all for me?"

"Not quite." He sounded cheerful at the prospect of the fight. Someone had to. We commandeered a couple of plastic chairs and ran through the staggering list of commitments. Coffee mornings. Suppers. Press calls.

Mannochie had excelled himself. "I'm counting on Will to wheel in some big guns. The Chancellor . . . or even the PM. Nothing like the big cheeses to make us feel we are on the map."

A little later, I got up to make a rally-the-troops speech. I knew I looked the part—unremarkable skirt, slightly more elegant black jacket, discreet jewelry. The uniform of the model political wife.

I surveyed the faces. They were good natured, expectant and wishing to be told that all was well. I had the choice as to whether to be honest—and the speech would run along the lines of: It was going to be hard and bumpy and there were no safe harbors and no safe out-comes to be had.

Or . . . I smiled. "Ladies and gentlemen. I know Will would have liked to have been here, and he will be just as soon as he can. Meanwhile, he sends his thanks in advance for all the work he knows that you will be putting in during the next six weeks. None of it will be wasted. We have the right policies, the right team and, if I may say so, the right person to represent you and to lead you to a tub-thumping victory. I live with him . . ." Pause for a ripple of laughter . . . "and I know that he spends every waking minute thinking about the con-stituency . . . even when I reckon he should be thinking about me."

More laughter.

"One of the things that I know concerns Will in par-ticular is, as a minister, how much time he has to spend in Westminster. But that does not mean that his con-stituency of Stanwinton is not engraved on his heart, and I hope you feel that he has always considered your views and put your interests at the top of the list . . ."

I sat down to enthusiastic applause.

"Very graceful," said Mannochie. "Thank you."

I was sitting in front of the mirror rubbing cream into my face and getting ready for bed when Will placed a hand on my shoulder.

"Fanny, I must ask you. I *have* to ask you. When Raoul came and saw you in Italy. Was that . . . was it?"

I knew exactly what Will was asking, and I knew he must have thought it over very carefully before he broached the subject. If it had not been for Meg, I am sure he would have tackled me earlier, and the long interval between my telling him that Raoul came to visit and this moment must have given him additional pain, for which I was sorry.

I continued to smooth the cream into my cheeks and neck and I watched my reflection performing this little everyday routine.

I had it in my power to square an old circle, to redress a balance. I could choose to tell Will the truth. I could say that Raoul offered me sweet and civilized delights, a moment of pleasure and sun, where I was not a wife, but myself . . . and I could add that I had wanted very much to accept.

Or I could tell Will that I had taken Roaul as a lover but he was not to worry. It was a terrible mistake and certainly was not going to affect our marriage. He would know what I was talking about.

Or I could say that I had thanked Raoul and replied that I would bear his offer in mind for the future. Keep it stored in the attic, so to speak, and drag it out every so often to dust it off.

I encountered Will's wary expression in the mirror and put down the tube of cream. It struck me that the politics of a successful marriage involved never asking too straight a question, and in never answering it fully, always leaving that tiny margin of unknowing. It was enough to know that each loved the other, and the rest had to be done with smoke and mirrors and more than a little trust.

I stroked in the final dab of cream. The mirror bore

the double burden of my looking into it and of its reflecting back the image of Will and me. My skin and my hair were satisfyingly glossy and chic. A girl had grown into a woman who, among other things, was a wife and mother. Making sense of what you turned out to be was much to do with determination of the will. And, above all, I had my inner room into which I could retreat and draw breath.

I got up and turned around to face Will. "It was business." I kissed his nose and drew a heart on his chest with my fingertip. "Only business."

"I've had an idea," said Will, as he threw back the covers and got into bed. "If there's any money left over from your father's estate, why don't you look into buying the Casa Rosa. We could do it up. I'll help."

I had heard that one before. I got in beside him and arranged my pillows the way I liked them. "There won't be enough."

He grinned smugly. "Did I tell you that Meg left me a small amount? I want you to have it." He reached out and snapped off the light. "That should do the trick."

Chapter 28

IN THE RUN-UP TO the election, I got up at six A.M., dressed up in one outfit, slogged through the streets on the stump, returned home, dressed up in another and sallied forth to teas, dinners and dances. I lost count of how many.

At each venue we were on together, Will and I slipped

into our double act, which we had got down to perfection. My neck ached from the adoring pose, and Will was going a trifle hoarse.

The national polls were not exactly encouraging, but the major slice of the local press seemed to support Will. Mannochie, however, was gloomy. "Can't put my finger on it. Economy is ticking over, inflation under control but it doesn't feel right to me."

Mannochie set me thinking. I am told that sea changes in the earth's composition take place underground and in secret. However hard they listen in with their instruments, the scientists can't work out exactly what has happened until much later. There is something in this.

The eve of polling day dawned. I had been on the stump for four hours. My feet hurt, and my wretched badge kept falling off. Our next-to-last stop was a block of flats down by the river where the concrete walkways were streaked with damp and corridors were littered with . . . best not to inquire. I knocked on a door that had once been bright blue.

A woman in a plastic apron stuck her head through the window. "What do you want?"

I launched into the spiel and she frowned. "You lot never talk to us."

"But I'm talking to you now."

"No, you're not. You're telling us."

Behind me, the junior party apparatchik trailing in my wake sniggered and I gave up. "Fine," I said and tried to stuff a leaflet through the letter box where it stuck.

I stifled a yawn, as well I might, for I had been woken at five-thirty A.M. by Mr. Tucker who had demanded to know if my spirit was in good working order.

Good question.

Next up was Mrs. Scott, my special assignment, who I knew would have spent most of the afternoon preparing tea for my visit.

The apparatchik and myself squeezed into her sitting room where a tray with legs had been laid up with a lace napkin and a jug with a beaded cover. In the corner, a television with the sound turned down winked and blinked.

"I hope you use yours." She whipped off the cover from the jug.

"I do, Mrs. Scott. I am very fond of it."

"Mrs. Savage and I are friends." Mrs. Scott addressed the apparatchik, "She sits in for the minister."

I glanced around the room. After much tussling, the council had replaced the glass in the front door after the violent neighbors had bashed it in. There was a patch of new plaster, too, where the window had cracked and the damp had got into it. "I am glad Will was able to organize to get the repairs. It's been rather uncomfortable for you, I'm afraid."

Mrs. Scott did not see it this way. "If those buggers hadn't bashed down my door, I would never have got to meet the minister."

Polling day dawned very stormy. I climbed out of our warm bed and pulled back the curtains. The rain rattled across the field, and welled into puddles on the road.

"Sod it," said Will from the bed. "No one will go out to vote." He picked up the phone and rang Mannochie. While I dressed, a conversation ensued where my name cropped up. I knew what it meant.

"Mannochie's ordered transport for the elderly." Will lay back on the pillows, already looking exhausted. "But we could use the second car and a driver."

I picked up my election skirt, not a garment of great beauty but it made me look reliable and approachable, and put it on. "Second car coming in useful, then," I said.

The polling station was the primary school where, as the roof leaked, voters dodged around buckets—which, it occurred to me, was not a good advert for Will.

The local press took photos of Will and me as we voted, and I went back to pilot the aged and infirm, and mothers with small children, to and from the polling stations. Every so often I checked in at one of the twenty committee rooms scattered over the constituency for an update.

The day vanished and, after a snatched supper of mashed banana and yogurt, the order came in—the Minister and his wife were called to the town hall.

I changed into a gray trouser suit and black suede ankle boots. I was, of course, wearing my tights. I masked the shadows under my eyes with foundation, blotted lipstick onto my mouth, and inspected my eyelashes. If it was victory, I was primed. If it was defeat, I wanted to face it at my feminine best.

Mannochie caught up with me as I threaded my way through the army of helpers at the town hall. He looked grim. "Exit polls are bad. It's possible that Will is going to lose his seat."

"Grief, Mannochie."

"We don't deserve it," he said.

"No, but Meg always said that at some point people got bored and wanted a change. Maybe this is it."

Will broke into a smile of relief when he saw me. "Thought you'd done a runner."

Like minor royalty, we stood side by side as dozens of people came up to discuss the situation, take orders, make a point. Every so often, Will squeezed my hand, and I squeezed back.

The ballot boxes trickled in. The voting slips were sorted, bundled and placed in lines on the trestle tables. I knew now to keep a sharp eye on those lines. Sometimes they creep, and sometimes they rocket along, and you can tell from the glances of the tellers which pile belongs to whom.

No one was looking in Will's direction.

"See," said Mannochie quietly. "Not good."

I helped myself to coffee from the Thermos. It was stewed but at least it was hot, and it gave me something on which to concentrate. At each end of the room, a television screen blinked and chattered.

At four o'clock in the morning there was a last-minute altercation with the Natural Earth candidate over spoiled ballot papers. Once sorted, the Returning Officer picked his way over to Will. "I'm sorry," he said.

Will's grip on my hand was bruising.

He stood on the platform, as upright and unflinching as he'd trained himself to be and, as always, I felt very proud of him. He did not falter when the final figures were read out, not even when he realized that the event that would rock him to his foundations had happened. Will had lost his seat.

The victorious candidate bowed, smiled and made a speech in which he thanked almost everybody in Stanwinton.

Will took the microphone . . . and I was transported back to the beginning, that bitter January in Stanwinton town hall. He spoke about change, the need to rethink and recharge, and how he had fought to hold on to his ideals. He thanked his supporters and told them that nothing was ever wasted.

At the end, head bowed, he listened to the applause. Then he stepped off the platform and I went up to him and said, "When you're ready, let's go home."

On the way there, Will ordered, "Stop the car."

He wrenched open the door and stumbled out. I followed him.

Then he was sick.

I held him until the bout was finished. "Sorry," he managed.

After he had got his breath back, I made him walk with me as far as the beech in the corner of the field. The sun was just poking above the horizon and, after the claustrophobic frenzy of the town hall, the air felt cool and fresh. We leaned on the gate and looked across to where the dawn was breaking, and the light picked out the hedgerows.

Will laid his head on his folded arms. "I always wondered how I would deal with it when it came."

"The answer is, fine. In fact, more than fine."

His voice was muffled. "We will have to think again about everything. How we live, all that. What we do."

Back at the house, I made him tea, which he drank thirstily. "Let's see what's happening on television," he said.

But I stopped him. "No, that's finished for the moment."

The dark eyes were dull with misery. "I suppose you are right."

Although I knew he had not had any dinner the night before, he refused to eat anything, and I led him upstairs. He submitted obediently as I unbuttoned his shirt and peeled it off. His body was soaked in sweat and, every so often, he gave a shuddering sigh.

In bed, I eased myself close and held him.

After a few minutes he fell into a twitchy sleep, but I kept on holding him until my arm grew numb. When I could not stand it any longer, I detached myself from Will and went downstairs to phone Chloe.

It took a bit of determination to track her down but, eventually, I got through. It was very late at night for her, and she sounded terrified when she came to the phone. "Mum? Nothing bad has happened?"

"Nothing so terrible, but Dad did lose his seat last night. He wanted me to ring you."

"Oh, poor Dad. Is he very upset?"

"Yes. He's sleeping at the moment."

Once Chloe was reassured that, basically, her family hadn't been wiped off the face of the planet, she sounded quite cheerful. "He can do something else. Tell him lots of people do. It's the spirit of the age. It's good for you to have a change. Tell him he's lucky to have another chance of doing something."

"Darling Chloe, I do miss you. I want to tell you about a lot of things and what I saw in Italy."

It was time I talked to Chloe about the family and its history. Some time, when she came home.

"Oh, Mum, I miss you too . . ." She chatted on for quite a time, and it was only toward the end of our conversation that she dropped in the following information: "Mum, I've met someone . . . his name is Paul . . ."

I surveyed my domain. I went into the sitting room and plumped cushions and drew back the curtains. This being the most formal room in the house, I made sure there was no dust on the mantelpiece and renewed the stagnant water in a vase of lilies.

I tidied the kitchen and assessed the food and wine supplies. Without a doubt, Mannochie and the team would be coming over in droves, and they would require feeding in defeat as much as in victory. I would cook bowls of pasta and open wine, and we could sit around the table and go over what had happened until it was sufficiently shaped to consign to memory. Then we had to move on.

I picked up the brown leather diary and leafed through it and resisted the temptation to score through the dozen or so pre-Christmas constituency engagements. That would be to snatch too small a victory from the jaws of defeat.

"Fanny?"

I looked up. Will was in the doorway. "I'm here. I'm not going anywhere."

"Good." He disappeared next door to turn on the television and returned with the news.

The nation had spoken. The party was out, and everyone was either licking wounds or looking smug or pious, or both.

We discussed what this would mean for various colleagues, and by how much this pushed back Will's dream of the Chancellorship. Privately, I knew that it was unlikely Will would ever realize it now. The timing was wrong. But it was not the moment to say so.

"I've rung Chloe," I told him. "You'll be pleased to know that she thinks you should look on this as the opportunity for a second career."

"Cheeky monkey," he said. He frowned painfully. "But she's right," he added. "I'd give anything to see her."

"More tea?"

"I think I've drunk more tea in the last few weeks than in my lifetime. I never want to touch the bloody stuff again."

"Nor do I." I inspected the rack. "Lots of lovely wine instead." Now that Meg was not here, I felt I was at liberty to say that sort of thing.

Will went quiet. We were both busy with our thoughts—and mine were principally preoccupied with how I was to shore Will up until he felt better.

"Will," I said gently, "you never know, you might like being free for a while."

He shrugged. "Easy to say."

It was not as though he lacked courage. Will had reserves of that. It was just that, at the moment, he was used to thinking along one set of lines. I would have to persuade him that trying out another set would be uncomfortable, but intriguing and perfectly possible.

"Thinking of change, there was a point when I didn't think you were ever going to come back from Italy."

I replaced a claret—a disappointing 1997 Haut-Marbuzet—in the rack and straightened up. "I might have done," I said. "I thought about it."

He ran his hands through his hair as if in search of the old Will, the one who had been so full of optimism and vigor. "I would have gone mad," he said, "or taken to the bottle."

"Not a good joke."

"Not a good joke," he admitted.

"After I'd gotten over the relief of being on my own, Will, I realized I wouldn't like being without you, either."

"Good." Will got up to check the latest figures on the television. "That's very good."

I picked up the full trash bin and carried it outside. Daylight was well advanced and a shaft of light fell on the garage door. With a curious half-painful, half-pleasurable squeeze of my heart, I perceived a suggestion—a hint—of the texture and color of the Casa Rosa.

"Francesca," said my father, "you live here in Stanwinton, of course, but you are a Fiertina."

Well, I was, and I wasn't. I cherished his metaphor and the story of making the hillside bloom. From bare hillside to the lushly fertile—"my grandfather's wood, my father's olive grove, my own vineyard"—in three generations, went the saying. But even he would have to concede that he had been talking about a time that was long ago. My father had not been in Fiertino when the workmen rolled up the road in the mechanical diggers and constructed the row of pylons that marched up the slope. Nor had my father been sitting in Angelo's where the talk was of olive subsidies and of house conversions.

But I would not think about Casa Rosa now. Not yet. I walked across the lawn. The house was behind me, an emptier house than it had been for years, in which the movement of things and people had dwindled. I turned around to look at it. After all, after everything, I had grown used to its spaces and awkwardness. We had rubbed along together, it and I—the ugly windows, the laurel hedge, the kitchen that never quite gelled. Like it or not, the house had been the *terroir* in which Will and I had conducted our marriage and made the effort to shape our lives.

Still stacked in the garage were Chloe's tricycle and a box of plastic toys. Placed neatly on a shelf in the garden shed—and virtually untouched—was a box of tools, which Will had bought to do the remodeling. In the attic, there were a couple of suitcases that, among other bits from the past, contained my wedding dress and a stool with a tapestry seat that had kittens embroidered on it. It was a castoff that nobody could bring to throw out, which Will had felt obliged to buy at a sale to raise funds for cancer research.

It was here, in this house, that our marriage performed its trick of turning from an abstract bit of paper—the bit of paper Caro had longed for—into the skin that clothed us both. Inside it, we lived and breathed, and smiled and wept, and drooped and flourished, sometimes all at the same time.

I went back inside and folded up clothes and tidied papers and unopened mail. As I moved through the rooms, I listened for that elusive trace, that tiny echo, of the presences that had once filled them.

Will had gone back to bed. I pulled my mother's quilt over us and put my arms around him. He felt cold and lifeless but tomorrow he would be different, and the planning and decisions would begin. There were many possibilities and we could look at them all, one by one.

I kissed his cheek and my hair fell over his face, and I whispered to him that we would survive, it would be all right, and that I loved him.

"I was thinking about Meg," he said. "And what more I could have done to help her. How do you think she would have felt about my getting kicked out? I know what your father would have said. 'Look at it this way.'"

I laughed.

After a moment, Will turned back to face me. "I like it when you laugh," he said.

Weeping Eros built a city and had ruled it and grown powerful.

That had been me.

The good wife.

Center Point Publishing
600 Brooks Road ● PO Box 1
Thorndike ME 04986-0001 USA

(207) 568-3717

US & Canada:
1 800 929-9108